Praise for Mia Gallagher

HellFire

'Takes screwed-up and scuzzy into hitherto uncharted territory…
Gallagher depicts a culture in despair and a society in irreversible
meltdown with tremendous compassion and energy… Remarkably
done; as is the unexpectedly weighted power and beauty of the
imagery… The vernacular rhythm is perfect… An extraordinary
ambition; a grand achievement, too.'

— *The Guardian*

'Mia Gallagher's coruscating debut novel is not simply an Irish
Trainspotting, though there are echoes of early Irvine Welsh in
the energetic joy of her language. Instead *HellFire* is a powerful
revenge tragedy, a glorious depiction of Dublin in all her dirty
glory, and an unusual love story… There have been few better
debuts in the last year.'

— *The Observer*

'A work with a strong social conscience, forcing the reader
to face up to the blindspots of Celtic Tiger Ireland… Gritty
realism interjected with poetic surrealism is not an easy stylistic
feat. However this is something that *HellFire* does effortlessly…
unique and innovative… takes the reader on an exhilarating
narrative and stylistic journey.'

— *The Irish Times*

'I am reminded of Laurence Sterne's *Tristam Shandy*… a
magnificent achievement, bursting with energy, full of wonderful
creations and telling a compelling, if unorthodox, love story. It is
a novel of Dublin to rank with James Plunkett's *Strumpet City*.'

— *Irish Examiner*

'Magic, drugs and rock 'n' roll... the darker, grungier, flipside to Harry Potter, Jonathan Strange and Mr Norrell, and all the other witches and wizards currently casting spells over willing readers.'

– The Independent (UK)

'Brilliant... easily compared to Irvine Welsh with its energy and raw, compelling narrative. You find yourself hearing Lucy in your head, telling you her shocking story and you find yourself staying up all night to be with her.'

– Sunday Independent

'Perfectly describes modern Ireland... a striking talent for storytelling and a subtly enchanting narrator... *HellFire* has the kind of episodic character that gives endless classics their power, the element of stories within stories... Mia Gallagher [is] worth getting excited about; something special, something different, something completely new, readable, talented and relevant.'

– Sunday Tribune

'Vividly and descriptively honest... striking, inventive but also raw-edged and authentic... a power-buster of a novel, rich in character and language.'

– The Edmonton Journal

'A novel as topographically significant as *Ulysses*... Because of the author's sheer ability with words and an abundance of characters that would have been the envy of Dickens, one reads on – perhaps white-knuckled!'

– Verbal Arts Magazine, Belfast Telegraph

'Powerfully told.' ... 'Brilliant narrative skill and lightness of touch.'
– Financial Times

'A powerful and brilliant book.'

– RTE Guide

'The whole sticky mess of humanity and inhumanity is here… a massively ambitious novel… it's hard to better.' … 'Nothing came near Mia Gallagher's *Beautiful Pictures of the Lost Homeland* for bravery and ambition this year. A skilful and fearless exploration of place, time and identity – it grapples the big themes to its heart. This is the Irish novel whose reputation will grow in the coming years. A new generation of Irish writers may well take their lead from it.'
– *Sunday Independent*

'It would have been easy for Gallagher to turn Geo's story into a blockbuster bestseller about transgendered identity. However, *Beautiful Pictures* is more interested in the binaries and doubleness of personal identity; the many lives we all live that produce the fleeting present moment… Comparisons with Joyce are inevitable… a gripping page-turner.'
– Sara Keating, *Sunday Business Post*

'Mia Gallagher's remarkable *Beautiful Pictures of the Lost Homeland* offers a flavour of past and potential lives. The story, which ostensibly centres on a transgendered film editor, takes the form of a montage, splicing together narratives from different periods to create a complex story about the binaries and doubleness of identity.'
– *The Irish Times*

'Gallagher has left us with a fearless and defiant book. Generous, reckless, revealing and baffling, you come away from it with renewed faith in what the novel can achieve.'
– Mike McCormack, *The Irish Times*

'Gallagher, I believe, with *Beautiful Pictures of the Lost Homeland*, has achieved some kind of formal evolution of the novel.'
– Oisín Fagan, *The Irish Times*

'*Beautiful Pictures* is no conventional door-stopper – it's more of a portal-stopper; it's no airport novel, it's more a rocket launch pad novel! Everything about this book is surprising... it's exciting and epic.'

'A voluminous book, sprawling and... absorbing, digressive and endlessly surprising... its rendering is incredibly vivid... her characters are isolated and enigmatic souls... shown with a delicate intimacy.'

'A tightly wound story, intricately imagined and expertly told.'

'Every page... is stuffed with prose of simple elegance that also displays human insight with brave, verging on cruel, description. Every permutation of family relationships is covered... We are all but individuals who each bear a certain private self we shall never reveal, for truth exposes us to more hurt than we can bear.'

Shift

Shift

Mia Gallagher

NEW ISLAND

SHIFT
First published in 2018 by
New Island Books
16 Priory Hall Office Park
Stillorgan
County Dublin
Republic of Ireland

www.newisland.ie

Print ISBN: 978-1-84840-669-8
Epub ISBN: 978-1-84840-670-4
Mobi ISBN: 978-1-84840-671-1

Typeset by JVR Creative India
Cover design by Anna Morrison
Printed by TJ International Ltd, Padstow, Cornwall

New Island received financial assistance from The Arts Council (An Chomhairle Ealaíon), 70 Merrion Square, Dublin 2, Ireland.

New Island Books is a member of Publishing Ireland.

For my mother
Miriam,
in memoriam

Whoso list to hunt, I know where is an hind,
    But as for me, *hélas*, I may no more.
    The vain travail hath wearied me so sore,
    I am of them that farthest cometh behind.
Yet may I by no means my wearied mind
    Draw from the deer, but as she fleeth afore
    Fainting I follow. I leave off therefore,
    Sithens in a net I seek to hold the wind.
Who list her hunt, I put him out of doubt,
    As well as I may spend his time in vain.
    And graven with diamonds in letters plain
There is written, her fair neck round about:
    '*Noli me tangere*, for Caesar's I am,
    And wild for to hold, though I seem tame.'

Thomas Wyatt, from the Italian of Petrarch

Contents

More Often in Future

She'd always been haunted. A devil on her shoulder, an infant demon with invisibly black eyes and breath like a blown-out match. Hey, it said, and whispered cold things in her ears.

Her name was Beatrice, but, weirdly, she was called Trish, not Bea, for short. Noelle, like everyone else, never queried that, not until it didn't matter anymore. She lived in a block of flats, in a part of town that as a kid Noelle only knew from sensational evening news stories and the number thirteen bus timetable. ANOTHER TRAGEDY JUMP. 65p, please. COT DEATH HORROR IN TOWER BLOCKS. You're not going to the terminus then, love? MOTHER OF TWO FOUND IN KITCHEN. No, I'm not thanks.

Noelle lived at the other end of the bus route. Her terminus had its own nightmares, a church where monsters prowled under the palm trees every Sunday and shook wagging fingers from the pulpit.

Noelle had had a thing for Trish's brother, once upon a time. She hadn't realised he was Trish's brother when she'd decided she had the thing for him. She knew Trish from school, though only vaguely, by sight and reputation. The closest they'd got to each other had been an audition for a school play, but they'd never spoken to each other. She'd got to know the brother through the other school, the Saturday morning drama workshop, with its colourful, clever, insecure members, quickfire slagging and no-holds-barred dancing at age-inappropriate nightclubs and end of show house parties.

In school, Trish was beautiful with her black hair and bright round blue eyes, her slim legs and shapely ass. Noelle, short, mousy and pear-shaped, envied her.

They were in different years, so Noelle had no idea how good Trish was, academically speaking. She knew she was bright. In those days, you could see her from yards away, radiant with her own knowledge. She went to university after school, with a grant. She was bright alright. And, thinking this, Noelle hears the lunch bell again. No sweet chimes; a long jarring scream.

Trish belonged to the elite. Dressed well, smoked, made fun of the teachers. She had it all. Christ, Noelle envied her.

She is washing her hair in cold water, gasping at the shock. What is she doing? you might wonder. Why cold water? Perhaps she's trying to wash her brain, and only cold water will do the trick, blast it back into something like normal. Perhaps she's trying to freeze it, too-fast brain, solid.

Stop. She can't afford a back boiler. Simple.

Her nails are bitten. Her fingers are longish. Her hands, like most of the rest of her, are thin and knobbly. The bitten nails dig into her scalp. Shampoo suds coat her forehead. The cold water makes the soap run instead of foam, so it drips into her eyes, stinging. She squeezes them shut and rubs off the suds, using the back of one thin, knobbly hand. Then opens her eyes again, careful, and eye by eye, picks the lather from the corners. The whites are bloodshot. She looks as if she's been crying. She takes a breath, plunges her head under the tap and rinses.

Noelle didn't see much of Trish during those long teenage years she was obsessed with the brother. Trish left the school just after Noelle joined the drama workshop, and they hadn't known each other, so there was no reason to stay in touch. The brother did mention he had a sister who used go to Noelle's school, but even though she knew their surnames, Noelle didn't put them together. She's always been a bit thick that way. So she never realised, those nights of sweating and dancing and hoping for a smile or even just a look from him, that this sister was Trish. Finding out felt huge. Like she'd discovered a new twig on her own family tree. Beatrice, he said, as they sat together without touching in the dark musky corner of a party, and the penny dropped, clunk.

Trish? Really? Isn't the world a small place? And so on.

How exciting. To find a legitimate chance to approach him, pretend they had something real in common besides their horny teenage bodies and their shared religion.

At fourteen, after ditching God the Father, Jesus and The Ghost, Noelle had needed a new idol. The path led her to a lodestar from the world of music. Was He rock, was He pop, was He other, was He art? He was David, and He was Divine. She wore His many faces on badges pinned onto an old waistcoat. The brother, she discovered, loved Him too. They discussed His new singles, His old albums, His intriguingly unclear future. One New Year's Eve they danced to the slow voice wilding as the wind, and snow fell outside, and it's true, she would rarely feel as happy as that again. After the dance, the brother took another girl's hand and Noelle drank and talked to others and fell asleep, and that was that New Year over.

He was thin, the brother, like Trish. Green eyes with a bit of a glint in them. He knew Noelle wanted him and he played her like she was a reliable but not very swanky guitar. He was popular in their world. Charming. And charmed, others scrambled into his circle. Eager puppies. He made enemies, or what they, with their naïve teenage hyperbole, thought were enemies. He would get restless, and play one friend against another, slipping through their cat's cradle allegiances unharmed, like mercury. Later Noelle would think he was a bit sick, because people who aren't sick don't do things like that. She imagined his mind a filing cabinet, with folders on those he knew, red-stamp Xs or tick-marks identifying who should be cultivated and who pruned away.

Oh, she was like the rest of them. She grovelled.

He's gone now. Somewhere worthy and interesting. Gone, with his guitar.

Occasionally, in the last year or so, he would flash across her mind, and she'd see him in a hot country, some place south of the equator. Trekking down a dusty road glaring orange in winter sunlight, hiking towards the horizon until he was lost against a backdrop of arsenic-green mountains. She would think, at those times, it would be nice to hear from him, even though they never knew each other that well. It would be fun, perhaps, to send him a postcard to make him think of her. Then she'd wrap her arms around her lover's sweaty shoulders and moan as he came inside her. She would feel a little sad at those times.

The first devil appeared during a school play, the one they'd auditioned for, a rural drama set in a famine cottage on a bog. She, Trish, got the lead. She was to be possessed. Back then, Noelle thought she wanted to be an actress. She yearned for Trish's part. Instead she was cast as a nun. The nun only appeared in the last scene so Noelle wasn't needed at rehearsals for ages. Word came back that Trish was good. Until the day she came into a rehearsal with scratches on her arms and neck. She claimed a spirit had done it. She'd gone to bed, usual time, nothing strange, and woke up covered in scratches. That was all, according to the people who'd been in the rehearsal room. She didn't talk about voices or spectral commands that sounded like radio interference crackling in her ears or a devil straddling her on her bed. Her evidence was admirably tangible. Another older, equally pretty, girl got the part. Noelle still played the nun.

The year after that, Trish left school and by then Noelle had met the brother.

Noelle grew out of wanting to be an actress. She told herself it was because of the magazines, body image, fuckability factor, all that, and Christ, isn't there enough pressure to be performing, all the time, in real life? She would be the first to say she wasn't good enough.

She sits in front of her window, looking down at the strip of green separating the concrete stretches below. The lights in the supermarket are offering Christmas bargains at slashed prices. She wears a towel around her shoulders like a poncho. Her wet hair lies on the towel, soaking through. Cold. She notices, she forgets. She smiles and the smoke from her fag curls into question marks over her head. She narrows her eyes, and forgets.

The long stick of white ash drips onto the floor. The electric bulb flickers. It's nearly dead. There are pots on the cooker. One is filled with some yellow muck that once lived in a soup tin. A pan of sliced batch waits in the cupboard. She could be hungry but she doesn't care. The hair near her scalp is drying a little. She is going out tonight.

She is going out tonight; she's no longer sure where. She forgets. She could be meeting a friend, or maybe someone closer. She won't be meeting the brother. He's gone. Her foot is blue-veined and purplish with the cold. Her toenails are a chipped orange. Her eyes are foggy. Remember, forget.

Once, about three years back, Trish had offered Noelle her flat. At that stage, Noelle was in college, not far from the tower blocks with their terrible reputation. Trish had graduated and was temping in an office on the quays. On a January afternoon, Noelle came out with her on the number thirteen bus to the wrong terminus, and looked at the place. It was cramped but comfortable. It had a lot of rooms, more than she'd remembered. A few years earlier, though it felt like a decade now, she'd rolled with the brother on a bed in the room at the back. A glorious summer evening. Noelle had still been in school. It was the first time she'd seen Trish in the brother's presence and – although the penny had already dropped, at that party where he'd said her name, Beatrice – in her thick mind she'd felt the pieces slot together again, like a puzzle from *The Crystal Maze*. Trish had come into the room, laughed at their fumblings, then gone out to make tea. Now she was showing Noelle the view, as if Noelle hadn't seen it before, pointing out the window at the shopping centre. All the amenities, she said. And then she made tea again, which they drank and chatted over, before Noelle had to rush back to her busy world at the other end of the bus route.

They had met by accident some weeks before, at Christmas. The brother had come back for the holidays and a gang of them from the old days had arranged to meet for drinks. The brother seemed different. His green eyes moved slowly in his tanned face, like they had seen things. Otherwise, he'd been in good form. Everyone was remembering, laughing, touching each other's arms, exchanging fond, meaningful gazes. He leant over and looked at Noelle and said her eyes were like everything. She felt her mousy skin flush under the red of the wine, and had to look down. She turned the talk to wordplay and showed off her newly gobbled education. He rose to it, adding to the banter polysyllables that she didn't know, that she was surprised he did, and she would remember admiring that, and telling herself, Yes, This is Why.

Trish was in another corner, talking to someone else. Her skin was pitted with the marks of spots Noelle had never noticed in their schooldays. She was wearing a jumper that didn't quite go with her jeans, and her feet were bare in her slip-on shoes. They all left the pub to go to a cinema and Noelle pulled a green scarf around her sore throat while Trish's feet stayed bare, white-blue in the plastic shoes.

After the film they went to a club and danced, like they were even younger than they were, and Noelle danced with the brother. All fast movements, hips and feet, hair. A mental beat and a saxophone, somewhere. He asked her to dance slow with him to the record they loved, and they did, and some sadness filled her. Trish was nowhere to be seen.

Noelle turned down Trish's flat and didn't see her for a long time. Then a year ago, they bumped into each other in the city centre. Both of them were waiting in the same place, for friends who hadn't turned up. Trish was wearing a wine duffel coat that was a little too tight. Her bony wrists stuck out from the sleeves. She suggested they go for a cup of coffee. Noelle couldn't make an excuse and say she was busy; Trish knew she had nothing else to do.

Over coffee they chatted. Noelle blathered what she thought sounded right, and Trish spoke intensely, and so softly Noelle had to lean towards her and cup her hand behind her ear. She wanted to be nice. She felt obliged to do the right thing. So she gave Trish her phone number, and got up.

Trish said, 'Oh, what way are you going?' and then, quickly, 'I'll come a bit with you.' At the park, Noelle noticed Trish was veering in the wrong direction, and took advantage.

'I'd better dash home. It's been great to see you.' Then, feeling like she couldn't push her luck, though later that wouldn't make any sense, because what she did was pushing it, wasn't it?: 'Do give me a ring sometime.'

Logical reasons.

Obligation. A sense of duty. Social conscience, even.

Noelle left her at the gate of the park in her too-tight duffel coat and sallow, marked skin. She walked, fast, a hundred yards or so, and then, once she was sure she was out of sight, relaxed and sauntered home, stopping at a market-stall to buy a bunch of carnations for her flatmate.

Trish started ringing her up, to talk, to arrange to meet. Noelle didn't know why, she told her flatmate. She couldn't see what she could offer her. The last time Trish rang they arranged to meet at three. Noelle arrived late. I got held up, she was planning to say.

Trish was sitting at a table, holding a cigarette. Her chin was resting on her hand. Her mouth was lipsticked, frosted pink. Noelle rushed up, as if she'd been running all the way, and said: 'Oh, you poor thing, I'm so sorry. Can I get you a cup of coffee?' Trish looked up with her round eyes that were like the brother's, though not the same colour, and smiled. 'Yes, thanks. That would be lovely.'

Noelle bought two decaffs, because they'd talked about caffeine the time before, and how important it was to eat healthily. She sat at the table and made more excuses, and Trish told her to calm down. Noelle thought: she's not resentful or angry or upset, that's good. She feels we have an equal relationship, even better. Good and better, because they hadn't, and Noelle knew that, and didn't want to know.

They talked about the rainforests, and unleaded petrol, and music, and their own plans, and the New Hippies, and the brother, a little, and socialism and hairspray. Then they talked about waste and evil, and love and good, and God and spirits and devils. And Trish lowered her voice and spoke of a presence on her chest one night and the fear she'd had in herself against it.

After the decaffs, they wandered around town, looking in store windows and second-hand clothes shops. Black lace, hats, satin and costume jewellery. In one shop they saw a heap of necklaces in a little glass bowl. The necklaces were all sorts, dull black wooden beads, shiny plastic geometrics, cut stones and glass beads in artists' colours: aquamarine, sienna, emerald. Noelle played with some turquoises on a gold chain, and Trish picked up a string of purple stones and held them against her duffel. The insides of the stones glowed pale pink against the wine coat. These are my favourite, she said. I love purple. The girl behind the desk made a small sound with her small nose and scratched her neck with her red fingernails. Trish swept a glance at her, and she was sixteen again, disdainful queen of the schoolyard. She dropped the purple chain back on the pile, letting her hand lie there for a moment.

They walked around some more. It was good, window-shopping, looking at things. Beautiful, isn't it? See that. Attention drifting, saving them from the twin awkwardnesses of silence and conversation.

Noelle left her to go to a party, held by people she didn't know well. Well enough to get drunk with, though, and argue with, and hug comfortably and mean it when they added to their goodbyes a Hope to see you more often in future. Noelle had hugged Trish too.

When she got home, she lay awake on her bedroom floor, still a bit pissed, for a couple of hours. Alone, thinking of Trish and the brother. Of the wooden hug she'd given Trish when they'd parted and not really wanting her to phone like she'd said she would. Wondering if it was the brother she wanted to come back, or just the her he used to like playing with.

She remembers. She is meeting a friend in town. She hasn't planned what she will wear. She doesn't plan anymore. She doesn't trust her judgement. Someone says: You look good in red, Trish, wear something red, and she wears red for a week. Everything red, down to her pants; all shades of red, abrasive, clashing, clinging red. She lets her mother buy her clothes, but with her own money, which she earns herself, from the temping. And her mother buys for a version of Trish that is too young, the twelve-year old she was before she started putting gloss on her lips and a razor to her legs. That's where the too-tight wine duffel coat came from.

She stands in front of a speckled mirror and pulls at the strands of nearly dry hair. She drags a nylon knitted jumper over her head. It's white. Stitched vertical columns line her chest. Her shoulders look bony underneath. White will do that. It's a bitch for showing up your flaws. Her skin looks yellow. She takes out her stretch denims. They fit except for the knees, which sag a little. She takes out a pair of socks. It becomes one sock in her hand. She frowns.

There were two socks. She always rolls her socks into pairs. She loses them otherwise and then her feet get cold. She had another white sock like this one, a little girl Holy Communion knee-sock with fancy stitching like a paper doily in a cake shop. Her mother got it for her. Them. She can't go out with just one. Must be somewhere. Maybe she'll find it when she eats her pills.

That night, after the coffees and the party, Noelle lay awake, still drunk, drowsing. And while she drowsed, she heard some voice come at her like a knife sliding through her skin, moving upwards along her legs, through her crotch and up her torso, until it reached her neck. It was as if it was travelling inside her body, but she couldn't feel it in any particular location. She thought of a devil and her head jerked awake, and all she could hear in the dark was her own breath. The luminous hands on her bedside clock said five.

Trish had told her lots of things between their silences over the black lace shawls, old hats and ornate rosary beads. She had been sick, she'd said. Her confidence was shattered. A man had loved and left her. She found it difficult to get up in the morning. She was taking pills. Her memory was going. Everything was bigger and brighter and vaguer and more and always more than before. When she felt down, she could kill herself, but then she was too down to do even that. She told Noelle those things, mundane horrors that don't mean anything really, except to the person who's experiencing them. A guilt in Noelle, a duty, sympathised. She wished it had been more than that. She felt sad for Trish and for what she'd been. So she put her arm around her while Trish told her about the entities coming at her in the night, during the day. Claws tearing at her from inside, baby demons scratching for birth, demanding she be mother. They were bad in daylight, but worse at night, when she was alone. She talked of fear, how afraid she'd been, afraid more than anything else of the fear.

Tingles at the end of a spine. Cold air around a neck. Cold feet, and a cold fear of the empty bed in the next room and the hands of the clock not moving.

It would be easy to be logical, and point to her bare purple foot in its pink shoe. To say, That's where the cold is coming from. But she's taken her pills and forgotten her missing sock and her foot could be ice or fire for all she cares. Anyway, the cold comes from some other world and no logic will change that. Always there, even with the duffel wrapped so tight. She turns off the light and walks down the piss-aromatic stairs into the winter.

Somewhere else, a place of perpetual summer, the brother is walking too, along an orange road. A truck with soldiers passes him, raising dust that stings his eyes. They might give him a lift. The sun might set over the mountain. He might be dead. So what. He's gone. A panorama. A strain of music.

Here, in Noelle's snug flat, Chubb-locked against the night, it's cold too. Because, logically, it's coming up to year's end. Decade's end, actually, and Noelle's got to go out. Places to visit, people to see, appointments to miss. The devil that once-envied Beatrice fears in the night, clawing at her chest covered in skin like the brother's, is waiting.

Standing at a frosty bus stop beside a vandalised phone box, remembering.

Polyfilla

The party had been thrown by a woman he'd met in college and who now worked in publishing. They'd kept in contact over the years; Seán had done a few jobs for her, she'd regularly plugged his business and, eighteen months ago, she'd drafted him in to oversee the renovations of her new house. She and her telly executive husband were childless and famous for hosting lavish dinner parties. Although Seán had been to a lot of them, he'd never met more than a sprinkling of the same people twice. He wondered if his hosts did this deliberately, blending their guests like paint colours, trying out different combinations until they hit the perfect mix. Maybe the choice was arbitrary, down to who was available and who had the flu. Up to now, it hadn't bothered him. He'd enjoyed them, the drink and the food and the mingling with whoever he happened to meet.

Tonight, though, was different. He'd felt it in his bones the minute he walked in. For a second he wished Lola had come, to buffer with her chitchat and smiles whatever discomfort was heading his way. Then he remembered, and the wish was gone.

He wasn't sure when he first noticed the woman in the blue dress. It must have been soon after he arrived. An ice-sweaty glass cooling the raging heart of his right palm. Bubbles of conversation rising around him, made meaningless by the thick membrane of his jangling nerves. His hostess dropping bits of him like breadcrumbs across the room as she ferried him through the crowd. He caught a glimpse of something in a corner – a swirling blue dress, a sparkling butterfly perched on a mane of red hair, a young bell-like laugh – and his hostess, reading the twitch under his skin, steered him in that direction.

'Seán,' she said, 'let me introduce you to Poppet.'

Poppet. Christ, what a stupid name. Though maybe...

Her dress was made of some floaty stuff that seemed to change colour under the lights; one minute the virulent cobalt of grotto Virgins, the next the soft turquoise of the Greek sea. It reminded him of the things Lola used to put on, in the early days when she was shy and sweet, before he'd got his hands on her. This woman was wearing costume jewellery, the sort that would suit a girl: bangles, beads, long silver earrings that brushed the white skin of her shoulders. Then she turned her head and Seán's maybes soured in a wash of irritation. Crows' feet. Flabby upper arms. Polyfilla make-up. Late forties, if she was a day.

'Seán's our architect, Poppet,' said his hostess, pressing her fingers into his upper arm. 'Very artistic. The two of you will get on like a house on fire.' She winked at Seán, released him and left.

A moment of awkwardness. The woman smiled. Then, at the same time, they both began speaking.

'Sorry,' said Seán, waving his glass. 'Go on.'

She laughed. 'Oh, nothing, just… You're an architect?'

Seán swished his whiskey, longing for the satisfying clink of contact: ice on ice. 'Mmm.'

'Wow.' Her lips curled, blow-job soft around an invisible straw. She had drawn a line around the upper one to make it look fuller. 'I used to be a dancer.'

'Oh.' He wondered if he should make his boredom more obvious, let his eyes roam over the room, yawn, pretend to check for texts. Maybe he should go the courteous route; offer to get her a refill and never come back.

'Aren't you going to ask me my real name?'

She was gazing at him, intent. Her eyebrows were drawn-on, manufactured like the rest of her face.

'Most people do,' she said. 'They don't like to think of a grown woman being called Poppet. They think it's silly.'

'Oh, I…'

'Sometimes they even throw names at me. Right in the middle of a conversation. Like a, you know, ambush.'

'Really?' His curiosity surprised him. 'What kind of names?'

She smiled. 'Why don't I leave that to your imagination?'

His own mouth, he realised, had begun to curve in a smile; his pirate's grin, Lola used to call it. He swished his drink again, brought it to his lips.

'Hey, Josephine—' he said suddenly.

The moment suspended between them. She laughed. 'Nice try.'

'Not Josephine then?'

She shook her head.

'How about… Phyllis?'

Her clumpy lashes flickered.

'No. I've got it. Bridget. Bridget.'

She laughed again. Her earrings tinkled. The skin of her shoulders was very white. Still laughing, she let her hands flutter up to pat her hair, as if it was a live animal she had enticed onto her head in the belief that it would be safe there.

He grabbed a refill from the tray and swallowed. Poppet had started to chatter away, punctuating her words with sideways glances, mischievous grins, dramatic twists of her fine-boned wrists. Half-listening, he smiled, laughed, making the right murmurings at the right time.

Everything about her was in motion. Her neck was full of little creases that opened and closed as she spoke. Her cleavage quivered, sand-dunes shifting in a sea of blue frills. She kept flicking her hair, touching it. Its bottle-red jarred with the changing colours of her dress, playing tricks on Seán's eyes, making the space around her shudder. When she lifted her hands, the flesh on her upper arms wobbled. Seán imagined how it would feel, that flesh. Soft and melting as a blancmange. He imagined touching it, gentle at first, then rough, grabbing and pinching and twisting so hard that in the morning she would find bruises. She moved and panic overwhelmed him. Was she leaving? She moved back. He grabbed another drink.

A bell sounded.

Dinner.

They'd been placed several seats from each other; too far away to continue talking. Maybe, thought Seán, his head already mushing from the drink, that wasn't such a bad thing. Yet every so often he would find himself glancing over at Poppet, or feel the weight of her glance on him and, if their eyes met, would catch himself smiling before looking away, as if he had just caught sight of an old, distant acquaintance on a busy street.

The food was excellent, as it always was, accompanied by a constant flow of talk. Seán listened to himself explaining cantilevers to a budding fashion designer and wondered if anybody had brought cocaine.

Dessert arrived. Chocolate tart and a sweet yellow wine from France. Seán left most of the tart on his plate. He was pouring out his second glass of dessert wine when he became aware of a change in the room's temperature. The stream of talk had begun to falter, breaking into lesser tributaries around an intense group on the other side of the table. Poppet's laugh faded. Seán caught sighs, murmurs, a sorrowful shaking of heads. Someone had raised a serious topic.

'No, no, no!' said a thin bald man at the centre of the intense group. His voice was loud, heavy with authority. Seán remembered being introduced to him earlier. A cancer specialist from the Blackrock Clinic. The last few bits of talk hushed.

'Of course, it's an awful mess. Inhumane. But we shouldn't think about it in simplistic terms. If we go back to Isaiah Berlin…'

The budding fashion designer was nodding. Seán dropped his mouth to her ear. 'What's he talking about?'

'Iraq.'

A grinding pain begin to throb in Seán's lower jaw.

'With hindsight' – the specialist was getting into his stride – 'it's very easy to be judgmental. But we have to remember it was an extraordinarily complicated issue at the time.'

Somebody laughed and Seán realised it was him. 'Complicated?'

The specialist glanced over.

'There was nothing remotely complicated about it.' Seán's voice seemed very far away; at the same time, louder than he'd intended. 'It's obvious the invasion was driven by economics. I mean, just look at—'

Murmurs began at the far end of the table.

The specialist lifted his hand. 'No, that's not what I—'

'Look at the figures. Take the death rates.'

'That's not what I—'

'Incredible. We call ourselves a civilised society. What kind of civilised society murders eighty-five thousand—'

Seán observed himself, as if from a height. He was leaning forward, teeth bared, index finger jabbing, statistics bulleting out from his tongue. Aggressive ape behaviour, Lola called it. The specialist was shaking his head, trying to interrupt. *That's not what I'm saying. No. no, no. That's not—* Two dots of red had begun to glow painfully on his cheeks.

Morality, Seán was saying, his voice resonant with indignation. Double standards. Greed, capitalism, cynicism. Blah blah fucking blah.

Shut him up someone, please—

'Excuse me,' said a third voice, loud.

The specialist, now cowering, hands spread in defeat, glanced at the doorway. Seán took the time to finish what he was saying, then looked over. The man who'd interrupted them was leaning against the architrave. There was something boneless about the way he stood there, as if he'd been flung at the wall like a piece of pasta thrown by a chef to check if it had been cooked enough. He had an expensive haircut and was wearing a Boss suit over an open-necked white shirt. Silver glimmered at his wrist.

Seán leaned back in his chair, eyeballing him. 'Yeah?'

'Well. See… What I was wondering…' The man's voice was slurred, messy, at odds with his expensive appearance.

Seán sighed, reached for his glass. The table's attention began to drift.

'What I was wondering was,' said the man, louder and clearer, 'was if you've actually met any Iraqis?'

Seán's hand stopped.

'Yourself, I mean. Personally. It's just you seem to know so much about it.' The man at the doorway slitted his eyes. They glittered at Seán, vicious little raindrops in a slack face. His mouth was a shark's; a thin-lipped triangle stained black from wine.

'All those numbers you keep saying. Very impressive. But you don't mind me…' He waved his hand. 'Asking where you got them from?'

Glasses clinked. Somebody laughed.

'Wouldn't be the internet, would it?'

Seán swallowed his wine.

The shark's mouth smiled. 'I knew it.'

Everything in the room sharpened.

Keep the head.

'I don't know,' said Seán carefully, 'what exactly your problem is—'

The suit laughed. *'My* problem?'

Voices rose; some aimed at the suit, some at Seán, others trying to resuscitate safer threads of conversation.

'Leave it, Seán. He's had too much to—'

'Let's just—'

'Has anybody seen the latest—'

'You're the one with the fucking problem!' shouted the man at the door. 'You're the sort of liberal shit thinks we should sit on our arses and do nothing. Fuck Rwanda, fuck the Iraqis. You know how many people died in—'

'Oh yeah?' shouted Seán. 'As opposed to—'

And they were off.

A dim part of him wanted to stop, but he couldn't. They had armed themselves, cherry-picking atrocities from opposing arsenals, and there was no easy way out. Rwanda. Bosnia. Mugabe. Hitler. Pakistan. Belfast. Kabul. No point having weapons if you don't use them. Their words flew, landed, exploded, maimed. Seán felt the back of his neck sear red, saw flakes of spit collect on his opponent's lips. Once or twice, their host, perched near the kitchen door, tried to intervene, but they ignored him, blinded to everything but the need to bully the other into submission, obliterate, prove *I am right, listen to me.*

In the distance, the silence of the other guests crystallised around the peaks of their conflict like a frozen lake.

'Okay,' said the hostess, standing. 'Brandy.'

They eyed each other. Seán's breath was ragged. The other man's eyes had become glazed. They could probably have taken it further but...

The suit slumped back against the door, spaghetti-soft again. Seán's shoulders drooped.

Truce. Nil all.

The hostess smiled a tight smile and laid the cognac on the table.

'Well,' said the host, 'that was lively.'

Timid attempts at conversation began to blossom. Seán sipped his brandy and let his gaze drift around the table. His eyes landed on Poppet. During the argument he had forgotten her. She had vanished, ice melting in hot water. Now she seemed all too visible, her imperfections stark in the candlelight, her garish colours hurting his eyes. He wondered how he could have ever found her, even momentarily, attractive. She was gazing at her plate, her finger chasing a last piece of chocolate around the gold rim. She looked up, catching him.

The unexpected force of her hate struck matches on his skin. Sickened, he looked away. His glass was empty.

An hour later, the party broke up, the night's mix too flimsy to survive the brutality of the argument. The guests made their apologies, shuffled into their coats and left in their cars, swooping down the driveway like participants at a secret wartime conference, their headlamps sweeping long beams of diamond-paned light across the dining-room wallpaper. The man in the Boss suit had been one of the first to go. Seán had stayed till the end.

He began to make his way to the door, his car keys flopping through his fingers like seaweed.

'Oh Seán, you're not driving,' said his hostess.

He turned and the room turned with him. 'I'm fine,' he tried to say.

'No, you're not.'

She was adamant. He had to call a cab. Eventually he agreed, sinking back into the leather sofa and letting her make the call because he couldn't get his fingers to push the right buttons on his mobile; couldn't get his mouth to form any sound except a grunt. The drink had soldered his jaws. His tongue was flapping around his mouth like a beached fish; disconnected, severed from its root.

His hostess put down her phone, made her way to the sofa.

'I'm so sorry, Seán, but they're booked solid for the next two hours. Can you believe it?'

He nodded blearily. 'Fucking country we live in.'

Through the blear he saw the other guests – the ones who'd had the foresight to book their cabs in advance – look on, smirking.

'Fucking country—' he said, louder.

'Maybe you could stay here?' suggested his hostess. There was a pained look in her eyes.

'Yes, do,' said the host. He didn't look quite so pained yet...

'No,' mumbled Seán, having sense enough left to do the decent thing. 'I'll hail one down on the street.'

Outside it was cold and murky, no moon. The air was blowing chilling little gusts up under Seán's lightweight mac, a bad choice he'd made earlier, deceived by the evening's golden sunlight.

He staggered down the driveway. Objects jerked into sharp focus, melted into a fuzz.

The footpath was a cold light blue, the colour of Picasso's dejected Harlequins. Wavering through the gate, Seán stumbled over a loose brick, straightened up, stumbled again. In the corner of his eye he saw his car, long and white and useless. He thought of going over to pat its bonnet goodbye – or maybe even crawl in and sleep there till dawn – but sense arrived again, a delayed, incomplete cavalry. He had a home to go to. Lola would be waiting.

He had been walking for about five minutes when he first heard it. An odd clacking sound, coming from – his ears found it, lost it, found it again. Ahead of him? Something wooden. Some wooden thing in motion, hitting off the ground. Disjointed, uneven, reminding him of something.

A children's story book, a—

Blind Pew from *Treasure Island*.

He stopped. The sound did too. He glanced behind. Involuntary. Stupid. Nothing. He let his eyes drift across the road, take in the empty tarmac, gaping driveways, sparse streetlamps. He could hear his own breath. Taste it too. Sour. He forced himself to squint up the road. The path was drowned in shadows, cast by a dense bank of beech trees overhanging a rotten granite wall.

Nothing there either.

He took a step.

click CLACK

The streetlamps under the beeches blurred, icy in their basketwork haloes.

Another step.

click—

Something was moving, under the trees. A smudge of black against the lighter black of the wall.

Seán stopped again. Silence ballooned into the night. His nose was full of the stink of his sweat, sharp and mushroomy. Maybe, he thought, I should turn around.

Yes. He could turn now, go back down the road to his hosts' comfortable house and their equally comfortable sofa and lie down and sleep the drink off and leave in the morning, after honourably refusing coffee and toast and marmalade, and battle through the traffic and get back in one piece and—

His hostess' pained face resurfaced in his memory.

Maybe not.

He tried to gather his thoughts. It was only a matter of minutes till he reached the main junction and then, Christ, surely he'd be able to hail a cab. Once he walked slowly enough, there'd be no danger of catching up with whatever was in front of him.

*What*ever?

Whoever. Jesus. What class of gom was he, jumping at shadows?

He started again, walking as slowly as possible, trying to ignore the clacking, the fucking clacking that had started up again when he did, the fact that it had slowed too, that with each step he took, it sounded nearer, like it was taunting him. His eyes strained. There, only a few yards ahead. The smudge, moving through the shadows. He still couldn't make out details. It looked like one mass of black, no limbs. Maybe it was wearing a cloak.

A cloak? Who would—

A sliver of light knifed through the branches, glinting at the place where the head should have been.

Seán froze. The thing mirrored him. Now there was only a couple of yards between them.

Seán's breath quickened. The thing began to turn, disengaging itself from the shadows. He could make out a grey oval – a face, thank God, a head after all—

Then a flash. A white hand, reaching for him. Seán jerked back.

His foot lost contact with the pavement, his spine whiplashed. Flailing, he crashed to the ground. His arse smashed into the gutter, landing him on a pile of sodden leaves. He groaned. His ankle throbbed.

Broken? Christ.

He looked up. The figure in the cloak was standing above him, silhouetted against the streetlight. Seán twisted, tried to scrabble away. Useless. Pain shot through his leg. He sank back, whimpering

The figure stepped back and tilted its head to the light. A pale face emerged, the same colour as the moon. A hand lifted, making an abrupt, almost absent-minded movement, as if it was stroking a small household pet that had got trapped on its head.

'Cat got your tongue?' said Poppet, and laughed.

Even afterwards, he couldn't tell whether she'd meant it as a joke.

She sighed, her sparkly veil slipping over her head as she bent forwards and lifted one foot off the ground. For a moment Seán thought that she was going to step over him, hike up her skirt and piss on his face.

Instead, she gripped her ankle and drew off her shoe. Her balance was perfect, the supporting calf strong, bunched with muscles. Cogs in Seán's memory whirred. *I used to be a dancer.*

She dropped her foot, held up her shoe. It had ankle straps and a stiletto heel, and under the dull lamplight was some dark colour that looked black. She pushed at the heel. It gave way, bending inwards at a painful angle.

Blind Pew equals broken shoe.

He giggled.

Hissing, she dropped the shoe. Seán twisted his head. The fractured stiletto sped past his ear, landing spike down in the gutter. Seán's nose filled with snot.

Poppet stepped forward. Her feet, inches from his eyes, looked like something from a macabre fairytale. The bare one was arched, her weight pushed onto her toes. The nails had been painted; the same noxious indigo as her shoes. The muscles in her leg twitched, rippling darts of black through her bone-white skin.

'You remind me of my husband.' Her voice was light in the cold air. 'I didn't see the resemblance at first. Did I tell you I once had a husband?'

Seán said nothing.

'Did I?' Her voice had hardened.

Seán looked up and gazed at the top of her head. Her shod foot lashed out, landing in his ribs. He grunted.

She laughed. 'No. I don't suppose I did. Then again, you didn't give me the chance.'

Her voice was chisel-sharp now, soiled with the same bitterness that had marred Lola's in the early days, before she'd learnt sense. 'I lived with him for twenty years, you see.'

Oh God, thought Seán. Now it's all coming out.

'He used to hit me.' She grabbed a curtain of her hair and pulled it away from her forehead, lifting her face to the light. 'See.'

Seán wasn't sure what he was supposed to be seeing. A tiny fault line where her nose had been broken? A slight wander in her left eye? A chipped front tooth? From where he was lying, she looked intact.

She twisted her neck, pointed to her left temple. 'There. That's where he used the glass.'

Seán saw cracks in polyfilla. Marks he'd half-glimpsed earlier through strands of hair; craters and bumps he'd taken for the leftovers of acne.

'I was always fast on my feet but the dancing wasn't much good to me when he got into his moods.' She smiled. The black lips stretched. The cracks widened. 'Maybe I should have learnt to box instead.'

Seán shifted his weight onto his other elbow. 'Look.' His teeth had begun to chatter. 'I don't want to – but – my ankle is—'

'You name it, I did it.' Her voice was light again. 'Black glasses. Headscarves. High-necked jumpers. Long sleeves. Excuses. I had them all. Walls, stairs, doors. Clumsy Poppet. Silly Poppet. Awkward Poppet. Poor Poppet.'

'Look, Poppet, I need to get to—'

Her foot lashed out again, the stiletto connecting with his breastbone. Seán crumpled back, retching.

'I knew what you thought, the minute you saw me. Look at the silly bitch. Who does she think she is, the auld eejit, going overboard with the hippy dresses, pushing fifty if she's a day. She's not fooling herself, is she? That she's got a second chance, the stupid—'

The stiletto jabbed again. Seán curved away. Her foot hit air. He grabbed it by the arch. It tensed under his grip, racehorse-strong.

'Let go.' She pulled. Seán, nauseous, clung on. 'Let me go, you prick.'

Her face was grotesque, eyes and mouth black holes in a Scream mask.

'I need a doctor.' Sean's words were coming out in clumps. Cold racing up and down his body. His mouth full of salt. 'I need to get help—'

Her held foot jerked, trying to shake him off. He gripped tighter, his other hand reaching for her ankle. She pushed back on her heel, shook again. The motion rattled through him, snapping his neck back. He released her. She tottered. The stiletto waved, an inch from his face. If she lost her balance, she'd send the fucking thing into his eye.

The sinews in her standing leg strained. The hem of her dress billowed, revealing the white shapes of her thighs, a flash of darkness. Energy surged through Seán, hardening his cock. He glanced down. Instinctive. The erection was pushing at the fabric of his trousers, tent-pole obvious. He heard a laugh. Poppet, her shod foot still raised, had stopped tottering. She was staring at his crotch. Cracks all over her face now, raking down the sides of her nose, digging trenches across her forehead, hatching fault-lines around her lips.

She lifted her eyes to his. Her smile faded.

And then, with infinite slowness, her eyes locked on his, Poppet began to move. The movement was so small Seán couldn't tell where it had started. A torquing somewhere in her hips, a curling of her raised foot, a slow bend of her knee. *Plié, first position.* Controlled, focused, her legs flickering marble as she lowered her spiked heel, letting it float towards his erection.

The tip of her heel brushed his zip. Seán made a small ragged sound.

The stiletto moved down, still light, tracing the length of his cock until it came to a rest on the ridge between his balls.

Their breathing was harsh. Little white puffs of air. Their chests moved. Up, down. Up, down.

The stiletto quivered. One jab, thought Seán. One jab and—

She lifted her foot and flicked it away.

Bile filled Seán's mouth. His erection collapsed. He twisted onto his side and retched. The sound tore into the silence, ripping it like soggy paper.

When he turned back, wiping his mouth, she was already hobbling away, a peg-legged ballerina sinking into the darkness. *Pad click pad click.* A few yards on he thought he saw her stop and bend. Then she continued, noiseless.

She disappeared.

Seán leaned over and puked into the gutter again, just missing her abandoned shoe.

He was woken by the growl of an engine and a blast of searing sunlight. A car, approaching. Groaning, he tried to push his torso up off the ground. Pain shot through him. He gritted his teeth and tried to call.

'Stop, please, help…'

His arm waved feebly.

The car stopped. A cab. Seán sank back and watched two feet shod in dirty grey runners walk towards him. Denim legs bent. A stubbled face with red-rimmed eyes peered at him. 'Jesus, pal. You been in the wars.'

Seán caught the smell of a mouth that had been awake all night.

'I've broken my – can you – I've got…' Weakly, he patted his coat pocket.

'Okay, no probs.'

Two hands wrapped themselves around his torso, lifted him, and he screamed.

'It's alright, pal. I'm not far.'

The world bounced past, red with pain. A car door opened. The hands slid him inside.

'There you go.'

The front door opened, slammed. The key turned in the ignition.

'Vincent's Hospital alright? It's the nearest.'

Seán nodded, his face pressed against the cool glass of the window.

As they pulled away, something on the ground caught Seán's eye. Standing upright in the gutter, Poppet's shoe. In the daylight it was red. He couldn't see the cracked heel. The cab swerved around a corner, and the shoe vanished.

A sprain, they said in the hospital, after making him wait for five hours. A few days' rest and you'll be right as rain.

When he got home, clinging to his crutch, Lola was sitting in the chrome and marble kitchen he had built for her, sipping coffee and leafing through the *Weekend* magazine.

He leant against the door and watched her. Shame crept red fingers up his throat.

'I'm sorry,' he said at last. 'I didn't mean…'

Lola sighed.

'Jesus,' he said. He hobbled towards her and dropped onto his good knee, ignoring his screaming ankle.

'Stop,' she said.

His head paused, an inch from her lap. He could smell her scent: coffee and Chanel.

'I'm sorry,' he said again. 'I never—'

She sighed again, silencing him. Her hand lifted.

Polyfilla

He closed his eyes, longing for contact. In the blackness he saw steam rise from her coffee cup, draw circles in the air, reflect silver on the dark Jackie O glasses that she always wore to cover the cracked and bleeding traces of their bond from the unseeing, meddlesome eyes of strangers.

Found Wanting

I dreamt of him again last night. Johnny O. Slick and lean as a piece of liquorice, black hair scooped up either side of his head like the plastic coiffure of a replica Elvis. I know that image is old now, outworn, maybe even dead, replaced by— What? A paunch, receding hairline, two kids, a four-by-four, a semi-d in Clondalkin (if he's lucky), some job I can't even conceive? But still.

I am wondering if I'll tell Carmel.

I first saw him, like the song goes, on Grafton Street in November. A cold mist up. The air just hanging there, waiting for the Christmas shoppers to break through it with their manic, unthinking urgency. He was at the Stephen's Green end of the street, dressed in a long black leather coat, doing nothing. I, on my way to meet Mark, thinking I was late, as I always was back then, touched his arm – 'Excuse me' – to ask the time. He turned, sweeping open a window in my reality, and I fell through.

Do I believe in love? I hate that question. I believe there are all kinds of love, but none, not even motherlove – and I know that one, intimately – means you get something for nothing. The messiest kind, with all it entails, jealousy and insecurity and so forth, is nothing but hurt; falling in it just an all-too common chemical high, Nature's sugar pill for genetic coding's cruel triggering of the replicate-slash-nurture button.

Yet.

See me, as he saw me, on that winter corner. Shaking like a schoolgirl, ice down my front, forehead to crotch, insides sloshing petrol, yearning for a match.

A long blonde rushed up, swung him away from me before he could reply, grabbing his arm with easy familiarity, covered him with kisses.

A long blonde rushed him away from me, extracting kisses before he could protest; loosening his arm with easy familiarity, swung off.

Mine.

I'll remember that, vivid, under my skin.

Sometimes it's hard to name what you feel. The rest of the day lay on me heavy and formless, lead cottonwool sucking moisture from my lungs. But that night I dreamt of him. I woke, craving, and there it was, as Francis Bacon used to say. Something had slipped sideways, setting me on a course. Sounds simple, but oh, its working was a worm in my code.

Dublin is a small town, was even smaller then. Inside its Viking walls, everyone is connected. I had many friends at that time – physical friends, not virtual ones, the type whose fears and evasions you smell in the moment, whose shame you sense prickling on your own skin, whose spoken utterings you pity for their unedited gaucheness, whose breasts you hug yourself into at times of need. I had lots of them, dear ones, in that late twentysomething way when you think you'll be friends for life because oh, they're so special, and because you're all immortal anyway, when you think that's what you need, friends and more friends, when you think that's all that matters. I was careful, I remember. Not too direct. I didn't approach everyone. I cherry-picked the nodes on the network, found different tangents in, feeding them lies and excuses while I drilled them for information. Though drilled, like lies, attributes too much consciousness to what I was doing. I would start off asking one thing: *you know that movie Mark said he saw when I was away…* But on the *Mark*, he would spark up in my mind, the guy from Grafton Street, and the question would become something else: *you know that blonde…*

I was tracking him, I realised. I can't deny the rush that gave me, the clean line it seemed to carve through everything that was going on.

Bit by bit, I felt him clarify. His name, his job. The O, apparently, was some sort of joke. He was English.

The music business bothered me, I admit. I should have known, what had I expected – the coat, that swagger – oh, fuck, oh dear. I'd slept with enough musos in my day to know it wasn't always what it said on the tin. All great from the mosh-pit, then you get them into the sack and it's selfish this or spaced-out that, or doling it out on brute speed-dial, as if force and vigour alone is proof of something, anything, everything.

Thinking (I bet): Groupie. Thinking (I bet): Take it, Slut.

Did that, I asked myself, have to be a problem?

I started getting impatient. I didn't want to hear any more details about his life. They felt banal, irritating, a distraction. Enough talk. I needed to make our paths cross. I thought it would be easy; the scene was tight in those days, like it probably still is. Selecting three from my circle – a college pal, a mate from work and Carmel, practical Carmel, who'd been my friend since we were tots – I began to frequent his haunts. I didn't let on what I was after. In the safety of numbers, I earwigged on his mates, mapped his movements.

Oh, that crooked smelly finger. Eat the apple, my dear.

On my way home from work I began taking detours, wandering coyly off the path. Like Red Riding Hood, I fancied, swinging a leash. I'd stop into aulfella pubs and sandwich bars or the new music centre where I'd sip a warming pint for a couple of hours, flicking through *Q* and *Wired*, pretending to be someone from A&R.

A certain desperation took hold of me. I realised I was thinking his name on repeat, as if trying to groove it into my cortex: Johnny, Johnny, Johnny. I began imagining him in the bed beside me, the far side from Mark. He became the blanket I'd sucked on as a kid, but soilier. In the theatre of my mind, we started acting out the big roles. I held him, kissed him, felt him naked on me, in me, around me, all that. And yes, though it's nobody's business, I began fooling around with myself to him too.

I cringe to recall this. I am mortified. It is pathetic, this thing. They say it's our animal selves. Give me a break. Animals, at least, have dignity.

The rush turned acid, ate at my stomach lining. I started to look like shit. The thought struck me that I was grieving. I struck it back, the useless thought, and found myself opening up to friends. Lorraine first, the pal from college, who'd done computer science before switching to marketing because that's where all the fun was. Ooh, she said, a wee crush? So that's why… How exciting. He sounds. Mmm. I know exactly how you feel, did I tell you about—

Then Carmel.

Christ, she said.

What was I doing? she said. I had a good thing going. I was happy in my relationship. Wasn't I? She looked a bit upset, the line that showed she cared ridging her forehead. Some people would give their eye teeth, she said. Mark was great, a great guy, what we had was great. We'd been together ages. Why spoil it? She paused, and I knew she was going to invoke Princess Di, who was everywhere then, with her head-tilting heartfelt confessions on BBC2, and Camilla, the ghostly wrecker sliming uninvited between herself and Chuck in the royal four-poster.

Go on, I thought. Say it.

'For Christ's sake,' she said, 'you don't even know him.'

I felt my face gurn like a five year old's, my fists clench.

I know, I could have said. That's the fucking point, Carmel.

That week, Mark had gone away to Brighton, to another Internet conference. Back then, people still spoke of the Internet in capital letters, and dotcoms were only twinkles in their begetters' imaginations. Along with Di's *Panorama*l confessions, digital superhighways were all the rage. To the rest of the world, Mark was hot. And to me?

Ah, please.

This, too, I find difficult. Even now, I can't pinpoint when it started, the erosion between us. I know it wasn't overnight. Becoming unimportant to someone, growing out of love – or whatever people call love to justify their commitment to each other – is slow and painless. Like being numbed to death. Everything's fine, it's always fine. Then one morning you discover you've been waking up on separate sides of the fence and the fence is so fucking high you wonder how you both scaled it in the first place.

I could go deeper. I probably should.

I could talk about childhood, his or mine, or our respective parents and their respectively fucked-up relationships, or our history as a couple, the arguments about my dad's money, the rushing into it straight after college, or even the man on the beach who let me feel his penis when I was three. I could rest longer on that word, *let*. I could talk about the things I should or shouldn't have done in my teenage years, the things I should or shouldn't have told Mark. But come on. It's simple. Mark was great, I was being a shit. Let's leave it there.

In the end, know this: it was Carmel's doing.

She called me up on the Tuesday, suggested we go out. We hadn't been on the tear on a week night in ages, just the two of us. I agreed and we scrambled into town in her little Fiat, honking wannabe wide boys out of the way.

It had been two months since Grafton Street. I was tense, wound-up. Carmel didn't seem to notice. Crossing Rathmines Bridge, I thought – desperate, yes – of suggesting one of Johnny's hangouts, see if I could steer us there without her copping. Then I caught her looking at me, just a flash, worried like she knew, and the whole thing seemed futile suddenly, silly. We ended up not being able to get parking in the usual spots, so we settled for a cheap tiles-and-piss pub on the quays. Well, said Carmel brightly. Pints on you. I looked around the squalid cell-like walls and although I knew she hadn't chosen this place on purpose – how could she? – my sense of futility deepened. Was this how it was going to end: in a grim sentencing chamber, with my best friend playing executioner?

I could already hear her words: Grow up, wise up, give up.

Can I blame her? I'd obviously become extremely boring by then. That usually goes with this territory.

I could feel what she was going to say. Perhaps, somewhere, I knew I'd asked for it, but I didn't want to make it easy for her. So I started bitching. Work first: my boss, the new girl. Carmel didn't seem to mind, welcomed it, in fact. Two drinks down, Smithwicks and pub crisps, we'd got quite relaxed, and because that felt better, after all the tension, I started bitching about Lorraine too. How flighty she was, how immature, what a gabber. And a bit thick. I mean, who would move from programming to marketing for *fun*? The problem with Lorraine, I said, and even Mark knew this, though he was too nice to say it, them being so tight in the old days, such good friends before I'd got to know her, was you could tell her something and think it was in complete confidence, but then she'd splurt it out to someone, anyone, and not even realise. She *was* thick, wasn't she? No offence, Carm, but she really should be the blonde. Or was I just being mean? Carmel laughed. Both, she said. I shouldn't say this, she said, but I've forgotten how much I love it when you're being mean. Look, she said, leaning in, worried again, and that caring line creased her forehead, and my skin itched, and I knew it was coming. Except then she stopped, her eyes focused beyond my shoulder.

Take note: she was the one who stopped, and let me see.

Johnny had come in, with a group of three. All boys, no blonde.

Wow, said Carmel weakly, and started to laugh.

Wow, I thought.

Isn't it always the way, with reprieve? The one time you don't expect and – wow.

They sat down, two tables away. I sneaked a glance. He was tall, but not as tall as I'd remembered, his face less symmetrical, a crease in his forehead over one eyebrow, a little scar under his right cheekbone. I was suddenly, foolishly, paralysed. See me as Carmel saw me: red as a beet, howlingly aware of hair, clothes, earrings. What age? Take a guess. Fourteen?

Carmel just happened to know one of his friends from her college days, or he knew her, and they struck up a conversation across the tabletops of emptying pint glasses. I concentrated on my Smithwicks. Someone half-shouted in my direction. An English accent. Johnny. He was looking over. His eyes were almost black. Was he interested? I smiled back, tried to make it casual.

We talked for over two hours. I can't remember much of it. He was from southern England, he told me. Kent. His accent was nice, deep brown like his eyes. It had me at a disadvantage. I wasn't sure if I liked that. I hadn't expected that, to be so unsure. He moved closer, saying he couldn't hear, and the edges of his consonants stroked the back of my neck. I thought of pulling away, but then I looked over at Carmel, still flirting with the friend, and stayed. We sat on the mottled greasy leather seating, thighs that distance apart where any closer they'd be touching, and went on with our illusory conversation. Bland synchronicities masquerading as fate: a shared love of the smell of roasting coffee, the taste of Camembert, the sounds of The Pixies. And throughout the silly chat and sudden stops and awkward, lengthening silences, we played the usual games. Pressing closer to share confidences, touching an elbow to make a point, accidentally – oops, sorry! – moving our pint glasses together so we'd have to brush each other's hands when we went to take a sip. Apologies: I say *we*. I have no idea what he was thinking. I mean, of course, *I*.

And Mark, Mark nowhere at the back of my mind.

At one point Johnny said 'Grafton Street'. He'd glanced away, at Carmel – who was laughing with both his mates now, a bit too bright, like she did sometimes, when she was stressed – and he'd spoken low. My thigh retreated. His face shut down. I went to the loo. I should go home, I thought. When I returned I saw he'd bought me another drink. His gaze stuck to me as I slid into the seat. And oh my god, I felt made by it. Never so real.

I recently watched a programme about people who have phobias about dogs and feathers and things. That's how I felt that night – heart, pulse, breath about to burst; an agoraphobic marooned in Kansas.

We found more ways of touching. The weight of his eyes on me made me ill.

We left the pub with the others. A party was supposed to be happening nearby. I pretended to follow. I could see Carmel down the street, turning. He pulled me back, gripping my waist. 'Stay here with me or I'll break your face.' I'm not sure which is more pathetic: him saying that or me with my half-assed outrage already melting, stillborn.

We fucked down an alleyway, like a bad noir. It was cold and the base of my spine ached from friction with the wall. The next day I found a bruise there the size of my fist, which I explained to Mark as an accident during aerobics. It wasn't good at first, no foreplay, too messy, too hurried. He kept slipping out and didn't find it funny. After all the build-up my nerves had turned giddy and I giggled, hard. But even with the awkwardness and panic, the cold and the pain and the stupid schoolgirl titters, there was something: a moment that surprised me, where I felt myself emerge to meet him in a way I hadn't met anyone before. I will not say if I thought of Mark.

He asked if he could see me again. I told him I was married.

'Shame,' he said, shrugging away from me as he buttoned his jeans. He started walking down the alleyway, his silhouette spiky against the oily lights of the traffic.

'No – wait,' I said. 'Johnny?' It was odd speaking his name. Too soon, too intimate; like calling a child, or a vassal.

He paused. I imagined him relishing the moment. The taste of power, the smoke of his cigarette. I hated myself. I pulled my tights up, skirt down. Closed my eyes.

His breath was warm on my neck. He slid his hand around, pressed it against my belly.

'Yes?' he said in that English way, polite and strange, inside my ear.

I lurched away. 'Nothing.'

His mouth made a little shape that was almost a smile. He swaggered off and the street lights bounced off his hair and coat, outlining him in glitter.

Oh, silly me. I had let the ghost into our bed and now I couldn't push him out. When I got home, I saw Johnny in every reflection, his eyes smearing me. We hadn't swapped telephone numbers. Back then, nobody had mobiles. I fell asleep, found myself trying to force his number into existence through a dream. Nothing manifested but my own date of birth in glowing neon and a cartoony Stephen Hawking, zipping over the Wicklow mountains in his motorised wheelchair, wearing a strange, long white beard and predicting the end of the world.

Two days later Mark returned. Doubt swamped me. Patches of guilt. Rage. Resentment. Fear. I became miserable, elated, miserable again. Useless at work, couldn't concentrate. I messed up an important pitch and was taken for an inquisitorial lunch by my boss. Twenty questions later I had him satisfied that I wasn't pregnant or losing my marbles. I told him I'd picked up some virus, something that had been at me while I slept. It wasn't a lie.

Oh, dear, said Carmel when I told her. The moment I saw the two of you together, I…

She bit her lip.

I haven't got his number, I said. I've no way of finding him again. And waited for her to say something characteristic, something wise, like this was clearly a distress call, or in time I'd get over it, but she didn't.

So I told one or two or – okay, three – other friends. Not Lorraine. They reassured me that what I was going through was normal, most likely only a sign of something, a communication meltdown in my marriage, an early mid-life crisis. Nothing to do with Johnny. He was just the superhighway that would lead me to a brand new I, me-and-Mark to a brand new Us.

I told Carmel what they'd said. I could hear her thinking down the phone. I waited for her to ask me if I'd told Mark. I had my answers prepared. Of course I hadn't. That would do no good. That would only lead to hurt. The timing was dreadful. Anyway, there was nothing to confess. It wasn't serious, like I was going to leave him. Christ's sake, it wasn't even an affair.

'I haven't seen him again, Carmel,' I said. 'I want to. I think. No. Jesus, I do. But—'

'He's a wanker. Stay away from him.' She'd interrupted me, not her usual thing. She sounded angry. 'Sorry,' she said. 'It's just. Mark's a great guy. I don't know why you're doing this.'

But it's obvious, I wanted to tell her. Can't you see it? Can't you feel it, the relentless compulsion of the cunt-mad need? You said it yourself: the minute you saw us together, oh dear.

They say stasis withers, but I remember the next four months as an infinite progression of vicious little moments, each lined up like a razor blade, me hanging over them, suspended. Death by a thousand papercuts. I had no idea what to do next. I told myself, and the friends I'd confided in did too, that this was good. The longer I didn't indulge the obsession, or distraction, whatever it was, the sooner it would retreat, letting the status quo claw itself back to where it should be. This didn't comfort me. I can't tell you how things were with Mark then. I was snow-blind, unable to see anything with clarity.

In May, I got a ticket to a benefit gig in aid of some charity. One of our clients had done the sponsorship and there were a load of freebies going. Mark was supposed to come, but he'd cried off at the last minute, some beta deadline to sort out, so it was just me and Carmel, and a cousin of hers over from Toronto who she'd insisted on bringing along.

The gig was fine, a muso pub, mediocre songs played too loud. I was at the bar, buying a round and swapping jokes with the guys from work, when I heard him through the PA. I looked over at the stage. Johnny was behind the mic, working the crowd while his band fiddled around, tuning up. The lights made him taller, flooding him in incongruous colours. Rose and amber. The music started. I've no memory of what it sounded like. As he sang, Johnny kept looking around the crowd. Sizing up the women, I assumed. He lingered down at the front, and I saw long blonde hair, arms held high, swaying. I half-turned to go and he looked at me. The lights changed. Humours coursed through my body, bile black, bile green, phlegm and blood.

We found a dingy little room on the top floor where the bands stored their riders. We cleared a space among the chilly cans of Heineken and Guinness and he lay on his back and I rode him. His body was soft, damp with sweat and adrenalin. I thrust myself around him with a grim determination, like I was willing myself to swallow him whole. It was more comfortable than the alleyway, a bit less messy, and that put me off. I felt any certainty that had been in me drain away into a black void that was telling me it used to be my soul, but just as I was about to lever myself off him, he did something – moved, relaxed, held still, impossible to say – and that surprise came again, freeing me. Though I can't, even now, articulate what I was freed of. He moaned. I imagined him absorbing it, whatever the act had sloughed off me.

Are you my bitch? I said in his ear after we'd come. He laughed, and that made me feel like a fool, so I bit his ear, hard enough to draw blood. He made an odd little sound with his mouth, like a baby's fart, and yanked me closer. I laughed then. You dick, I thought. He pushed what was left of his erection deeper inside. I stopped laughing, let him come down. For a while all I could hear was his breathing.

I reached for my clothes, started to get up. He locked his leg around my ankles. His fingers touched my back. I could feel his plectrum nail digging at my skin.

'Same night next week.' His voice was too crisp for the dank room. He mentioned a pub I knew vaguely, on the northside. I grabbed his hand, the one at my back, and squeezed his fingers, willing them to break.

You are only here, I said to him in my dream last night, because I want you to be.

Every week, more or less, for six months. I look back and am staggered by my bloody-mindedness. Any gap longer than a week was iffy. We – sorry, there I go again, I mean I – would go from sated to restless to hankering to fearing with tedious predictability. Eight days in, the fear could turn to guilt, or doubt, and that would be a recipe for disaster. Shorter gaps were dangerous too, leading to a risk of discovery, though on some weeks Mark was away, I let us meet more than once. We picked different nights, so I could come up with a range of alibis. What kind of idiot would do it without one, out in the open, run the risk of being caught? I don't know what Johnny told his blonde. I never asked. We did it everywhere. Outside, inside, grass, sheets, stone, concrete, pine needles, cushions. In the dark as much as possible, and always with our clothes on, getting at each other through fabric or zips or under elastic, as if we were teenagers. Sometime we hit, or bit, or scratched, or kicked. Vanilla, nothing to write home about. I'd expected that the moments of connection between us would turn out to be part of some game I was playing on myself, that they'd reduce as time went on, but instead, that side of things only got more intense. Not consistently, but any time I felt the need to end it, fuck right off, something would happen and bang, there I'd go, surprised again. I knew about tantra and mild S&M, roleplay: this didn't feel like that. This just felt weird, off. But interesting. How could so much surprise come out of so much mess? At times I almost believed in it. That other shit, I wanted to say to whoever would listen, that crappy story we've all been fed – eternal companionship, fucking affection – it means nothing, not compared to the intensity of an individual moment.

Was this enlightenment, I wondered, my hand pressed on Johnny's chest, feeling for his breath. Was I Siddhartha?

After those evenings, I would go home and sleep. Like a baby, no dreams.

By then, only Carmel knew. I wanted her to. I needed it: for my friend to hear, and by hearing, get caught up. In it; in me. At times I nearly had her. No! Leaning in, eyes bright. Cheering me on, almost. Complicit, like we were back in school, fourteen and into Iggy and the Velvets again, enjoying the thrill of a meths-dipped needle spiking our pale earlobes. But it was a struggle. I felt it off her, smelt it off her. She'd be fine for a few minutes, or half an hour, and then she'd have to bring Mark into it. Did he not even have a sense of what was happening? A suspicion? Was I sure? How would I feel if, you know, the boot was on the other foot? Jesus, Carmel, I said. This isn't about Mark. This is about me. Yes, she said, but. Hadn't I thought about the future of our marriage, what I might be doing to it?

'I can't answer that,' I said. We were upstairs in the mezzanine in Bewleys, when Bewleys was still Bewleys, having coffee and carrot cake. She was picking at hers, moving it around the plate with her fork. An irritating habit, though it had never bothered me before. 'I don't want to think about that stuff. That's not why I'm telling you this.'

'Oh, come on.'

'What does that mean?'

'Aren't you even a bit guilty?'

I exploded. 'Of course I'm fucking guilty. I don't want to hurt him. Like you said. Mark is such a great guy.'

'But?'

I didn't answer, just ate more cake.

'I don't know,' she said. 'I really don't.' That line on her forehead looked painful. Between the tines of her fork, her cake was babymush, grey and oozing.

Mark was being attentive, but I couldn't tell whether that was because he suspected, or just how he was, how he'd always been. I hadn't lied to Carmel when I'd said I didn't want to think about him, about us. I felt stuff around it, sure, lots – guilt and doubt and fear and yes, pity, even – but I was done thinking.

We never talked, Johnny and I. No point. We just fucked and sensed it, that thing that kept us bound to our meetings in backrooms and scruffy parks and dodgy pubs all over Dublin. We. Us. Apologies again. *I. Me.* And each time I felt freer. As if more of my self was being pared away, but whatever was left was more me. Essential, perhaps. Is that the word?

A paradox. As those moments added up, collecting mass, exerting force, I began to feel less and less substantial around Mark; like I, not anyone else, was the spectre in our bed.

It finished in early November, about a year after our first encounter. Maybe things like this have a natural timeframe, as mappable as mammal gestation or the growth-cycles of crops.

We met in the Gravediggers pub in Glasnevin and walked out into the cemetery. The sky was dark except for a thin skin of early evening clinging on in the west. It was bitter. Johnny pulled me down onto an overgrown grave. We lay facing each other, his hand on my hip. Through my skirt I could feel his skin, soft and hot from the pub. Succulent. A strange word, the word you'd use for a houseplant, but there you are. I grabbed his fingers and pushed, rolling him onto his back as I lifted myself up to straddle him. My palms bore down on his, forcing his fingers into the earth. The ground beneath my shins was icy, my knees warm against the lining of his coat. I went to kiss him but he held my wrists so I couldn't, pulling me in so our faces pressed against each other. He said my name into my ear, then something else. I twisted my mouth around. 'What?' He repeated it. I froze, then stuck my tongue into his ear, began licking.

He twitched. 'Stop. You heard me.'

'Stop?'

'Yeah.'

'Oh.' I moved to get off.

'No.'

'No?'

'No,' he said. 'That's not what I mean.'

I didn't want him to talk. I was afraid of that, the talking. So I moved forward, trying to kiss him again. He pushed me back. Then he said it, the other thing. It hurt. Oh. A blow to the chest. I think I might have flinched.

'Fucksake,' I said. 'That has nothing to do with anything.'

'But it does. You know it does.'

No, I wanted to say, it doesn't. Instead, I pulled myself off him, turned my back. His voice kept on, too crisp again, for the night, for us, for the stupid words he was using.

Look, we're both feeling, um, it.

This, um – this thing.

It's. Good.

And I um, don't want it to stop—

Real!

It's real, yes. And, you know.

I've been um, going over it, in my head, Christ, whenever I can and – I don't think I can be with anyone else anymore, with…

Don't say her name.

And you. I know you can't either, and—

He'd sounded nervous to start with, but was getting confident as it went on. I stared at the ground and kicked at a stone at the edge of the grave, some unworded swear boiling in my gut.

'No,' I said.

I made myself look at him. To do otherwise would have been unfair. I am nothing if not a fair person.

Then I explained.

I could see something like a question in his eyes, but it flickered out fast and all he did then was make a little laugh and shrug back into his coat. A slinky movement. He moved well, I remember that. He started to get up, then stopped. Took out a cigarette. Lit it, inhaled. Leant forward and looked at me.

I looked back.

We stayed like that a long time.

When the cigarette had finished, he lifted my chin and kissed me. The burn of smoke on his tongue. Then, somehow, he had moved, or I had, and I was straddling him again. Please don't ask why. Oh, silly me. A tendon in his neck. Mouth opening. Teeth small knives, stalagmite spit. An unbuckling. The work of fingers, tongue, skin. Melting, fusing, all that, the usual. Lunge, grip, flesh, cloth. In and out. He pulled back my head by the hair. Ouch. That was new. Something – chemicals, chemicals – down the spine. Hip sockets straining. Knees grating. Will I be doing this, I thought, when I'm sixty—

Ah, there it is. Snake from tail to crown. Grabbing, let it ride.

He was about to come when he groaned and pushed me off him. Held my waist with one hand, like he'd done after we'd done it the first time, and pushed me into the ground. I tried to turn, but he shoved my head back, away from him, arrogant, English, the prick, even on his knees, his body crossbow-tensing away from me. I kicked against his thigh, awkward and panicking, found that tender spot above his knee. An old football injury or something; he'd never said. He grunted, ground. What a beast. The cunt. Yet. See me as he saw me: sinking down in myself. Inviting. Pathetic. All gowl. See me holding. Waiting. The nasty feeling: eat him up, spit him out, the two-faced lying swine. He tried to avoid me, I could feel it, the attempt to hold back, make me meat, but the habit was too strong, the moment had too much mass to it, and neither of us had much choice by then. I held him and wouldn't let go, and there we went again, like we always had.

He left before I did, without setting up another meeting. Don't ask me if I doubted, thought of calling him back. I watched him go through the bones and the weeds, my mouth full of dirt, my nails black with his blood and tiny pieces of his skin.

When I told Mark, ten days later, I never mentioned Johnny's name. He confessed immediately: he'd been sleeping around too. His words. Trendy girls from San Francisco, he said, programmers he'd met at his conferences. But they hadn't made him feel any better. They just made him want to come home. He took my hand, kissed it. By then I was exhausted from it, the lies and the manipulation and the not knowing and – if I'm honest – the stuff with Johnny too, and he's good at sentimentality, my old Mark; pictures of wrinkly everlasting love in a rose-covered cottage. Wasn't that why I'd married him in the first place? So I duly fell apart and agreed with everything he'd said. It was the same for me. He, Mark, was the one I really loved. I was just looking for excitement because I couldn't handle what had happened to us since we'd got married. I loved him, always had and I really wanted us to work.

I didn't mention Carmel, or seeing them snog on Grafton Street, that moment Johnny swept his coat aside like a highwayman's cape and turned to face me. Nor did Mark. I did drop Lorraine's name a few days later. And got it straightaway. The smell, the prickle on my skin, like I'd got around Carmel that night in the pub before Johnny walked in, the other times too, when I'd been baiting her, or guilt-tripping her, or god knows what. I knew I'd been right about Lorraine being their go-between. She always was a tight-mouthed sneaky little cow.

We fell into bed and fucked till three in the morning. You can call it an exorcism if you want. The next week, we began to go to counselling. A few months in, when the counsellor looked like she was going to hit a seam, I began to talk about needing to have a baby and we dropped out. I got pregnant pretty fast. Good genes. Our kids are beautiful.

I would kill anyone who tries to come between me and that.

I'm a pragmatic person. I don't like to regret and I rarely let myself think about might-have-beens. But I'm only human. When I've had one or two too many or the kids are, you know, or I look over and I realise I hate the man I'm with, I can't resist it, pulling at the scab. For a while, it was all silly adolescent stuff. The two of us haring around the world on his motorbike – though I never even knew if he had one – stealing from banks to get by, sleeping rough by the side of French roads, with nothing but fucking to keep us warm. When the fucking got boring, I saw us selling each other's bodies in Bangkok, playing mindgames with respectable colonials and disenchanted Americans, relieving them of their last, dearest-held beliefs along with their wallets. When that wore thin, my fantasies turned moral, and I had us fighting for freedom in Nicaragua and Venezuela, cracking code and Yakuza in Tokyo, climbing to the top of the Statue of Liberty and holding it hostage on behalf of the global dispossessed. Idealism palled, as it always does, so I turned us anarchic, capricious: fomenting discord in the Arab world, assassinating dictators, singing with Elvis in Vegas, where Johnny's accent would have gone down a storm. Then, in the end, caprice ran out. I backed us into a corner, put us living in Berlin like rats, underground. My mind is a limited thing. I desiccate with age. My visions now are just as silly, if less operatic. Walking on a beach together, snuggling in bed, eating good food, the odd christening.

I'm glad I never asked Johnny what he had in mind the night he asked me to be with him. I'm glad I gave it to him straight. Let me explain. I am using you. You are only here, you vainglorious boy, because I want you to be. That stupid phrase. I love you. He had no business saying it. Even though, after nights like this, when that stubborn ghost has crept back in under our covers, I wake and am once again found wanting. Thinking: come back. Oh, Jesus, come back.

I will tell Carmel tomorrow, like, eventually, I always do. Wow, she might say. No! she might say. And I'll wait for her to say something else, something characteristic and wise, while that terrible line in her forehead deepens, and her fork moves uneaten cake around her plate, crushing sweetness into failed grey babymush.

Christopher de la Rosa

She'd been sitting at the PC for days. Let's go for a walk, suggested Finn. Okay, she said, sick of pixels. It was Hallowe'en, a gorgeous cool, quiet morning balancing on that slice-edge between autumn and winter. Sky pale; air hanging over the earth, a blanket about to fall.

The Park felt like some place out of time. Browns and greys, a few last bits of gold. They went to the bandstand, and Finn sang *My Way*, sending echoes bouncing off the broken roof.

Then she saw him. A figure in a green combat jacket, skulking in the bushes. He wore glasses, an odd woollen hat.

Let's go, said Finn, though she'd said nothing, hadn't pointed him out.

They were halfway up the hill when the children appeared, rushing out of the undergrowth like Peter Pan's

Lost Boys. Three of them. Two fair, one dark, all wearing superhero cloaks.

The smallest, the dark one, had large limpid eyes and a grazed chin. The two fair ones were freckled, crew-cut. Brothers, she thought. The oldest wore a necklace made of seashells.

'Excuse me?' he said. 'Have you seen our friends?' He wasn't more than nine but spoke with a grave precision that wouldn't have been out of place on an elder statesman.

What do your friends look like, they asked. Details. No, we haven't.

The leader shrugged. He didn't seem that bothered. 'Can we walk with you? Maybe we'll find them on the way.'

Finn looked at her. In this day and age, adults, children, health and safety. But it felt okay to her and must have to Finn too, so they said yes.

They walked. Grassland, woodland, gardens. Occasionally the boys left to search in thickets for their friends. No luck. They'd always come running back, fall in line with them again. In the rose garden, she struck up a conversation with the oldest. Christopher. His best friend was a girl, he told her. She was one of the missing ones. He fingered his necklace. 'She gave this to me.'

Zöe loved that, how he wasn't embarrassed having a girl as a best friend. How he wore her gift with such derring-do, like a pirate's treasure.

'My name's not Christopher,' he said suddenly. Finn was a few feet ahead of them, humming to himself. 'It's Stephen.'

She could have walked with them for ever. They were sweet. Not like icing. The sun rising, the sound of heather bells, a still Hallowe'en morning.

When it was time for them to go, they left as easily as they'd arrived. No warning, no goodbye, they just took off, running down to the lake in a wild, shambolic chase that only children that age understand. Or maybe lovers know it too, in the early years, when they still define themselves by that verb of intangible doings.

As they walked home, Finn asked if she'd noticed him. She said nothing.

'The guy in the bushes,' he said.

'Yes.' She was thinking of Christopher's necklace, and the best friend, the missing one, the girl who he'd said had given it to him, and wondering if she was real, or like his name, a patron saint summoned from his imagination to protect him on his travels. She was trying to remember what Saint Stephen had been martyred for, but couldn't, and was glad.

Hello My Angel

I am a city boy. I should say man. The walls of my house are thin.

That is not the house's fault. Or, indeed, a fault of the walls. They're proper walls. Fired brick, lime mortar. Built, as people often say, to last. They can't help that they're only two bricks deep.

It is modest, our house, like all the houses on our terrace. We live in a neighbourhood that was built for workers but is now on the up-and-up. You can imagine what it was like in those early days, at the turn of the twentieth century: a few small rooms behind every front door, grimy uneducated children packed like sardines in the same bed, a chilly outdoor toilet, a patch of earth to grow spuds and cabbage. Now there's just two or three, or max four people in each house, and we all have indoor toilets, usually installed in the built-on extensions. Some extensions are two-storey. Ours isn't. Everybody's extensions are built of concrete, not brick. These walls, too, are thin.

Our neighbour's house, the house to our right when you are standing on the footpath in front, also has a single-story extension, but it's not designed the same way as ours. I don't know whose extension was built first, or if there was a time-lag between them. I still can't tell if they share a wall, or if there are two layers of concrete-and-mortar, snugly running side-by-side. The point is, our indoor toilet is at the back of our extension, while the neighbour's one is ten feet in. As a result, our toilet is right beside their kitchen. One might assume this was by accident, not choice. But after the trouble started, I was on the loo one evening and the thought struck me: while they eat, they can hear me shit. I had never had the thought before this particular neighbour moved in. It offered some comfort.

We often hear this neighbour. She has a child. She calls at him. Often the call takes on the quality of a yell. More than once I've heard her tell him to be a man, that only babies wet their bed. He is three. I don't listen on purpose. Nor does my wife. This neighbour has a very loud voice, with a deep timbre. When she is agitated it cuts through the party wall like an angle-grinder. I should say, in the interests of fairness, that I also hear them laugh together, this neighbour and her child. Though in the interests of absolute fairness, it must be stated that the laughter doesn't happen as much as the yelling.

My wife is a country girl. Woman now. She hates the thinness of our walls. The neighbour's cries and yells make her jump in her skin. But so does the laughter.

The neighbour on our other side, the left-hand-side, doesn't affect her in the same way. Or me either, I must say. He has always been very pleasant.

Some people.

There was a party once that this neighbour held, the neighbour with the angle-grinder vocal chords and the three-year-old child. Then there were more parties. By parties, I mean loud voices and singing. The kind of events where it sounded like cocaine was involved. I say this not because I'm an expert on contemporary drug usage, but because the voices and sing-songs – and there was a lot of swearing too, and laughter of a raucous quality, and people running up and down the stairs, and the stairs in these houses are wooden, so you hear every step – would start around two in the morning and go on until nine or ten. Usually on a weekend, but not always. It's hard to imagine people could find the energy to keep up that volume and intensity for so long without the help of some kind of stimulant.

We need to say something, said my wife. She was raging. Pretending to be calm, but underneath that, very angry in the way calm people get.

Look, Fran, I said, let's wait and see. It might only be the once. Though at that stage there had already been two parties, or maybe it's more accurate to say two-and-a-half. We hadn't really counted the very first party. It woke us later than the others, slipped us by, almost. We hadn't been primed for it. We hadn't realised this was a thing that would need to be counted. Anyway, everyone's entitled to a house-warming. Aren't they?

Before this neighbour, others had lived in that house. People who had fucked at two in the morning – the house next door seems to like that time of night. These were women, the ones doing the fucking, and they went on for hours. One of the women, the one the house was officially leased to, was on the run, according to local gossip. She had a pitbull. That wasn't gossip. We saw it, and heard it too. The feral cats my wife occasionally feeds didn't like the dog very much, but they are cats and good at keeping away from trouble. The fucking from the pitbull owner and her various lovers, and their accompanying loud waves of pleasure, used to keep us awake. I was fascinated, I have to say. That probably puts me in a bad light. My wife giggled at first, but as those nights went on her face adopted a look I couldn't quite read. Jealousy, or suspicion, or judgement. With a calm overtone, as is her wont. If it was any of those things, jealousy etcetera, I don't blame her. It's been years since we went on for hours.

Come ON, says this neighbour now, the one with the child, and calls his name. One of those first names that sounds like a surname, or the name of a household appliance, or a boxer. You're not a baby. Be a man for fuck's sake. Though sometimes, the times when she does the laughing, she calls him endearments and *baby* is one of them.

We let three parties go – or maybe it was three-and-a-half – and then my wife got her way and it was me who stood at their doorstep at 4 a.m. and said, politely – I'm a polite, citified man: Can you please keep the noise down?

I'd massaged my request with a few qualifiers: e.g., I know what it's like to be your age and needing to let off steam and so forth. I'm older than this neighbour, but not that old. My work often puts me in contact with younger people. I do guided tours of the local attractions as we live in a historically interesting area and I get a lot of younger people on the tours, sometimes even from local schools. I've always prided myself on my ability to talk to just about anyone.

Only having a few quiet drinks, said this neighbour now. Crossing her arms against my polite request and looking down at me from her step. No law against that in my own home. She seemed very certain.

It's my fault, said my wife. I should never have welcomed her to the area. That's what she'd done, the day this neighbour arrived. Knocked on the door and said, Hi, I'm Francesca, welcome to the area.

This neighbour just looked at her and said: I grew up round here.

Oh, said my wife, and gave one of her charming smiles. We must have seen you so, when you were little. We've been here for twelve years.

This neighbour said nothing.

There were several more parties. Four, to be exact. By then we were very good at counting. The landlord was called. It was at this point I began thinking of events and actions pertaining to next-door on the right in the passive voice.

I hate this house, my wife said. She had loved it when we'd moved in. Now the rooms were too small, the door too ugly. The garden, Kevin, she said. You call that a garden? Though she was the one who had done all the planting and made it beautiful.

These walls, she said. They're like paper.

Which was not completely fair, I thought. Not to mention inaccurate.

She began to speak about sound-proofing.

One afternoon I found myself stroking the plasterwork of our sitting-room, near the junction between the original brick wall and the concrete wall of our extension. There was a crack in the corner; it went all the way up the wall to the second storey, right to the ceiling of our bedroom. Rising damp. Or maybe it was to do with a leaking gutter and was the falling sort of damp. Perhaps, I thought as I stroked, the noise was coming through the crack. Perhaps it was a fault of the plaster, not the structure. I stroked again, and the emulsion paint flaked beneath my finger. I wondered if it should be filled. But I am not a plasterer. I am not very handy. My wife, believe it or not, is more adept with power tools. When we'd moved in, I had done some bits and bobs. I had removed the exterior paint from our front wall and I had allowed myself to have some ideas about lime-rendering which had felt quite exciting at the time. The prospect now of filling the crack with a synthetic substance had a disappointing flavour to it. It seemed disrespectful to the house, like careless stitching on a wound. Though would it be, I wondered, as drastic as sound-proofing?

Other neighbours in that house had been loud, not just the woman with the pitbull. A family from Romania with a sick baby girl, who, my wife said, never stopped crying. I had been working with the newspaper then. I used to be a printer and on Saturday nights I worked very late shifts. There was also a trio of Chinese students, all girls and very quiet. And a refugee from Algiers who had two small boys who would wake in the middle of the night and howl in unison.

She didn't tell her kids to be men, said my wife, meaning the refugee.

But, I said. Come on, Fran.

Live and let live, I meant.

After six months of relative party-less harmony following our initial contact with the landlord, the arguments began. A boyfriend. We were woken, again in the wee hours, by shouting, and could not make out the gist of what was being argued about, though we could identify certain swear words, in a pattern, almost like music. We didn't care that we couldn't make out the gist. We didn't want to know. Over several weeks, there were further instances of swearing, shouting, and the banging of doors.

You see, said my wife. She was losing weight and I wasn't sure if it suited her. Shadows were crawling under her fine grey eyes and her skin had taken on a translucent, rather gorgeous quality. At moments I fancied I could see her bones underneath, a coral reef prodding through the sea of her humours.

The Algerians never did this, she said, and they were refugees. It seemed to me that her voice was losing mass too, becoming frail and wobbly. I would never use the word screeching about my wife's voice – she has a beautiful voice, rich with a burr of Galway about it, it was one of those things that initially attracted me to her, along with her magnificent hindquarters – but if you could imagine something like a screech that wasn't actually one, then you'd understand what that once-attractive voice was starting to sound like.

Sound-proofing, said my wife. She brandished a file I hadn't seen before. Purple plastic with popping buttons. In it were brochures and even one or two quotes from manufacturers.

Anxiety was felt in me. Exactly like that, in the passive voice.

Let me have a word with the landlord first, I said. I texted the number. The house had been sold, came the reply. To this neighbour. The one with the child.

Well, I said.

Okay, said my wife.

I wasn't imagining it. Her bones were definitely showing through. When she turned from me suddenly, or if I came into a room without warning, I sometimes did not see her.

I could tell what was happening.

The parties started again. Though really, it was only a few voices and, although they were loud and began at three in the morning and went on till nine, and included sing-songs and took place on week nights, not weekends, they only happened on two nights before we did something, albeit two Monday nights in a row, which felt like the commencement of a new pattern, and with no recourse to the now-defunct landlord, and being unsure of our rights and also hesitant to contact the Private Residential Tenancies Board because we assumed they would be unlikely to help in the case of a house that was occupied by an owner, not a tenant, and besides, with the current homelessness situation and news stories about young families on the street, you could understand the growing anxiety that was building on our side of the wall and my wife wanting quite fervently to nip things in the bud. Sound-proofing was being suggested again, more than once. At this stage all the materials in the purple plastic file had been read and it had been established that a professional job would result in, at the very least, a two-inch membrane being layered over our wall. Besides interring the original bricks and plaster under an arguably less attractive surface and blocking them from access, rendering stroking and other acts of contact impossible, such an installation would eat away at our already constrained space, present a health and safety risk in the narrow stairwell, and prevent the erection of bookshelves or any structure that required fixing with a screw, nail, rawlplug, or other penetrative fitting.

Besides, the money was not there.

We could try to ignore it, I said. I mean—

I'm going to talk to them, said my wife. Her jaw was set in that way of hers. There was no option but to agree.

Invitations were offered. A knock on the door. Come round for a chat. My wife essaying a friendly tone. No, I'm busy. Reasons were presented for this neighbour's unavailability: work in the morning, a bath, the need to put the child to bed. Then we left a note. Again very friendly. A chat and a cup of tea. Our first names, shortened in a friendly way – Fran and Kev. Our mobile numbers. The invitation was not responded to. At least not directly to us, by this neighbour. Instead, loud voices were heard raised in anger, with much swearing, through the walls. By this point, I did not want to take it any further. Come on, Kevin, insisted my wife, I'll explode if we don't do something. I could see by her growing insubstantiality that *explode* was not quite the word, but that a transformation was imminent, and if I wasn't to lose her, action must be taken.

Therefore it was not altogether unexpected that an argument was had on the doorstep of this neighbour's house. It was a Sunday afternoon. I am reluctant to say who started the argument, but if you must know, it was my wife. She drew herself up very tall, Fran's a tall woman, and the March sun shone through her exoskeleton as she stood at their doorstep and asked, again, to have that conversation. I ducked and shied behind her. I grew up in a city. I know this type, this neighbour's type. This is not the type one can have a rational discussion with.

I am sick of the pair of yous, said this neighbour. I have nothing to say to yous. Closing the door. For Christ's sake, Kevin, be a man, said my wife, and I looked at this neighbour's child, the child with the surname-firstname, clinging to the hand of his mother who by then was starting to raise her loud deep voice and make accusations.

Because my wife had placed her foot on the doorstep of a house that wasn't hers.

What followed included further accusations and much finger-pointing. Oh, you've dirtied your bib now, said this neighbour, and – though do not take my word for this – there might have been glee in her eyes. To her credit, my wife did not point any fingers, though she had started the argument by insisting on communication with someone who did not want that and had then stubbornly exacerbated things by placing her foot on another person's doorstep, though admittedly not bringing the mass of her entire, if increasingly insubstantial, body along with it. Now communication was being forced, she was content to spread her hands and say in a reasonable and calm tone of voice, more than once, that all she wanted was a conversation. As we were going to be living next door in the long term. Indefinitely. Just a chat. All we want.

Take her away, screamed this neighbour to me.

My wife did not listen to me.

I will call my mother, screamed this neighbour.

Fine, said my wife, and stepped back.

We waited on the front path, beyond their gate, with the neighbour behind her door, and then the mother arrived, and more shouting took place.

Don't patronise me, said this neighbour's mother. Pointing her finger in my wife's face.

I'm not, I don't mean to, said my wife, spreading her hands again and stepping back. Which was now too late and a bad move, as any city person would know, because the thing to say, when accused of something like that, is: How exactly am I patronising you? But I was shying away from it, and she wouldn't have listened to me anyway, because she didn't before, and I was shying away because with that type, once it gets to that stage, there's no point trying for conversation. The best you can hope for is a stand-off, and something like that did happen after the argument, for a while.

My wife stood her ground. She was gauzy with rage. She was a candle-flame. Plasma. The purple file was brandished, along with the phrase *these type of people*. I could see where this was going and that night, following the argument, I made a pact with the house, more specifically, its walls.

I don't mind you, I told the walls. I get you. I'm a city person. But she…

I thought of the red-brick semi-detached house where I'd grown up, in what is now regarded as a very desirable part of the city, and the loud, cheerful family beside us who had played jazz at all times of the day and night, including sometimes the wee hours, and their occasional arguments, which we never discussed in our house, but which I took to signify a healthy sign of life, and the father of that family, who had always greeted my own mother with a glorious *Hello, my angel* anytime they'd bumped into each other on the street, or he'd seen her coming out of our house, or vice versa. This man was, unambiguously, a city man. I had never thought of him as *these type*, the same type as this neighbour, the one who says Be a Man. My wife, however, who did not grow up in a city in a red-brick house, either terraced or semi-detached, and therefore possibly did not know what she was talking about, was beginning to lump everyone into the same basket. How easy it is at those times when, through lack of sleep, one's capacity for just about anything is strained to a fine, stuttering filament of drool, to make assumptions.

My wife was shrinking. At times she would resemble an exceptionally long leaf, waving in a breeze I could not feel.

Have you heard me? I asked the walls.

This neighbour watches TV on a small screen, and eats. I am speculating about the TV because I can't see it. I am not there yet. Nor can I hear it. But nearly everybody watches TV, so this is probably an assumption that is not offensive to make. This neighbour's TV may be streamed on a smartphone, and she might be wearing earbuds. I can't hear her child either. Maybe he is staying with his grandmother, the woman of the pointing finger, as he often does these days. He could be asleep. What I do hear, with my ear against a cup and the cup against the wall, is the sound of my neighbour's teeth meeting each other and squashing her food and her tongue slapping against them and against the inside of her mouth too. The liquid clicks and gurgles of suction and spit inside her oral cavity. When she speaks, though, I hear nothing.

There was, as I have said, a lot of finger-pointing on the part of the neighbour's mother, and a lot of arms crossing and flat eyes and protective covering of the child's ears and *I have had ENOUGH of yous* repeated at length by the neighbour herself. There were indirect accusations of harassment and insinuations of voyeurism and the word abuse was mentioned several times and there was the painting of certain people as innocent and others as bullies who listen in on young women and want people to take their shoes off at night and some people – for example, my wife – might say that's exactly what you might expect from that type of person. A veiled threat was made about our dog and what wouldn't be done to it if it was caught shitting where it shouldn't. Though we don't have a dog, so the reference might have been to the feral cats who my wife occasionally feeds.

Later, sitting on our loo, I would think of that dog and wonder if, in some parallel seam of reality, I was actually it.

And though in the heat of the moment, after the foot had been retracted, there was mainly calmness on the part of the other type, i.e., my wife, and a reasonable tone of voice and only one instance of swearing – Oh, this is fucking ridiculous! – which not totally unexpectedly was greeted with a *You see, you see, it's all coming out now*, later there would also be other reactions on that part, i.e., the part of other type, i.e., my wife. Namely, outrage and finger-pointing of the incorporeal kind and crying and panic.

Not to mention the shrinking and so on.

By the time the veiled threats to our non-existent dog's life were being made, I wanted to be shot of the whole situation. I could see what it was doing to my wife and I had had enough. I was surprised that others couldn't see. By others, I mean not just this neighbour and her mother, but also the police, who were called down to, by us, on the evening of the argument in order to clarify beyond a doubt who was the victim and who the bully. None of these people could see it as I could, how transparent my wife was becoming. One young policeman said all he could see in the situation was a mother, meaning this neighbour, protecting her child. Though some members of the force did offer calming, if not exactly tender, words, others told us this was not a criminal matter so they could not help us. But by then I had more or less lost hope in that strategy.

Little man, the neighbour had roared at me, while the mother pointed a finger and told my wife not to patronise or bully her. The mother stepped up to my wife with her finger extended and – little man, the words burned my ears – my wife, practically invisible at this stage with fury, the texture of a flattened jellyfish, stepped up too. It was then that the mother uttered accusations of being threatened, *Oh oh oh I see you, I see you* all the time pointing the finger, while the neighbour, her daughter, cupped her three-year-old's delicate ears.

I stood at our bedroom window later, before we went down to the police station, and watched the feral cats bask on the roof of our shed. They looked back at me with amused green eyes.

When I started working as a tour guide, after the newspaper closed down, I put in some time at Glendalough. It was not local and I didn't enjoy the long trips there and back on the bus with the tourists, so I didn't work there for long. But while there, I became interested – I wouldn't say obsessed, just curious – in the difference between hermits and anchorites. Hermits are outsiders, but they still maintain contact with others; they can move around and have been known to work at real jobs – mending roads, building bridges. They are, you might say, handy. Anchorites such as St Doulagh, who burrowed himself away in what is now the oldest stone-roofed church on the island, are a different kettle of fish. They usually don't have a religious profession before they find their calling, or it finds them. But once they have, they withdraw from society and spend their lives walled up. A hatch for food and drink. One small window to look out from onto the world.

I would do anything, I said to my house that night, long after we'd come back from the police station and my wife had gone to bed with a handful of sleepers washed down with a slug of Powers. I stood in the patch of railing-enclosed footpath at the front of our house, which, like all the front so-called gardens on our road, had been illegally commandeered from the city council by an early tenant or, more likely, owner. A worker, perhaps, needing to marshal more soil for the spuds to feed his family; or the worker's landlord, seeing an opportunity to raise the rent. Anything, I said again, entreating our friendly windows with their wooden frames which my wife had installed at great cost, our brick that I with my own unhandy hands had scraped free of the leprosy-red gloss paint it had been covered with when we moved in, because that's what the type of people who grew up in this neighbourhood do, to protect their houses from the seeping rain they paint the brick with flat colours, sometimes emulsion but often gloss, the tones approximating but never matching the original brick because how can paint, a liquid medium, ever match brick, a solid ground? Not only does this paint not match, neither is it effective at serving its original purpose – i.e., to keep out the damp – because, as my wife, who grew up on a large farm with lime-rendered buildings, used to point out, it is plastic, this paint. So it traps the moisture in the body of the brickwork, rotting the grout and making the plaster on the interiors crumble and fall, spreading damp across the structural and party walls and around the single-glazed aluminium-framed windows commonly used to replace the wooden originals since the 1970s and, occasionally, this seepage can even lead to cracks in the walls – though probably not our crack, the one at the corner that I had found myself stroking – and, if let go unchecked, may eventually, and fatally, result in subsidence. I pleaded with those exposed bricks, the ones I'd scraped by hand with a triangular scraper and had also sanded, which was a mistake in the end, because along with the ugly scabrous patches of rosacea-coloured paint, I had sanded away the fine protective coating granted the bricks when they were being kiln-fired. And in that respect I was no more effective, and perhaps a lot less, than the people who had been living here all their lives and back even a few generations, people like this neighbour and her mother. Please, I said. Help.

It is quiet here. I don't hear her eating anymore.

Our neighbour's washing line is in their back garden. Unlike our washing-line, which is a single cord stretched between two of the trees that my wife planted after we moved in, the set-up next door is far grander. They have one of those inverted-pyramidal contraptions easily found in DIY or hardware shops: a symmetrical and rather pleasing design of green nylon cord filament in a transparent cylindrical casing, suspended from a central metal, or perhaps plastic, pole that can be contracted, like an umbrella, when not used. The landlord installed it. For days after their departure, a damp dressing-gown hung from it. An adult's dressing-gown, grey like rabbit's fur. It tilted and swayed in the wind as the contraption swung around its metal axis, and it flapped pale at night when the big light at the back of the neighbour's house, the light my wife used to call ignorant, snapped on. If one wanted to, one could imagine a person inside the dressing-gown, leaf-thin and insubstantial as memory, dancing or dangling from the ropes. At some stage the landlord took the dressing-gown down. I say landlord because it was revealed, in the end, that the house was not sold to that neighbour, the one with the child, and never had been. I didn't see the dressing-gown being removed in person, because I was too ensconced at that stage. What I did notice was that my wife suddenly stopped calling it names and the silence landed on my ears like velvet.

I didn't hear them go. I don't know where they moved to. They were there that evening and in the morning, when I woke, they weren't and I was here.

Now the landlord can't get anyone to stay longer than a month, not even people who aren't the type to point fingers or land unfounded accusations against their neighbours.

It's haunted, said the young man who was the last to move in. A pleasant enough chap: Spanish. I had the feeling he was gay, but he didn't stay long enough for me to find out. I saw eyes in the kitchen wall, he said. Give me back my deposit, I wouldn't stay here to save my life.

His English was very good, with a certain mastery of the Hiberno idiom.

But I'm not doing anything, I would have told him, if he'd asked. I'm just sitting here, having a few quiet drinks in my own home. I am proud, I admit, of how certain those phrases now sound in my mouth.

My wife grows sturdy and content. The feral cats fight over her leftovers. One or two have died since I moved in, but there are always more. You can count on that in a city. One of the new cats has begun to enter the house that used to be ours but which is now my wife's. My wife doesn't seem to mind. She takes lovers from time to time. Occasionally, they go on for hours. Sometimes that's because she is with a woman.

Ageing will suit her. Sooner or later, in one form or another, like the feral cats, she will leave this neck of the woods.

The neighbour's house is still empty. I tend to keep to the extension, at the back of the house, the party wall whose precise nature, double or single, continues to remain unrevealed to me, but there are times when I am feeling particularly relaxed and in the mood to luxuriate, and then I allow myself to spread myself through into the original section of the wall, the double rows of yellow Dolphin's Barn bricks laid and mortared at the turn of the twentieth century. The other morning my wife walked past just as I was in the middle of all that, the spreading. The blinds were up. I saw her face, puzzled, in the narrow rectangle of the neighbour's front window. And then, I swear, she smiled.

Shift

Gas, clutch up to biting. Hold it there. Let her move forward, roll, easy does it, easier on the gas, bring your revs down, that's it, no, not that much, ah—

Fuck.

He's awake. Sweating, tasting of salt, mouth bitter, heart thumping, acid in his veins. Pillow's soaked, a soft wet lump under his ear. His ear's soaking too, and the bits of hair he's still got left, little strings ready for the comb-over. His knees locked together, his jaw a rictus.

He looks over at the clock radio, a present from Ritchie seven years earlier, when he'd given up the van. That's an awful yoke, he'd thought then, looking at its smooth gunmetal-grey shell.

It's a joke, Da, Ritchie had said. Keep you on time now you don't have me to get you up in the morning.

Cheeky pup.

01:41

The dots between the numbers are blinking on and off. How can you expect to rest with a thing like that blinking all night long? Make no mistake, it's an awful yoke, but Sandra thinks it's the dog's bollox.

Ah Ritchie went to all that bother you wouldn't want him disappointed Dessie.

She's way too soft on the lad; always was. She's on her back now, snoring. Soft and round, an eiderdown in woman-form. Or – what's the name the Yanks have? Comforter.

It must be stress, getting to him. The teaching. That young McFadden one has been doing his nut in. Thinks she's Mario fucking Andretti in a dress. Nice-looking girl, sure. Slim. Elegant, that's the word that came to him when he first saw her. Moves like liquid, he'd thought, watching her slip into the driver's seat.

She's blonde, and it looks real, though you couldn't count on it. Shoulder-length, curled under at the ends. It put him in mind of those black-and-white films he used to watch on a Wednesday afternoon in the eighties when he was on the dole. Veronica Lake. Lauren Bacall. All legs and hair, eyes gleaming, cigarette just resting there on the little round red mouth. McFadden smokes. He's told her God knows how many times since she started that there's no smoking in the school cars – the sooner they bring in the laws they've been talking about the better – but she's never listened. Must think, and this barbs, oh it does, he came up the Liffey in a bubble.

Twenty-six, maybe twenty-four. He's guessing. The kids all look like grown women these days, with their chests and implants. And the women look like kids. Are you not into all that? said Sandra once, a real dig in her voice. The youth, Dessie? She'd just started the change. No, he'd wanted to say, I'm not, love. But that dig had an edge to it, so he let it stay there between them, sharpelbowing both of them. Back when he and Sandra were courting, women knew how to get old. Take the ma and her like. They'd let go of the finery and the pencil skirts and moved into the flat shoes and housecoats no bother. There'd be the odd one who'd still dress up, but on the whole that generation didn't fight. Now, pushing forty and they're all in tight trousers and tee-shirts that wouldn't fit a kid, the hair dyed so they look grand from the back, and the chests sticking out even more than the young ones, or God forbid, if there's no bra, off they go with the beacons drooping down at their waists.

The other day McFadden came in wearing a skirt. It just about reached her knees when she was standing but it rode up the leg when she was sitting down. Not too far, just a few inches, and only at a difficult junction, when he was giving her loads.

over my side, clutch down to second, that's it and steer to the right, more on the gas, more, no, okay, gently on the brake, clutch down, brake fully, that's it

She gets rattled, McFadden. The legs move too much, too fast, the feet still only with an L-plate on them, not knowing if it's gas, brake, clutch. The left knee bends, jerks, jerks back – making the Punto hop forward with a shudder – and there's the skirt, on its way down. Over the creamy stocking – it's all tights now, he knows, but he likes that word stocking, nice old-fashioned word – down, down, or is it up, up, to the – no, not that far. Just enough to show him the top of the thigh. Trembling, muscled, her tights, stockings, whatever, shiny, little sparkles on top, woven into the fabric.

Soft skin, hard bone underneath.

He'd started off, like a lot of his buddies, with nothing. Bits and pieces: security guard, shelf-stacker, potato-picker out beyond Swords three summers in a row. Then he'd got the forklift number in the parts factory off in the Glasnevin Industrial Estate. That was a grand thing, while it lasted. Training, certification, regular money. A man with a skill. It gave him and Sandra the chance to tie the knot and get a decent gaff in Cabra on the never-never. They had the first three: Ritchie, Lorcan and little Triona. Then bang. The economy hit the wall, and the country was down the tubes and into the godforsaken nineteen eighties. His job went, along with his pals', and in no time they were queuing up outside the foreman's office on a misty morning in February, waiting to get the P45 in the brown envelope.

Sandra was bulling. Jesus, she said. I've enough on my hands with the kids without having to go off and skivvy. Though if she'd brushed up on the typing, she could have got something good. Even tempwork would have been better than nothing.

Because that's what was in store for him. Pushing thirty with not a skill to his name outside the forklift. Nothing for it but to head off to the Navan Road and sign on the scratcher. Hatch Two, 10 a.m., Tuesdays.

He was entitled to Benefit, which was more than what he'd get these days. You wouldn't get pin money now, and at the same time they're still handing out all class of stuff to you-name-it. He's not a racist, never has been, but he can't help thinking there's the government talking about this new recession and austerity measures, and you have all these people that weren't even born here, with God knows what diseases and a rake of kids and their mots up the stick with another one to make sure they don't get turfed out, and the powers that be are still tripping over themselves to give them a luxury apartment and a tidy little pay packet. And for what? For your man to sit on his arse, getting up to all sorts with his robber pals. Ritchie hates it when he talks like that: Da, you can't be saying that stuff. You're generalising. And he knows that's true, to a point, but once he starts, he can't stop. Yeah, Ritchie, but most of them have police records back there. No smoke without fire. You have to ask why they're on the run. Our own kids, hard-working, not able to buy their own home, or if they do, mortgaged to the hilt, having got to live off seventy odd quid a week, if you're lucky. You know what I mean, Ritchie. And the fuckers in power are telling us to tighten our belts?

Ritchie can never say much to that, though his wife, sour-faced young one, always stares over at Des when he talks like that, like she wants to kill him.

In many ways, it was better then, even though they'd be queuing for hours, all the men with strong backs and strong hands and no university degrees, while beside them, the young ones with their babies would be up two at a time to get their Unmarried Mothers. In and out like a relay race. Des' hatch was cursed with a slowcoach culchie from Donegal, thick as two planks and she had it in for the jackeens. Laid on the mucker accent twice as strong, just out of spite.

He had time, though. Even if, like most young men, he had no idea of its worth. The games of poker at Holy Joe Fenton's on the Tuesday after the scratcher, the pints in the Hut. The films on a Wednesday, him in his jocks and vest, watching Lauren Bacall blow a kiss at Bogey. And he loved getting up late, though Sandra was always at him.

It was her who drove him into it. He would have been happy enough just getting by. He wouldn't have picked up that paper and he would swear on his bollocks he would never have looked twice at that ad. It's funny. He can still remember every word, though the number's gone clean out of his head.

He'd been three years on the rock'n'roll. Sandra was up the pole again, with Jason. And, like every time before: Nag nag bleedin nag.

Why don't you look at the jobs pages again, Dessie? We need to get the kids their books and uniforms. There has to be something there, Dessie. Part-time, nixer. We can't survive on that welfare. Is it you don't want to look, Dessie? Is it that you don't want to be a good father to your kids? Is it you're thinking you'll keep heaping the pressure on me and I'll break?

Pressure? Break? Fucksake, he'd thought. But anything for a quiet life, so after the midday pint, he picked up a copy of the *Herald*. It was the first thing he saw.

Strong experienced driver needed for deliveries, house removals etc. Must be willing to work late. Cash in hand.

Underneath, a number. Southside.

He gave them a bell. No choice, he told himself, not with Sandra breathing down his neck. While in his mind *Southside* was whispering, drawing him. She wouldn't be able to keep tabs on him from the other end of the city.

A husky voice answered, a woman's, with a touch of the foreign to it that was unusual back in them days before the migrants started. She asked a few questions and that was that. Afterwards he would think it was lucky it was he who rang, because they might have been landed with some ignoramus who'd have walked straight into it and then maybe taken it all wrong.

Near the end of the call she asked: Are you of open mind, Mr Maguire?

Funny question, but he put it down to her being foreign. Open mind, he thought. Christ, love, he wanted to say, I'm open to anything that'll put a few extra pound in my pocket and get the missus off my back.

Of course, I am, he said, using the good voice he used at interviews. No worries there.

The line went a bit funny – P&T, useless at maintenance – so he couldn't catch what she said next.

Yeah, great, no problem, he said anyway. Thinking: any job's better than none.

Only afterwards he copped she'd been talking about Christo.

They lived in Sandymount, in a lovely little place on the seafront; dainty from the outside, though it went down deep at the back. There were just the two of them. Isabella and Christo.

The van was in Christo's name, so it would look like he was the one taking care of business. But it was Isabella who did all the book-keeping and handled the orders. She was Italian, she told Des. Used to be an opera singer. She'd come to Ireland before the war and fell in love with a doctor. Had Christo, stayed on, never went back. The Communists, she said, with a sad smile, though Des hadn't been about to ask why. He never found out what happened to the doctor.

A nice lady, he thought. Not wealthy, but grand in her own way. Very. And *glamorous* was the word that came to him later, when he was making his way back to Cabra on the 122.

Jet-black hair, eyes like Sophia Loren, an ivory silk dressing-gown barely clinging to her shoulders.

She was upfront – he had to hand it to her.

My son is a depressive, she told Des. He is a good boy but he has problems. He can be moody. It is influenced by the weather.

Uh oh, thought Des, but she was staring at him with her Sophia Loren eyes and her cleavage was moving with her breath like God himself had put it there.

It's just, she said, and paused.

Uh oh, thought Des again.

Her black eyes flickered, made a decision.

Sometimes, when his mood is not happy, he likes to dress up. That's why we need…

No worries, said Des, interrupting, feeling his teeth stretch in a smile. Didn't ask: Dress up as what, Missus? Just added something about the world being a boring place if we were all the same and all God's creatures, and she smiled, and even laughed, showing her own teeth, beautiful as a row of pearls.

He hasn't thought about it for years. Not hard, the past is the past. But there was a programme on the box the other evening that had flashed up while he was looking for the Arsenal match. It's very difficult, they were saying to the presenter, to get the hands and the chin right.

He didn't realise how hard he was staring till:

Jesus, Da, said Triona, over for the Sunday dinner, never would have pegged you for—

Huh, he said, and zapped. That's just wrong.

With Christo, it's not that he didn't notice, or wasn't bothered. You'd want to be blind back then not to take a second gawk at a young lad wearing tights and a handbag. He didn't look brutal, exactly. When he wasn't dressed up he was good-looking enough. Twenty odd, slim. His hands were small for a fella, but that programme was right; they did look wrong when he was dolled up. And a bit too narrow in the hips for a real mot, though from the side he was grand. Long legs, shapely. Like an ad for stockings. That part was alright. But the make-up. Christ on a bicycle. And even without that, Des would have never mistook him for anything real. The chap would never have inspired him to – you know.

You'd wonder sometimes why he'd stayed on once he knew. He'd only done a couple of jobs by then, so it wasn't as if he owed them anything. There was no contract. They'd no rights. Even before Christo came down that morning, Des hadn't felt too easy around him. The lad was very shy. But you can put that to one side, can't you? A job's a job. And when he appeared that first time on the landing, in the green dress like an Aer Lingus trolley dolly, with the wig and the slap, even though it was a shock – Des felt a bale of bricks land on his chest, his gob slack as a halfwit's, down at his knees, because what was it, exactly, that he was looking at? – he was somehow able to put that to one side too.

There was the money, of course. And Sandra.

It was awkward. You couldn't deny that. Des was bothered not so much on his own account, but more how was he going to explain Christo to the customers? That first time, they were booked to do a removals job for an old doll living near Leonards Corner on the South Circular. She was moving out to Ballinteer to live with her niece, and it was a worry, he'd admit that, how she'd react. Heart attack, he kept thinking. Whatever about the niece.

Before they set off from Sandymount, Christo went down the road to sort out the van. Des was hanging on behind, standing on the front steps of the house, having a fag, catching his breath after the shock. Then Isabella came up behind him. She'd headed out of the hallway before Christo had come downstairs. Afterwards Des realised she'd wanted to see what he would do – a runner, or stay put? Now she was just inside the hall door. He could hardly see her, they kept it so dark inside, with all those green plants like a jungle. But he could smell her perfume, and hear the rustle of what she was wearing, another satin dressing-gown, black, very classy.

She leant over to him so he could feel the breath on his neck, and put her hand on his arm. It was then he figured out why she'd left him on his own with Christo. He'd never been into any of that psychic crap, but it was like one of those premonitions, that déjà vu Sandra was always banging on about.

All Isabella said, though, was a whisper: Keep him in the van, Mr Maguire.

So that's what he did. All day, kept Christo inside the back door of the van, loading and unloading while he did all the carrying. He found it easy and that surprised him. No, no, he'd say, there's a load of work for you to be doing here. I'm grand, son, not a bother. Hardest day's work he ever did but in a strange way, it was worth it. The old doll wandered out a couple of times, worried about her china but, God bless her, she was no Inspector Morse. Couldn't tell a green light from a red one, let alone a not too bad-looking young fella in a dress from a real mot. And on the other end, the niece was a lazy dose, stayed inside her semi-d the whole time, said she was down with the flu. Normally Des wouldn't have taken that guff, but that day he'd have been prepared to offer up a novena to keep the waggon inside. So in the end, they were right as rain.

They found their groove. Little rituals, warning signs. Isabella used to give him black coffee and cucumber sandwiches on the days Christo wasn't feeling too good. That was how she put it.

Christo isn't feeling well.

Looking at him with her sloe-black Sophia Loren eyes, the eyeliner at the edges peeking up, little cats' tails, and Des would nod, eager almost, like it was their secret together.

She never waited for Christo on those days. Always skedaddled, leaving Des on his tod, as if everything was alright as long as she and her son weren't in the same place at the same time. She didn't want to have to see it, and he could understand. Someone else gawking at her boy when he was like that. If she didn't see him witnessing it, she could let on that everything was AOK. And

Des found he wanted to help her keep pretending, God knows why, but he did.

03:56

That fucking McFadden one.

Up to a couple of weeks back, she was grand, bearable at least. Then, coming up to the pre-test, she told Des her 'partner' had shown her how to steer. Oh, you're all the same, he found himself thinking. Coming here looking for help, trying to weasel all my little tricks out of me, acting grateful, making me feel king of the world. Then you start picking up a few tips from your fucking 'partner' and before you know it, it's all gone to the dogs.

He told her as much: You know, Miss McFadden, he said, I'm not doing this for the good of my health. I'm doing this to impart information, to protect the safety of the public, and your own.

Not even a thank you.

The other day, she turns to him at a traffic light, ready to go into first.

Mr Maguire, she says, I wonder if you could tell me what to do with the steering wheel instead of moving it for me the whole time.

He looked at her. Her skin was shiny over the make-up, like her stockings. Her mouth in a round 'o' shape like she was about to kiss someone. He smiled.

Of course, that's absolutely fine, Miss McFadden. Sure we all have to learn by doing, don't we?

She nodded and before the nod was even halfway over, he was off.

And into first, foot on the clutch, let it up. Mirror. Mirror. MIRROR. Wheel to me. My side. Hold the clutch. Hold it, hold

*it. Handbrake down. Wheel, your side. More revs, more, hold the
clutch – ah – No.*

The car shook, stalled.

He heard himself tut, a grannyish sound like Sandra
started making after the change.

Her pink mouth a tight line. Still annoys him now,
even after today, just thinking about that. And he knows
he was being a fucker, but he was Jesus-damned if he was
going to let that little bitch think her so-called partner
could teach her things he couldn't.

He began to call her Isabella Loren. Not to her face, but to
himself. She looked like the movie star in her prime, lush
and ripe even though she was pushing forty-five. Forty-five.
Now that's youngish. But he always thought of Isabella as
the Older Woman. Because he was hanging around mostly
with Christo, probably, and he was a good bit younger.

Hanging around at work, now. It wasn't like they were
pals. He had plenty of his own compadres: Arthur Regan,
Holy Joe Fenton, his cousin Eddie. The odd poker game on a
quiet Tuesday, the Hut or Doyle's most evenings. And Christo
was so shy, even on his good days, it was an effort to be around
him. Des felt he had to be doing all the talking. That would
wear anyone out. You wouldn't call someone like that a pal.

Though he did grow on him, especially once the
summer started. That was how it worked, Christo's
depression: it changed with the weather. It didn't have a
name back then, but only recently, Des saw an article about
a young one who had the same thing. Poor young one.
She'd topped herself on account of it.

There was a photo of her and she kind of reminded Des
of someone but he couldn't figure it out at first, because

she was different, of course; a young one for starters, and a stunner. Not obvious, but she'd get to you, dark and miserable like Winona Ryder. It was her eyes that made it click into place. They were just like Christo's. Big and sad.

Seasonal Affective Disorder. They call it by the initials, the article said.

Gas, thought Des, having a sickness that's called what it means. Instead of, say, pneumonia. What's that – Scotch Mist? But SAD, that's like Ronseal.

The summer lengthened. Christo was doing A-One-Ball by then, going weeks at a time without dressing up. Fine by Des. Meant he could get him out of the van and carrying more, saving the stress on his own back. As the sun shone brighter, he started opening up as well. Not exactly chatty, but not so clammed up.

Then this one day, they were driving along towards Clonskeagh, at the junction of Milltown and Eglinton Road. They were just about to take a right, when they spied an old fella on a bike. He was wearing a dirty old cap and a mac, belted round with a piece of string, shoes falling apart, and his bike had no jaysus tyres. Christo said something then, out of the blue – for the life of him, Des would never remember – and it cracked Des up no end.

It was the first time he'd heard the lad make a joke, and he realised he was laughing as much for that as for the joke itself. Christo seemed very pleased, a pinky colour on his cheeks, and he gawked down at the dash, still shy, like he was knowing Des was looking at him and laughing, not at him but with him, and it was then Des saw—

Him, he supposed.

His eyes were half-closed, those long lashes just resting on his cheeks. The sun was shining off his hair, making it a silvery colour – he was browny-haired but went blond in the sun – and: Fuck me, thought Des, this young fella doesn't need to dress up to look like a young one, he's got it already. He's more like a mot the way he is now than with all the slap and high heels.

He wasn't thinking anything sick, like that he – you know. Just that, of a sudden, he could see why Christo did it, going to all that bother with Isabella's make-up and the wigs. Except he also saw Christo didn't need to do it at all. And he knew then why he got so low with the SAD. It was because he thought he was never going to look like what he felt on the inside, he was only able to be a – the word stalled, then burst inside Des' mind – a mockery.

Christo looked up then and Des would have sworn there were tears in his eyes. They were probably just from laughing, on account of the joke. But in that moment he wasn't so sure. So he looked back at the road and beeped at some woman driver – probably frightened her off the road for life, too fucking easy to do that with the mots – pretending she'd cut in front of them. He kind of knew Christo saw what he was doing, that he was letting on he hadn't – you know – but somehow it didn't bother him.

He was surprised it didn't get more awkward after that. On the contrary. Christo made a few more jokes and they weren't bad, and Des didn't mind thinking of things to say to him in between. Christo seemed to be listening to him, like whatever Des said was spot-on, pure expert, and what's more, he'd a few things to say himself, like about the diesel tanks they use on old Fiats in Italy and how Bonner would work out as a goalie in the European Cup. It was a nice afternoon, very sunny, and they went for their first pint after, to the Horse Show House in Ballsbridge.

It must have been a good night because Sandra was fuming the whole next day. Des struggled in close to 2 a.m. – had to walk all the way back to Cabra because there were no taxis, it not being a weekend, and the ones that were, weren't going to stop and pick him up the way he was walking everywhere in a zig-zag. Not like now, where morning noon and night they're all using them. He's lost count of the number of wasters and smackheads he's seen jumping out of a cab to sign on. As for the young ones, they'd hail a jo to go to the bleedin jacks.

Sandra thought he'd been on the razz with the lads. Didn't believe him when he said he wasn't. Though it was thick of him to say that because then she thought he'd been off with Avril Dempsey who'd only turned eighteen and was already the local bike. She was climbing the walls, Sandra, three weeks to go till the birth and those hormones driving her doo-lally. That weekend he had to make it up to her by foregoing the pints with the lads and staying in to watch *Blind Date* and Noel Edmunds with the kids.

After that they went for a jar regular. The jobs were picking up. It's a seasonal game, he'd end up working it close on twenty year and it's a fact: people do more moving in summer. Christo knew every pub on the southside. And – something that didn't tally with Des' first impression of him – the barmen knew him too.

'Lo, Christo, they'd say, or just give him a nod. He wasn't doing hardly any dressing up then and Des was glad of that because, even with everything, there's no Jesus way he'd have walked in with him in all that gear. The job was one thing, but the pub? Fuck no.

Des didn't know how much the barmen knew. Some of them would give Christo a queer look when they came in, and that vexed Des. What happened to good Christian thinking and Never judge a book by its cover? In fairness, though, they were always polite. No one made any nasty comments, or said anything that could be taken up wrong in any way.

He knew a lot of things, Christo. Once he had a glass or two inside him, he'd open up. Tell Des loads of stuff about poets and dreams he'd had. He was well into the astrology. Talked to Des all about Isabella too and the lovers she'd had. It was a tad spicy, not the class of thing Des was used to hearing. It was different after Bertie came along, but back then people didn't have lovers. You were either married or you weren't and if you got restless, you kept it to yourself. There were a couple of young ones, that little Avril Dempsey, who'd do the honours, but not for Des. He wasn't like some in their area who had a rotten name for messing around. And to be fair to most of Des' pals, it wasn't for them either. A decent man wouldn't do that, go around taking advantage of a young one. So Christo's stories weren't the sort of thing he was used to hearing. Still, he listened.

There was a side of Christo that was very on the ball. He knew when Des was uncomfortable or when his mind would start to wander and, almost without you spotting it, he'd change the chat round to something more of a common interest to the both of them, like Everton's chances in the FA Cup. Before then, Des had thought he'd no interest in football, anything like that. Mad how you can be proved wrong.

04:48

For fucksake. He was almost under when Sandra started it, the old shifting around. She hasn't been the same since the change. Though that's the Ronseal too, isn't it? They wouldn't call it the change if you stayed the same.

What we know, Mr Maguire, Isabella used to say in her husky opera-singing voice. Is life changes. So we plan. If all fails, plan.

He didn't take much away from that job, but that advice has stood to him. He'd never have managed the teaching without it. Thirty-five students now, excluding the German – with five coming up for their test. They grade you on your percentages and even though he'd like to see them grade Bertie or Cowen or those other tools sitting on high, his average is eighty percent, and that's not bad. Do the maths. Four out of the five will hack it while the other poor eejit won't.

McFadden's pre-test was two days back. You're in the twenty percent miss, thought Des. No way ready for a licence. She was looking in the rearview all the time, though he's told her fuck knows how often it's the side ones that count.

You won't see a cyclist in the rearview, love.

She hates being called 'love', like it's an insult, or he's having a dig at her liberation bollocks. Back in the day, young ones loved it. Made them think you had an eye for them. Sandra included. But now, you give them a 'love' or a 'pet', never mind a tap on the elbow to help them into the car, and it's fucking harassment.

The problem with McFadden is she thinks she's better than she is. He's spent hours, days, years – and that's no exaggeration, he's coming up to seven now at the instruction – explaining and showing her kind the basics, but it just doesn't go in. They don't know how to feel, they don't know how to do. They want it all broken down for them, in words.

Then I do this, Mr Maguire, and then?

It's not Maths, he tells them. It doesn't work like that, a then b then c. It's timing, it happens at once, you've got to feel it. I'll tell you what to do as it's happening, you just do it, and you'll see, you'll remember.

He was going to start telling McFadden that at the pre-test, but he couldn't bring himself. It would be a waste on that young one's ignorant brain. If there is a brain there. Letting on she's a cleverclogs with her Interior Design job – she wouldn't know clever if she met it on the street and it give her a slap. Just like Bogey used to do to the girls in the old films. You wisecracking me, sweetheart? he'd say. And bang – a belt. Didn't do them any harm. Sweet as pie afterwards, all over him in their tight skirts and them stockings with the lines up the back.

Clever, shite. Edel, his youngest, only twenty and blazing through that psychology degree, she'd wipe the floor with McFadden in the brains department in a snap.

She was all in black at the pre-test. A sweater that left nothing to the imagination – though thanks be, there was no show there. No stockings but black leggings, tight too, like a glove. Hair loose in front but done up at the back so he could see her neck, a light brown colour, like a mushroom. Glasses with a black rim, not bad, though he's never been partial to the four-eyes. Her lips dark red.

A change in season, he thought.

While she was grabbing at the gearstick and making a hames, yet a-fucking-gain of putting it into third, he clocked the ring. Left hand, fourth finger in. A sparkler. Engagement.

And not a word to him. He gave her a hard right turn up Maxwell Road, Rathmines. Very narrow and she tends to go wide. She panicked, too much gas, up too soon from the clutch, they shot around, a Honda Civic – metallic green, oh-four reg, flash but would have been a sight flasher if it was oh-five or six – had to do a sharp swerve not to get hit. A young fella was driving, mid-twenties. Des got a glimpse of snazzy suit, slick hair, put him in mind of Jason when he was working for that estate agents. Honked like a bastard, he did. Raging in a way Jason would never. Des braked for her, a little later than he should have, just so she could see what went wrong.

Live and learn, Sandra's always saying. Practise what you preach, that's what Des prefers.

She'd been happy enough for the first couple of months. It got him out of bed, and out from under her feet and, even better, out of Holy Joe's poker sessions. But after Jason was born, around the same time the work picked up, she started getting antsy. He wasn't home enough to help with the kids' homework. There was a mountain of odd jobs needed doing around the house. Who was going to do all that if he wasn't there? No matter how many extra spons he laid on the table, it was never enough. Then she started at the business lark. How he'd be doing much better if he ran a van of his own. Why didn't he do that, start saving and then they could move on, instead of wasting it on a sunshine holiday?

Des told her it was their first sunshine holiday ever. He'd been looking forward to it ever since he'd booked it in May and there was no way after all that work lugging other people's stuff around he was going to get himself in debt trying to run a business of his own. Now everybody's used to setting up their own businesses, they even have special courses for every scrounger and junkie on the giro, but in that day, nobody had money, and worse, nobody had courage. And if you did try to set up something for yourself, they'd be down on you like a ton – the taxman, the welfare, the health board – no cushy allowances, no way José, and as for your two-weeks' holiday paid by the scratcher, you could kiss that goodbye.

What made it worse was all his stamps were used up by then, so he was back on Assistance. No laughing matter. All the lads were in the same boat, except Arthur Regan the cute hoor, who'd talked himself into a part-timer spray-painting in a mechanic's shop. No sooner than Sandra finally gave up on the van, up again with her like fucking Lazarus on another whinge. Why didn't he get himself a decent, ordinary job with a regular payslip like Arthur, instead of snivelling around taking backhanders in someone else's van? It was coming at him all quarters. Sandra had a vicious tongue in those days. But there was no way he was going back on the holiday.

Christo had been late that morning. Des was worried he was in a mood, or worse, a dress – but Isabella said no, quite the opposite: he was having a shower. A shower? Des said. Very la-di-da. You didn't have showers then, except after football.

They were sitting in the kitchen downstairs, Isabella smoking a long black fag. She smoked one every morning, Christo had told Des, but no more than that. Terrified of losing her voice – though the opera days were long gone and she was only on the cabaret scene then. She was made-up, perfect, like always, wearing her black shiny dressing gown. Underneath a white silky thing, half-top, half-dress, see-through so, if Des wanted to, he could have made out the shape of things beneath. Her hair was in a double wave, out then in then out again, very Loren, and at one point she turned away to look out the window and Des saw she had the same eyelashes as Christo.

She was asking him about the summer and his plans, and he told her he was thinking of a trip away because of Sandra and the kids; he'd never brought them anywhere farther than the caravan park in Brittas.

Ooh, said Isabella. Away?

So Des mentioned Spain, and how his cousin Eddie's sister-in-law had said it was very exotic, though the food wasn't up to much, and Isabella cracked this great husky laugh. She said something in Italian which sounded a bit vulgar, and then said: No. You must go to Italy, Maguire.

What happened to the Mister, Des was wondering, though the dropping of it had made him feel warm inside, like that secret they were holding together had got denser, like that rock he'd seen on the telly being melted in a volcano's belly. And she was already telling him where to go, what travel agents, the best hotels at a good price, all that jazz. He got the tickets on the QT, not a word to Sandra, and laid them on the table. He almost laughed at the gob on her. Surprised was not the word.

And mirror, indicate right, look out of your window, not too much. Mirror, clutch up. Hold. Hold. Give it some gas, over your right shoulder. Let it up. More gas, and into the right mirror and—

Fuck.

06:02

Off like a light for forty winks and now he's awake again.
Is there no justice, he thinks. And tells himself he can't hear a
husky voice saying, None for the wicked, Maguire.

When he filled in the form for the hollyer, the young
one at the Assistance hatch – from Cavan, lacking in the
looks department, but sharper than the Donegal yoke,
they always put the clever ones on Assistance – gave him
a load of grief. The nerve, because he was entitled to
it. Had he any other income? No, he said. Why was he
taking the family to Italy? Relations, he said. Where was
the travel money coming from? A loan from his uncle,
he said. Bulling because they hadn't been hassling Holy
Joe, who was doing odd jobs as a mechanic, and was way
more flash with the cash than Des.

The summer was at its peak, so hot you couldn't
breathe. Christo and himself would be wringing with the
sweat, backs and arses glued to the front seat of the van.
On their breaks they'd be shirts off, lying in Herbert Park,
chewing the fat, throwing crumbs to the birds. Christo
was really coming out of himself. Had this mad sense of
humour that it took a while to get, but once Des got it,
he'd be bent double with the laughing.

They'd just finished a break and were comparing tans
while pulling on their shirts. Des was a reddy colour – he
could tell he'd be sore that night – but Christo was a dark
even brown, like the best sort of toast.

Jesus, said Des. Your daddy a nignog or what?

It just slipped out, one of the things the lads would say
to each other on the potato farm. Christo looked at him
odd and Des thought, *oh fuck I've crossed the line.*

He was trying to figure out how to say sorry when Christo let out a laugh and punched him in the stomach. Not hard, just messing.

Des grabbed his wrist and over they went, rolling on the grass. Jesus, it was hot. Christo had his tee-shirt on by then, an old Pink Floyd one torn at the arms, but Des was still bare. He still had his hair in those days and didn't look his age, hadn't yet gone to seed with the belly and all, and he had this funny thought, just for a second, that the people watching would think they were – you know.

Because what with the long hair and all, Christo looked like a – well, a bit like – a young one.

Des was grabbing onto his wrists. The skin was very soft. Bone hard underneath, but soft on top. He would remember that.

But God – no.

It wasn't as if – ah, no.

Then the musical clock went, from the castle-y church on Clyde Road. Time to go.

He should have been keeping an eye out. He knew that shower were sniffing around. He should have been more careful.

They must have followed them all the way to the house they were working at. Dunville Avenue, Ranelagh. Moving to Raheny. Even took a few pictures, including a couple of tasty ones of Des pocketing the cash from Christo.

And that's what he got from the Cavan girl, the next day down on the Navan Road when she was supposed to be handing him out his holiday money. A bent finger, a *Come over to Hatch 16, please, Mr Maguire*. Her voice wasn't too loud but he got nosy looks from everyone in the queue.

Over at 16 and she slid them out onto the ledge, one by one. Pictures, eyewitness accounts, you name it. He had to act the eejit to get out of it, say it was only the one job. Then she said they'd been following him for a month. He said it was a friend – that part was true, wasn't it? – that he was helping out, he'd done it for free all the other times.

She raised her eyebrows in that Oh yeah? look they're all trained to do. He milked it, played the gobdaw, told her he'd nothing better to do, he was taking it hard being laid off with no opportunities, a father of four with a young wife, if there was no steady work he needed to do something worthwhile with his time and – trump card – his pal was a bit on the handicapped side so he'd felt obliged to help him out.

He felt bad about saying that last bit but it seemed to work. Arthur Regan grilled him afterwards, said he couldn't have thought of a better line himself.

Can you prove it's true? she said, but Des could tell she'd already bought it. They didn't have other pictures of him getting the wad from Christo. So he said, not too cheeky but confident, Can *you* prove it's *not* true? Then he said, Look, Martina – that was her name – if it's going to cause problems, I have the solution. I won't help out my pal any more. She nodded, chewed the pen, thinking – he could see the old sprockets going around behind the glasses – then she said: Mr Maguire, if you require continued financial service from the State, you'd be wise to follow that course of action.

Sandra was fit to be tied. Lamb of Jaysus, how many times does a woman have to say I told you so? Point taken. But oh no, she had to keep reminding him how she'd known it was a rotten idea, and so on and so forth. Des had always thought of himself as a mild-mannered man, never hit a living thing in his life, but on top of everything in the last couple of days, the heat and all, he'd had enough. He knew if he didn't get out of that house he'd kill her.

Christsake, it was only a fucking job.

07:00

Five hours. The birds are singing now, in time with Sandra's snores.

It felt strange, coming over in the evening. Sandymount strand was blue and white, striped from the shadows of the houses across the road. Fingers, he thought. The long arm of the law, said Christo, when Des told him. He was good at that. Finding a different angle to a normal everyday thing.

Isabella wasn't there, so Des broke the news to Christo on his own, in the wooden kitchen downstairs. He seemed calm. Des wasn't expecting that, though he wouldn't be able to tell you why. Okay, said Christo, and went to the drinks cupboard at the side of the room and took out a big bottle with green stuff inside. Three-quarters empty. Des didn't catch the name; it sounded foreign, like crème de menthe. Christo poured them a glass each. It didn't taste like crème de menthe. That was a mot's drink but this stuff was hard, liquorice mixed with paint stripper.

It will help us to forget, said Christo, and knocked his back. Then: Excuse me, one moment.

Des knew what was coming next and really wanted him not to do it. He should have stopped him, he thought afterwards, though he didn't know how he could have – or maybe he did – but he didn't. While he was gone, Des poured himself another glass of the green stuff.

He didn't look as brutal as Des thought he would. He'd left the wig off and Des was glad they hadn't knocked back too many because even the make-up was alright, not as much as usual. He had on that white silky thing Des had seen on Isabella, with a slip underneath and faded jeans. It looked good on him. He looked sort of in between the way he usually looked in all the rigout and the way he looked when he was just Christo. He poured them each another glass. Des felt his belly go on fire.

Ready? said Christo.

Des wasn't completely AOK with the situation. But he didn't want not to go out with him, it was their last night, God knows if he'd ever see the poor divil again, and you have to mark these things. Respect. His head was turning a bit from the green stuff, and – he didn't think this in a sick way, but – he liked the feeling of being with Christo, the way he was just then, not all dolled up and not just himself either, and Des didn't know if that was good or not, so he just went along with it.

They started in Sandymount – Byrnes – then up to Ballsbridge, pints in the Horse Show House, chasers in Bellamy's, down to Jurys, whistle stop along Baggot Street – Ryan's, Henry Grattan, Doheny & Nesbitt's, O'Donoghues and the Baggot Inn – tried to get into the Shelbourne but couldn't, then down to Dawson Street – Dawson Lounge, smallest pub in Dublin – and Kehoes on South Anne Street. They were regulars in Kehoes because Christo liked all the young people. Des was fairly fluthered by that stage but he was pretty sure nobody there recognised Christo that night. Even the barmen thought he was a mot. Then onto the Pygmalion, they call it something else now, or maybe it's gone, packed with young ones wearing black lipstick and no bras, young fellas acting like you know, not normal, drinking girls' drinks outta long glasses.

Des knew he was well on the way to pallatic once they'd hit the Dawson Lounge. Christo, though, just seemed to get better as the night wore on. He had this shine about him. People laughing at him, with him; Des was too gone to tell the difference. He pulled Des into an alley and they – you know – had a jimmy riddle, then across over to Bartley Dunnes. Faces, music, heat. Christo's eyes, mad and glad in his brown face. White teeth. At one point, he brushed the inside of Des' arm.

Soft.

He woke up with a headache the likes he's never had since – not surprising because that was the last time he drank – and it was all over the news. It had happened at the back of Fleet Street. Near one of those clubs. They didn't show any pictures. Des was glad. He wouldn't have wanted to see what they'd done to him.

He went to the funeral but didn't stay long. Isabella pressed his hand. Her face was wet with the tears and she was mumbling in Italian. She seemed terrible old.

Some of Christo's pals, the funny sort, turned up but nobody recognised Des from the pub crawl. In a way he wasn't surprised. Christo had been shining that night, he was the one they'd all been looking at. Des wasn't anybody. In the long run that was probably for the best. It would have complicated things if they'd remembered him – or worse, told Isabella. Because on the news, they'd said it wouldn't have happened if he'd been with someone. To protect him. Isabella not knowing would make all that easier. Plus with him leaving the job, it would be tidier, maybe, to keep it like that.

He got the van a few months later. Isabella had put theirs up for sale and he saw the ad in the *Herald*, recognised the phone number. She hadn't a clue about prices – it was going for a song – but he didn't want to call her. Water under the bridge. Then his cousin Eddie found him a fella who was looking to emigrate and Des bought his van for a good price, nearly as low as Isabella's. Set up the business, got it on its feet. Had Arthur Regan do a lettering job, all lovely neat black letters. Name, phone number – no mobiles back then – then, underneath, in a beautiful curly script: *Services Rendered*. It was Sandra came up with that one.

He stayed fifteen years in the business, then once Ritchie got the hang of it, took a raincheck. He'd never felt fully comfortable in that line of work. He was doing it only because Sandra had wanted him to, and it did make a definite improvement to their standard of living. But with all the buying and moving and what have you in the Boom, Ritchie started bringing in enough for himself with a good bit going back to Des, so it made sense to change gear. He's never looked back. Took to the instruction like a fish to water. Chose the southside because it gets him away from home a bit longer, and he likes those big roads with the trees. Reminds him of summertime.

Of course, they ended up not going to Italy that year. Between one thing and another, it just didn't happen. He thought after it was for the best. Sandra wouldn't have liked it. They tried Spain a few years later, when the business was nice and settled, but Italy, never.

08:24

It's a bright day. Going to be a scorcher. He's starting to feel a bit, not great, but better. Hot and prickly like he's been on the booze, but sleepy. Maybe he'll get some last-minute kip in. He'll need it for McFadden this afternoon.

She failed. Second time round. No surprises there. Twenty percent. He could have told her. Came in straight afterwards and booked another set of ten, with him. She didn't dare look at him, kept staring down at her feet, twisting the belt on this dress she was wearing, grey wool like a nun's. He couldn't help thinking of her thighs under the habit, soft skin, hard bone, the goldy ends on her screwed-up brown hair, those lashes long on sun-darkened cheeks.

Well, he said. Third time lucky?

The dots on Ritchie's alarm clock blur and mesh. His eyes are closing. Sandra whimpers, throws out an arm, pinning him.

And into third. Lovely. Keep checking the mirrors, into fourth. On the dual carriageway now, free as a breeze.

He left him at the corner. A shout. Des turned, nearly falling flat on his arse in a puddle. Christo was laughing. Des started laughing too. Another shout. Des blinked. He could just about make out Christo's lips moving. 'Coward!' he was saying. Des' head was melted by then, with the booze and the taste of Christo's mouth, but he still knew, even in the middle of all the mess, that Christo was – not that he was right, not that, but that – fuck me, he thought. Maybe? Christo pushed up his lips and blew a kiss. Des put his finger to his own mouth. It was still wet from Christo's tongue. He let his finger go somewhere in that direction, then turned away, still tasting, and swayed for home.

Departure

He was my first. There would be others, though I didn't know it. But the question is always the same. Why? Then it's sorry, I wish I had been there. I was there, though. I wasn't too. That's why, I used to think. Now I'm not so sure.

I heard the news on a rainy July afternoon. I was wearing a red scarf around my head. I wanted to look like Grace Kelly in a sports car. A red scarf, and sunglasses in spite of the rain.

We met up on Good Friday and the two of us went for a walk. The sky was very blue, a perfect April sky. It was warm, the beginnings of summer; insect life darting and flipping through the air. The leaves on the huge sycamores were a fresh green, like the grass in the park only not as sharp. A lovely day.

We walked along the long road several streets up from my house. As a child I always thought of the trees on that road as big and friendly, like people. My mother used to take me for walks there. In my pram, or later on foot. The houses were big too, full of exciting windows and cream-painted ceilings. The windows were exciting because they had ten little panes in them, not like the two big panes in the windows at home. They looked like something from a story, especially in winter when they filled up with Christmas lights.

We walk along the big, friendly road. We are talking, of the things we talk about when we're together. He does most of the talking, but he listens to me too, carefully, with an open sad grace. He speaks of an idea for a book.

Two children dart by. The boy grabs the ball, red striped with a blue like the sky, and runs on. The girl scrunches up her face and kicks a pebble against a tree. Vicious. In the park we sit on a bench. I like the way he talks, shaping the air with his hands. I remember him as quite unsure, and yet, when he spoke, his words had a certainty mine didn't have. Still don't, a lot of the time. He has an idea for a film. He is writing a lot now. His ideas fill sheets of white unlined paper with blocks of handwritten text in capital letters.

Sun gets in my eyes, so I have to shield my face with my hand when I look at him. I feel good, squinting this way. Summery.

He talks about the girl he used to go out with, the one who left him for someone more handsome, a guy with a louder voice. He is still in love with her, he says. He wants her to act in one of his films.

I lean back against the bench, and the wood is warm and hard. The paint is peeling from the heat. It's strange. This is only April and it's so warm. The sun and the leaves so bright, their colours talking to each other. I love the way the kids are playing around on the swings and the seesaws. Their mothers and minders soaking up the sun, sinking back onto their coats spread out on the grass and closing their eyes. Beautiful, I think.

I listen to him talk about the girlfriend, the actress who wanted to be a dancer but learnt too late, and I nod. He tells me that she refuses to see him now, but he can't blame her. She has her own life. I nod. He tells me he cried thinking of her last night.

We walk back to my house in silence. The sun has moved around the sky, it's later in the afternoon. I smell the sweet and cinnamon of hot cross buns.

We drink coffee down in my parents' kitchen, and the black cat jumps up on his knee and rubs the side of its head against his jeans. He touches it – he always had a gentle way of touching things – and begins to talk about cats and witches. His new film is about a witch. His new film, the reason why he came to visit me in the first place.

We go upstairs, to the room everyone loves to sit in, and talk some more. The film will be good to work on. I've already helped him, I've a very helpful side to me. I've looked up stories about white mares in mythology books, I've scoured *The Occult* and *The White Goddess*. You've been a great help, he says. I've got loads of ideas now. He explains the plot. It sounds a bit strange, a bit mad, but exciting.

The doorbell rings. It's my boyfriend. Introductions in gold sunlight. We chat.

He goes and my boyfriend stays.

Aftershave lingers in the warm beam of motes streeling in through the two window panes.

That was summer. But winter was the beginning. Two, maybe three years earlier. Coming home after the drama festival. Ten of us squashed into the little van, wrecked from dancing and performing and laughing, from writing names in the sand on the beach on the rainy second afternoon, from drinking coffee at two in the morning and talking about acting, movement, voice projection.

In the van, darkness collapses around us. I put my head on his girlfriend's knee, and hold her hand. He holds her other hand. Warmth. I feel, I am, very young.

Coming into the city, I sense flashes of light strobing in through the windows. Hot red bands striping the every-colour black of my shut eyes. An arm shakes me awake. Gentle. We pile out, stretching cramped, exhausted legs. We got to a café and eat mounds of fish and chips and hamburgers.

He comes down to my bus-stop to wait with me. His girlfriend comes too. It's bitter cold. It'll be warmer once it rains or snows. I get my bus, and look out the back window at them. She waves, he puts his arm around her, they walk off. They are dressed in identical green trench coats.

That trench coat. It always comes to mind thinking of him. He had other coats as well. Who doesn't? He took me to a film, and he wore a brown leather jacket with a sheepskin collar. The handsome man his girlfriend left him for had a jacket with a sheepskin collar too, only his was denim, not leather.

The first time I risked saying I love you, instead of just thinking it, was at Christmas. An easy time to say it. An easy time to blame the drink or the season or the sentimentality of wrapping paper.

I never said it to him. Because, I told myself, he was my friend, nothing more. Because it would have been taken up wrong, because that's not what I would have meant. I meant a spiritual love, nothing more. It's a pity spirit is so hard to find without a body. And no fooling around with Ouija boards will change that.

Someone told me that his girlfriend was a bitch; she went around telling people that she'd never gone out with him at all.

It was summer, a different one, when he took me to the film in his good leather jacket with the sheepskin collar. We'd met up beforehand in a record shop. He was buying a cheap album, second-hand, some ancient band I'd never heard of, so he could learn more guitar chords. He glanced up and the edges of his eyes crinkled.

Look.

He had a white scarf wound around his neck. He looked like a fighter pilot from World War I.

It was a great film, even though the cinema was tiny with an even tinier screen. The imagery was beautiful, blues and neon, with warehouses and a lighthouse, an opera singer and a godlike man in a white suit. I've seen it again since, many times. The first time I saw it after hearing about him was a Christmas, on the television.

That night, he walked me home, and on the way he told me about his dancing classes and the group he was in. It takes him out of himself, he said; it's good to meet people, he doesn't get as depressed.

Rock and roll. There'll be a party somewhere sometime after that, and he'll swing me around under his uplifted arm, smiling, and I'll remember. Dancing classes.

The road is washed in clear blue light. The sky is velvet dark and the stars glint. It's still warm. I feel a bit wary. I'm worried about that. I like him a lot, we're very close, but I don't want anything to happen. I hope he will understand.

We walk up the road my parents' house is on and our bodies collide as we take mismatched steps. I move away from him. Not too obviously, I hope.

He asks will he walk me to my door.

I shake my head. I'm fine, thanks for the evening, the film was brilliant.

He nods, slowly.

I move to hug him, and he backs off. A little, not too obviously.

It's okay, he says, and I remember again how gentle his voice is. He smiles, and lifts one hand in a little movement. I smell his aftershave as I walk back up the road.

His brother died near the beginning. The day he heard the news we were rehearsing a play he had written. His girlfriend walked in. Her face was strained.

Afterwards I saw them on the stairs. She had her arm around him and he was looking at the ground. I went up to him, to hug him, to hold his hand, and when he raised his face his eyes were wet.

Rain.

On the day of the funeral, he met us to talk about the play. We all sat around a café table that was covered in dingy white plastic. My fingers messed with salt and pepper sachets; his held a cigarette and shook all the time. His other hand, the left one, cradled a mug of coffee. He sat in his black suit on an orange plastic chair, and reassured us: yes, yes, our performances were all fine.

His brother was young and lovely, he told me once. His poor mother.

I can't remember exactly the last time I saw him, but I know it was after I returned from Germany. He came to see me in a play, and visited me at home once or twice after that. So any last conversation would have been in my parents' house, in the comfortable kitchen with the round table and big corner window. We would have talked about his films, the many ideas he had, the ones that fell through, the ones that could never have happened, the ones that would have been easy and, maybe, right to do. He would have talked about Transcendental Meditation, his social club, girls he'd met who'd let him down, the night courses in the social sciences, the job two evenings a week cleaning offices. He might have talked about his brother and his medication and his poor tired mother. We would probably have talked about the future.

He sits at the table, his back against the window. There's a candle burning, and the kitchen is warm. I see my face reflected twice in the two large panes of the corner window. His face has only one reflection, a profile. Grains of sugar spill on the wooden table. I play with them as he talks.

He tells me about the night course he's doing now. A class in philosophy, and they were asked: Who is the centre of your universe? He figured it out. It's me, he says, and points. I'm the centre of my universe.

Later we walk into town. It's December and my feet are cold. He's pushing his bike, a blue racer with gears and brakes and all the rest. The stars are sharper than in the summer. My nose is cold; I hope it won't get too red. He tells me about a trance he went into. A bit strange, I think.

An old man with a peaked cap and a long dirty mac shuffles on in front of us. We pass him, and he grunts as the bicycle handle gets him in the back. Sorry.

Strange? For a while I thought: Oh, no, that would be different now. That wouldn't be strange now, but wonderful.

Now, this now, I'm not so sure again.

I heard in the rain in July, on a grey street made greyer by the sepia plastic of cheap sunglasses. Why. If. Me. I. So many questions.

What is his face like now? What are his eyes, and his gentle thin hands?

No more hugs goodbye, I wrote. He must have been so lonely. Live with that.

A small white room. Drawers full of paper and capital letters, a guitar, a record collection and a scent of aftershave. An empty bed and a chair knocked over by dying feet. A lot remains.

You First

Overweight, Adam had thought, four weeks before. Then – Woman.

Overweight Woman Strides into Ward.

She'd walked past his bed, only changing course when the nurse pointed in his direction. A mistake, he thought, looking up at her, puzzled.

A motherly type. Green eyes, brown freckles visible under streaky orange foundation. She had a slight frown that seemed as if it was always there, as if she was constantly trying to work things out.

'Hi Adam,' she said.

Something in the way she named him.

A small smile. 'It's George.'

He stops breathing, hating his bad lung as it tightens, lifts, soars in his chest, a prima ballerina held high by fear.

Later, Adam thought he'd have known her just from the way she said his name. Some people hold your name in their mouths like a jewel. When it drops out and lands in your hearing, it leaves an imprint there, a fossil shorthand for their presence. Nobody else, when they call you, makes quite the same mark. But she had named herself before he could respond, stripping even that last test from him.

So this was what had become of her.

No, he thought. *Go away. Get back to the past. You should not be grown.*

'Good to see you,' she said at last. She smiled again. Bright, this time.

Good to see you. Adam looked down at his shrivelled body under the snot green blankets, the plastic tube feeding life into his disappearing veins, and wondered what had made her, his gorgeous piratical George, so fucking stupid.

They sit in the corner of the children's room. The playroom, Adam's mother calls it. There are brown tiles on the floor. Cork. Safer to play on than wood, his mother says, and far more practical. They play marbles. George's idea. It's an unusual game for a girl, but then, that's George all over.

Adam's favourite marble is the one that looks like a miniature universe. It sparkles. Deep, deep blue, speckled with silver. Adam loves that deep, deep blue. But George says it's a useless marble; it may look pretty but it's cheap and won't roll. Her favourites are catseyes, especially the greenish yellowy ones that really look like the eyes of cats.

Adam thinks she's way off. Who would settle for a cat's eye when they could have a universe instead?

As usual, they agree to disagree. They value each other too much to make a fuss. George is not just a cousin; she's the big sister Adam never had. The big brother too, all rolled into one. At times, Adam thinks George *is* him. She owns so much of him that he can't tell the difference.

It's early afternoon, visiting hour. She pauses at his bed, as she always does, as if she needs his permission to sit. Under the fluorescent lights, she looks even more wrong than usual. Her face is drawn, the skin stretched tight, her freckles vivid orange. She's lost weight. Too many angles.

She looks better with flesh on her, thinks Adam, surprising himself with the thought. No. With the *flesh*.

'How are you?'

He says nothing. Something flashes in her eyes – regret? – but she quickly smooths it over. 'Phew,' she says. 'It's hot outside.'

She plumps down on the bed, carefully avoiding the place in the blanket where the tiny mounds of his knees poke up, mocking his lost mobility. Her movements are still clumsy, tomboyish. The springs of the bed recoil. Adam, slowed down by morphine, imagines the bedclothes lifting, floating, settling. Like feathers, like dust from a bomb blast.

Stray bits of hair cling to her forehead. It's unlike George to sweat. Despite her lion's heart, she's always been—

What's the word?

Phlegmatic.

Dust holds the amber room together. Dust. Separate but together, like ants. It turns the light in the room into great big honey-coloured slabs. It carves yellow slices out of George's face, making Adam want to touch it. Adam is absorbed in the game, the chuckling of the marbles as they roll over the cork, but still he sees this. Her face, scarred golden.

She takes out a cigarette. Long, slender and black. Adam can't remember the name. It hovers at the edge of his memory but then something catches his eye, a dying fly on the windowsill, and the word disappears. Just like that.

He stares at the cigarette. She glances down, shrugs.

'I know,' she says. 'Terrible habit. I'm trying to give them up. It's easier to pretend.'

Adam, yearning for nicotine, swells with dark hunger.

He sees that her fingers are trembling. Quivering on the black stick of tar like the innards of a watch, the wings of a butterfly in a museum, an electroscope's gold leaf.

He watches the movement, fascinated. It seems like all the movement in the world to him. In the distance, he hears bells ring, wheels whirr, curtains rustle. Further away, children's rhymes, the flap of a bat's wings against the slate roof of a church. Further still, his heart, beating.

She is seven and he is six. It is afternoon, early summer. Bright. No school. The quarry is ten minutes away. It's always seemed like a great idea to go there but they've never had the opportunity. Then something happens, a mother's migraine, warm wind blowing in through the open hall door. Possibly a visitor. The stage is set. The chance is upon them. They take it.

They walk up the road and through the palm-studded grounds of the gloomy church, imagining the thunderous saints in their grey arches sneering at their disobedience. George sticks out her tongue. Adam waits till the coast is clear, then throws a handful of gravel at the granite wall, under a stained-glass image of a shrunken bleeding Jesus. A violent gesture. Sacrilege, indeed.

On her second visit, he'd tried to speak. But before he'd got even one syllable out, the vicious crab in his chest crawled upwards and clawed at his words, forcing them back into his throat.

He coughed. He coughed.

'Jesus!' she said. He could see pity and panic fight for space in her face. He wanted her to call the nurse but instead she lunged towards him, sliding her hand under his head.

'It's – it's okay,' she said. 'It's okay.'

He spluttered and gasped, a dying fish, as she lifted his head, raised a glass of water to his lips. The water tasted tart. His blood, of course. Her hands were rough. Fuck off, he wanted to say. But all the words were gone, scared off for good, coughed out of him along with his rotting body, leaving nothing but a man-sized tissue stained all the reds in the world.

The disused tram track lies predatory brown in the sunlight. Across it rises a bridge, curving over the ancient sleepers and smooth green lawn like a set of false teeth. Adam likes cycling over that bridge, even though there's always the risk of going down it too fast, of smashing bike and head and bones into tiny pieces of red-spattered chalk, twisted metal, sending the grey sauce of brains everywhere.

The air hums. Adam can tell it is alive and hears insects everywhere, crackling with the promise of summer.

The cigarette makes things worse. George keeps fiddling with it, weaving it through the one-sided conversation like a conductor's baton. She caresses the black coating, taps the white filter with the calloused pad of her thumb. At times he thinks she's going to rip it apart, send the precious tobacco flying across the ward like gunshot.

He can't understand why she's tormenting him. Light the fucking thing, George. Get it over with. His irritation surprises him. Funny he should care, even now.

She doesn't light it. Hospital rules. Besides, she's giving them up, isn't she?

She talks. Christ, she talks. Coffee mornings. Tennis lessons. Weather. Headlice. Home helps. School fees. She avoids politics. As usual. Though what is she afraid of? That he'll suddenly jolt into life, start ranting on about human rights or the shitty world we're leaving the young, or worse, prod a latent reactionary nerve by disclosing an unwanted intimate detail from his cruising days? Some hope.

He sneaks a glance at her watch. Fifteen minutes five seconds. Ten. Twenty. Thirty.

She doesn't notice him looking. He would. If it was the other way round, and he was sitting at her bedside, he would take note of her every sideways glance. And he'd wonder why. Why count any more, Adam, when all it does is take you down?

But he's always counted; he's a scientist, comfortable with numbers. Besides, everybody does it, don't they? Parcels out their life; if not with coffee spoons, then something else. Adam's parcels used to be schooldays. How he longed for holidays – Easter, Christmas, and best of all, summer. Then, one September, he realised that he could long for the rest of his life until one day there wouldn't be a life left to long for. Realising didn't stop him.

She talks. Oh, she talks.

At the bottom of the quarry is a pool of black water. They look down at it from a height. Their reflections in the pool look funny, like bad photographs. Adam asks George what's in the pool to make it so dark. She hesitates – then, with conviction, says, 'The tar baby.'

Adam shivers and prays they won't fall in. He's heard of the tar baby, the black sticky mess fairies leave in your bed if you don't do what you're told. It eats you up, says his uncle. It sucks out your blood and grinds your bones for porridge. Then it turns you into tar too. Adam couldn't bear that, to have to squelch from bed to bed when the fairies tell him, just to teach some other poor boy a lesson.

He doesn't tell George he's scared. She won't understand. Besides, she's the girl. She's the one who's supposed to be afraid.

A silence. She swallows. Adam has glazed over, is staring at the middle distance, but the sudden movement in her throat drags his eyes to her face. She blushes and looks away. Idly, she taps the cigarette against the *New Scientist* she's brought in as a present for him.

'Do you remember?' she says.

Something twists the blackened seersucker surface of Adam's right lung.

Stupid question.

Still, the noises around him stop.

They lean over, staring at their alien, distant reflections.

'Jump in,' says George. 'I dare you.'

Huff, puff, bluster. She is seven, he is six, remember.

'No way!'

'Go on,' says George. 'I dare you.' Her freckles are brown rain on her face.

It's then she pushes him; a little push, but it feels like more. Years later, at times of stress, he feels her fingers at that point on his arm, embedded into his skin.

'You're not afraid, are you?' she says.

'Course not.'

What else can he say? He looks down at the tar baby's pool.

'Okay,' he says. 'But you go after.'

'Okay.'

A crude pathway leads from the crest of the quarry to a broken, sheared-off drop halfway down. He'll have to jump from there. The height isn't the worry. Adam's good at diving. It's the tar baby he's thinking about.

He curls his lower lip in under the gummy ridge where his baby teeth used to be. George looks at him, green eyes candid. Adam lifts a foot and climbs over the rusting rail they've put up to stop people going down the path.

The rail wobbles, but he's over.

Adam looks down as he runs and sees the yellow ground flash past, flaking stone from under his feet in their navy runners. The two white stripes on the sides of the runners blur, making him dizzy. He skids on the loose stones. George wouldn't skid. Her runners are much better than his. But then, everything that George has is much better.

He comes to the edge, pulls himself to a stop. Strangely enough, the pool looks much farther away now that he's closer. His reflection doesn't stand out as much. He has merged into the cliff behind him. The city hums in the distance.

'And then—' she says, and stops, suddenly confused. 'Christ, Adam. Do you know, I can't remember what happened next...'

Her face concertinas; a mixture of disbelief, amusement. Sadness?

Adam lets the moment hold, treasuring the silence. He is an ivory hull in a sea of snot green but he can still treasure silence. Just before it passes and she starts off again on another, safer, subject, he speaks.

'George?' he says. It's the first time he's called her name in thirty years. It's an effort. He's forgotten how ugly he sounds.

She flinches. He can smell her tension. Fight or flight. I dare you.

'Yes?' she says. Adam lifts his hand. It's an effort.

Puzzled, she glances where he's pointing. When she looks up, there's a glint of something familiar, tigerish and yellow, in her green irises.

She looks around. Then she gets up, making the springs creak, and pulls the curtain along its casters so it encloses the bed. In the cool green cell it's strange to hear the noises from the rest of the ward continue to filter through, unchanged. She sits down, close to him, and puts the black cigarette into her mouth. Against the black, her lipstick is a garish salmon pink. Some of it has flaked onto her teeth.

She takes out a golden lighter, flicks it. The small blue flame eats at the black tip. She inhales. As soon as the smoke is in her mouth, she stubs the cigarette out on a folded tissue.

She leans over. He smells her perfume. Citrus. Sweat. Under the neat preppy collar of her blouse he catches a glimpse of her cleavage. Her breasts are brown, freckled. Fleshy. She places her mouth on his. Her lips are dry.

She opens her mouth.

He looks into her eyes. Green, speckled with gold. A catseye. A universe.

Adam stares at the pool. He tries not to think of it but pictures of the tar baby crowd his mind. He sees himself falling, sinking, but never rising again to the surface, sucked down by the bottomless dark into the arms of the white-eyed thing with gnashing teeth.

What if he doesn't jump? George would understand. She knows him inside out, after all. And—

No. Even if George doesn't mind, the tar baby will. Oh yes, it will come for him, if not tonight, then soon, snuggle up to him in bed and taunt him for his cowardice. It will put its sticky black hands over Adam's eyes and in the darkness tell him, *You are mine. I own you.*

He glances up. She's waiting.

You are mine.

He parts his lips. He is aware of her tongue lurking there, somewhere in the background, as much as he is aware of his own. She lets go, closing her eyes, and he inhales. The smoke creeps past his teeth, into his ruined throat, down to wash the mottled surface of his dying lung where the cancer waits, counting down.

Adam runs, falls. He thinks *No!* as his cheap navy runners leave the path but it's too late to go back. He drops, a half-baked Icarus, flying past the orange cliff.

The world tilts, the black rises to meet him. Adam lands with a boneshattering thud on his knees. The pool is three inches deep, full of damp leaves and muck.

Worms writhe around his screaming kneecaps. Adam sees the twist of their pale pink bodies in nightmares for years afterwards.

Her eyes blur, overlap in parallax, too close for him now to make out the individual glints and specks. He sucks the smoke in, greedily.

It starts raining. Adam picks himself up, muck and blood streaming down his arms and legs in dirty streaks, and turns to face the cliff.

She is gone.

Footsteps squeak on the linoleum. George pulls her mouth off his, sucking his breath away, and scrambles back to her usual spot on the bed. She pats her hair, fixes her clothes, doesn't meet his eyes, looking for all the world like a guilty lover.

The thought makes Adam smile.

She looks up, smiles back.

They kneel on the playroom floor. The marbles roll. Crash, bang. Stars collide.

At the door of the ward, she pauses and looks back. Her hair is amber in the evening light. She blows him a kiss. Then she vanishes. Adam's bad lung screams. He knows he and George aren't the same person, has known this ever since the day she pushed him, but it still hurts when she goes.

From the corner of his eye he sees the small gold watch on the nurse's wrist. Thirty-two minutes and twenty seconds. A minute for every year he has known her. More or less.

He closes his eyes and drops, towards the waiting blackness.

Lure

It's those little bitches start it, sniffing her out at the Black Horse. The rain helps. It's pissing again, hard, third week in a row, and the waters under the city are high, squirming for release. But were there no bitches, or no sniffing, or sniffing at a different stop, the chain of confluence may never have led to me. They get on at Fatima and go tracking up the tram, baying and hooting as they sway past the commuters, on the prowl for prey. It's that feral intent first disturbs my sleep, down in the gravelly bed of small, sweet Camac. Though it takes a while to rouse me – they're distracted too, sad little cunts. Chatting in capslock and exclamation points, middle fingers Snaptweeting Facetagram, stroking and flicking clever as a loverboy's.

Nine of them, groomed to the last inch. Hair glossy and smooth, nails dripping charms and studded with sparklers. Eyes decked with thick black liner, Kardashian-style, and lashes – the best ones, seventy squids a side, bought, not robbed, a point of pride, with first disco money begged from their nans. Dressed in silks that sort of match: hot-pink puffa jacket over grey schooltrousers. The same trousery type-things their quarry's wearing now, though – hah, such wilfulness! – she hates them.

Better that you blend in, Margaret, they've told her at the House. *We don't want a repeat of what happened last time. We can't afford for you to be so*

v   u   l   n   e   r   a   b   l   e

Soft nursey pat on the arm, but between the lines she can read the beancounter eurosigns.

Shame. She loves the glamour, this Margaret, no, this—

Magpie.

Had a bright blue coat once, like a kingfisher's plumage. Velvet, with a fur collar. These days it's granny clothes, granny colours – sedge-grey, sludge-green, to match the oldlady cough and swelled ankles. The only swank she has left is her hair, and under all the *nicey-nicey no pressure, in your own time, Margaret* she can tell the House is itching for her to chop that off too. Blend? Don't make me laugh. Cunts is cunts. They'll never see a blending, no matter how sludgy she makes herself.

The tram hisses up the canal. The bitches' voices grow nearer. She shifts her weight towards the window, hunching small as she can behind her mountain of bags. Proud Magpie: stubborn lady of the hoarders and gee-gaws, Magpie who used to light up the dance-floor. On her other side, a bulky Afrohair is arguing with a phone. No, No, No, she says, each No a nail. Opposite, an easterneuro with razory cheekbones watches, grommets of plaster itching under his fingernails now the booming is back in business.

'Fucksake.' The bitches are only three seats away now. 'This is boring. Can we not just leave it?'

'Wait.' Their leader, a lanky ginger, sniffs. 'D'yous get that?'

Oh, *eau de Magpie*, distinct as the whorls of her most unusual brain. Under the silt and gravel and river-weeds, my sleeping nostrils open, caught by her scent, that coaxing mix of meds-sweat, coffee, rose attar and fagbreath.

Up goes her elbow. The action is sluggish, sticky as honey. The pack lurch forward, all nose.

Blackhorse, says the lady on the speaker, and the easterneuro reaches for his bag, Leap Card sweaty against his palm. The ginger's eyes swerve, find the seat he's about to empty.

Magpie's mouth is bone-dry. I taste the salt thirst of her dread—

Oh, woman, you will be mine.

And come myself awake.

'Ah!' yelps everyone, even the bitches, as outside the Camac bursts its banks. I ride it, powering through the young saplings lining the towpath at the top lock, and flood into the canal. Magpie's eyes are open. Does she see me?

A lithe flash in wetsuit black, straddling the foaming waters under the bridge.

Does it matter? I see her.

The doors chime. The easterneuro sits back down. 'Wrong stop,' he says, but no one is listening. Magpie has a finger in her mouth. Teeth against bone. The tram slicks away from Stad Capall Dubh to curve up the Naas Road. The bitches lunge forward, all gabble again. I tense, I dive, back into little Camac's depths, under her bed into the spiderweb fractures of the water table. Around my throat, something glints.

At the terminus, she dismounts, sticking close to the large woman with the Afro. I'm looking on from a height, sucked from the mouth of Camac's sister Poddle into rain vapour by an unseasonal swatch of hot air. The bitches cluster, scramble, unleash. They're heading for the Square, their usual spot: ground floor entrance, Tesco.

Magpie gnaws at her finger. I smell the thoughts as they glitch, clusterfucking the pathways in her most unusual brain. They say she has no insight, a byproduct of her blahdiblah, but even with the medload it's not all upstairs for dancing with Magpie. She knows well as anyone what's safe to do.

The House, with its secure door.

Its secure door. Its tedious telly, its ohnonothinglike-Magpie headcase Housemates, its aren'tweralldoinggreat arm-patting nurses, its yetagainthesameoldboring shite.

The long walk there, ten minutes up the avenue.

Darkness and rain. Alone, exposed—

My turf. My balls twinge.

The leader of the pack stops, looks back.

Magpie's finger leaves her mouth. She lunges after the Afrohair and hurries across the tracks in her shadow, clunky and awkward, making for the other entrance, the one the bitches never use.

Oh, the faith you small-minded beings place in the camouflage of crowds.

Don't suggest I am leading her there. Quite the converse: if I had my limited wits about me, I would stop and consider, because such places rarely lend themselves to my kind. But I am gagging for it. What's a chase without a challenge? And I'm a cocky fuck, long where it matters but short on memory, blinded my own gorgeousness, the conviction that if I want a ride, she'll want it too, my lady of the desperado pheromones. So I fall as rain, swoosh as puddles towards the nearest drain, slide down gravity's pipe and squeeze, through a hairline fissure, into the centre's concrete foundations.

It wasn't always like this. Once, long ago, after the move, one of them, the ginger, was nice to her. Called her Missus, asked her if she wanted help across the road. When Magpie said no, the ginger switched. Full of compliments, finding her weak spot, pressing hard. I like your coat, Missus. Very stylish. Where d'ya get it? Your hair's a lovely colour. Is that real? Later, the questions expanded: did she have the time, a light, a couple of euro for the bus. They would have a laugh. *You're great craic, Missus.* Her guard lowered. Nice kids, she thought. Little pal, she would think when the ginger, Redser, crossed her mind, because – *that's what we are, Missus, pals, yeah?* – the bitch had said so herself. She can't remember when it turned. The ginger starting to call her names, sly invective over the traffic. The others joining in, laughter and whistling. Words she could parse but not hear. Then they crossed. Clustering up behind her. Jabs and digs. A shove. Nails in her skin. Tugs at her tangle of crazy-coloured hair. That night, on her way back from the library, a shock as the bag got pulled. She didn't pull back. A choice. Her fingers flapped, useless, as the girls shook it out, all her precious stuff tumbling to the footpath. Mags, picture books, make-up, notebooks, her very photoID self.

Fuckers.

The word comes up from nowhere. She stops, halfway down the make-up aisle in Boots.

'Fuckers,' she says aloud.

Under the concrete foundations – unh – I stiffen and jolt.

The whitecoat at the med counter glances over. Doubletake, then a smile. Lovely smile, full of teeth, full of pity.

'Can I help you?'

Magpie smiles back, bland and sweet. The same one she gives to her rellies – *Poor little Maggie* – at the insufferable family parties.

The pearly fangs waver.

I begin to hurry.

I come up against dead ends, blocked plugholes, air-pockets. Foam gathers at my mouth. My watery teeth begin to gnash. I am backed up now, blue-balled. Around my neck, my bridle gathers mass, link by link. Can I feel it? Hardly. I lie. Not at all. Do you lot ever sense your own source of life, or power? All I feel is need, and her, its maker.

She's itching, from the inside out. The place is off, and so is she. The coloured lights she normally likes so much are hurting her head. The sounds too: that smarmy yapping of the man on the tannoy, the different musics tempo-clashing beyond the red end of the spectrum. The electronic crackling through the air, so loud she can't even hear the little kids asking *Why?* as they trail after their mothers, though here, they never ask a *Why* like a question. Too dazed under the tinny buzz. Here, everyone's—

a word she loved in school

—unmoored.

She clings to the shadows near the casino and watches them, a mass of plankton drifting up the travellators, drifting down. Pushing buggies, pushing trolleys, catching their breath on leather sofas and blondwood benches, stretching like catapult elastic past Dealz and Jackie's only to fling back again, seduced by the eternal promise of the special offer. On basement level, she can see others, lonely little sealice prowling the empty lots. Underneath them – though she can't see this – the water nexus of the Tamhlacht plague-pit, and me, bucking and scraping for a way out.

That finger's between her teeth again. Her throat is aching. The thirst is worse now, killing her. She'd murder for a Coke, but on this level it's all fastfoods, and much as she appreciates their warm grease chomp, cosy-cosy, dancing days again afterthepubbeforetheclub, she's not so off that she'll risk queuing in their white glare, a big obvious look-at-me sirencalling through the wide windows.

'Fuck *you*!'

A laugh. Two lads, skin pure Americano-no-milk, hurtle out of the casino. She shrinks back, but they're so constrained by their own youth and vigour she doesn't even flicker on their peripheral. She's just Crazy Old White static; formless. My heart rips. Woman, you need someone who will see beyond that. The lads begin a mock-fight, their arms flailing like bishops' maces. She ducks between them, then—

Dearie me.

Realises she is out in the open. A flicker of ginger hair, coming up the travellator. Dread washes her mouth again, seasoned with a vinegary undertone I have no word for that sends hardening shivers down my watery cock.

stupid stupid stupid

When she does that—

Oh, woman, you are mine.

I find a conduit. I ooze towards it. I'm in.

She edges back to Boots, fast as the meds allow. White coat looks over. Out. Dunnes. Not a soul. Out again.

Past the glassesplace, keyplace, candyplace. Her breath is shortening, her lungs aching. Another flicker of ginger. Now the pack is on the same level as her; across the chasm, beyond the white sails, sucking shakes from toxicplastic Mingles beakers, laughing.

She swerves, her arm thumping into a button on the wall. The lift opens with a ting.

They look up, across.

She shifts back, bumps into glass. Her eyes dart around. And—

Ah, I sigh, as her vision snags on a place that's new to the routeways of her complex perception, and up from the soggy underground of the Tallaght marshes, carried on the travellator by mist and sweat and tears and cum and blood and eyeballs and the black stuff deep in bones and the yellow stuff crusting on the hidden corners of clothes, and all the other juices that flow through close-pressed human tissue, because where there's water, there's a way, I canter, her drop-dead gorgeous answer to prayer.

She has backed herself up into the doorway of an empty unit. The door is closed but there's no *Closed* notice. A lazy patch of water seeps out from under it, as if a cleaner knocked over a bucket inside and forgot to mop up. No name above the doorway, no shutters. No shutters on the windows either, just themselves, misty with half-dried Windolene. Behind the mist an ancient sign. *Don't fall in, we need the business.* Three exclamation points, like it's a joke. Under the sign a glass ball, swirling with colour.

Alluring. Another word she loved. It made her see things, but not in the bad way. It evoked. That is what good words do, Maggie, her teacher used to say. They make you think of other things. So: this fisher's ball in a window. Evoking bright feathers and glinting metal bending under river water. Her father, wandering Duncan, on the canal bank. The fishing rod. Slick as a whip, laughing through the air. The trout he caught for supper, greedy mouths sucking for the hook. The other small fish too small to have names, sucking at the trouts' bellies. Her hand in his, sticky with the dregs of ice-cream.

See that, Magpie?

A plume of white foam leaping from the lock. Flaming mane, wild tail; full of life.

That's a kelpie.

Her fingers extract, reach to touch.

Ah-ah, Magpie. He's a cocky wee lad, and handsome, but your waterhorse is not like other horsies. He can bite.

She seizes the handle.

It gives and, with a click, the door opens. I seep under its frame, across the puddle, and lead her into a place of failing light.

The sounds outside have disappeared, sinking under a blanket of silence. The smeary windows are portholes, the world behind them a bright blur. A tap is dripping somewhere, or maybe a burst pipe, she thinks, or the rain. Her eyes adjust. She makes out the fuzzy edge of a countertop, covered in dust so thick it's filth. Old posters are stuck to the back wall, peeling at the corners. She can't see what's on them, but gets a sense of her father's homeland. Tumbling water, lochs and mountains. She steps forward. Her foot touches something.

Ah, I sigh, and flow myself along the wet lino into the ragged pile on the ground.

She freezes. I give her space, stay still. Hear her neurons spark, connecting as I take on the shape of my guise.

I am a man, she sees, but one that's in a fair state. Covered in torn rags and smelling of river-weeds, with long dark hair matted in dreads. I am lying on the floor, on a heap of useless crap. I appear to be asleep. I feel the headline labels swizzle through her mind. Vagrant. Migrant. Mendicant.

Mendicant. The fuck? I open an eye.

She jerks back, but doesn't run.

We take each other in.

I shake my head, let the dreads lift. I know her well enough to tell she has a weakness for men with wild hair. I turn my whirling eyes fluid and soft, let my nostrils flicker, my skin quiver. A hint of vulnerability can work wonders with the chicas. I stay prone, but edge my elbows back, artfully dislodging the rags so she can get an eyeful of my bareness, and prop myself up on my arms. Makes the biceps look good. Strong. Knotted ropes over a grooved and scar-pocked six-pack. But with the legs a bit arseways, she can see I'm no threat.

Her stare softens, slides down my legs to my feet. Oh, dirty girl. You know not what you do. I hear her father's voice.

Know how to tell a kelpie from a real horse, Magpie?
Uh-uh.
Its hoofs.

I let my breathing match hers, shallow, as if I'm afraid.

My guise clarifies in the mirror of her pupils. I'm youngish, she sees, not old, but not young either. On my collarbone glistens my bridle, a medallion dangling from silver links. Nice touch, I think, watching her pores flare. My bones angled under the skin in a way she hasn't seen before, and my skin itself most strange. A deep colour, green-blue. I am – I have to credit myself – damnfucking handsome. She must know now she wants me, even if she didn't before.

She pulls her jacket tighter around her belly.

Fuck him with his looks, she thinks.

And oh, I groan, for in her arrogance she has made herself nineteen again, pale and lush and irresistible in the moonlight.

I snort, hardening. My chest moves. My bridle gleams. Her face changes and I smell her need, rank as rivermulch. I hoist myself up, scrabble to a sort of standing. My legs are shaking, their muscles twitching, a newborn foal's. I tilt my head, exert my glamour. She steps to me, and – hah! – she is fluid as a mermaid. We stand, body-to-body. A molecule of space between us. I smell the mud of her sweat. She lifts a finger, her left pinky. It's a nub, two joints shorter than the others. The heat off her skin is unholy. I shudder, my edges splintering. She stops.

Thoughts fight in her face.

Yes No

Oh fuck.

Are those arms, she is thinking. Or—

Yes, Magpie, they are. Shaking as they bear my weight on the counter.

Are those feet, she is thinking. Or—

Yes, Magpie. Bare. Look. They have no—

And I invoke him again: wandering Duncan, the useless, adored father.

Kelpie's hoofs, Magpie, are always the wrong way round.

She staggers then, flooding. Her father and mother early on, kissing, fumbling. You are so. I will always. The things people say to each other on soaps. I've never. Only you. I need. And dancing, a boy with yellow hair, sex more than once, and it's mushing now, the years held in her mind, so I can't tell if this was the dancing days before her beautiful neurochemistry began its journey beyond the norms of quotidian balance, or, naughty Magpie, the tricky self-medicating times when she was sure she could manage on her own, and oh, she could, and oh, that sex wasn't bad, not bad, not bad at all—

Her teeth lunge for a straw that isn't there; her pinky shoots up, clamps in. Her throat is a bone funnel, her eyes itching pebbles.

'You know me now,' I say. I let my words be what they are, bubbles in the underwatery silence between us. She watches them rise, up to the infinite heights of the empty unit's surface, and the look on her face makes me almost come again, like I did waking from the canal. I hold back. It's an effort.

'Let's get out of here.' I offer her my hand. A gentlemanly gesture. 'I'll take you for the ride of a lifetime. You'll never think of that fella with the yellowy hair again. Stupid bastard.'

Her face softens. Her hand approaches mine, then drops to the springy place between my not-right legs. She grabs.

I hear myself giggle, a shocking whinny, high and weak. No, woman, I should say. Not here, I should say. Or something equally masterful, for in my dumb watery awareness I know it's risky here, not enough in my element, not enough wet to do it the way I do it. But I'm a creature of action, not great with words at the best of times, and—

there's puddles here, she's whispering, and dripping taps and coiling wires

and

take me, she's whispering

—and her mouth is lowering to mine, and that smell, her breath, her ageing body, I want, I will, I open my gnashers to suck her air.

She stops.

Laughter?

I look up. Vague pink shapes have gathered outside, their foreheads and palms pressing clammy patches of zombie-black against the window. A stink rises in Magpie: smell of old rivers, sweet underland flowings dirtied by shit and chemi-dump. Smell of her brain. Smell of fear. She gags.

Fuckers.

Look, I should say. Ignore them, I should say. Just— Keep— I'll sort them if—

Sweetheart, I should say.

her weak spot

Beautiful lady of my lonely nights, woman of the majestic arse and queenly tits, sweet little fanny that I love to lose myself in, clever Magpie, brilliant Magpie, most superior Magpie—

But she's too busy looking around, looking around, looking around to hide.

And: Ah, ah, ah, I groan, furious, because this is bollocks, not how it works, do the usual thing, the same old thing, fuck that, no, and I send my frustration through my cold skin into her blood. She stumbles. I grab her wrist in my knife-and-hook barbed fist. She pulls, but I'm too strong. I reach for her throat, the throbbing pulse. I hate to do it like this, no finesse, but my cock can only take so much teasing, and I know no means yes, I know she wants me, and now – ah – she knows that too, her gaze sagging, her fingertips wilting against the links of my bridle, and—

'There!' Redser's voice.

The bitches' eyes have broken through.

Magpie's irises sharpen. Two points of light, gleaming silver.

Fuck, I think.

And: Fuck, I scream, pulling back too late as she yanks at the bridle, using the rusty edge of my own index finger to slice the chain free from my neck.

In all fables, there comes a point. The porridge eaten, the granny's door knocked, the key turned in the bluebeard's door.

The handsome kelpie tricked, his glamour broken by the maiden – or vice versa.

The point of any fable, Maggie, said her English teacher in school twenty-five years earlier, when she was seventeen and doing her Leaving, eighteen months before the chemical coding she got from wandering Duncan's sister and his mother before that and a great-uncle before then and you name it back to the start began carving those interesting new paths in her brain, *is to make you think.*

The point of a tale is to offer up an alternative vision of reality.

Discuss these statements, with reference to the text.

The point of the telling is a compass, she wrote. *Here sweetheart, find your way*.

Sprinkles of glass caught in a net.

Rags and cloths. A grill. A tarp. Knotted ropes. A bundle of fish-hooks. A gutting knife. Six Dutch Gold empties, dented and bashed. A rusting angler's rod.

My guise's bright eyes reduced to maggotcans, cartwheeling along the grooves of her brain.

You know how to master a kelpie, Magpie? Take away his silver bridle.

I lose charge.

My ions rupture from their opposite poles. My droplets wheel into space, howling for their stable, their nearest body of water. The boiler system coiled in the services room behind the empty unit makes a sound like a shriek as the heated rainwater inside it, hearing my call, balloons around an airlock. The rivets creak. And she, she—

What?

She has grabbed her bags and is running.

No, I should say. You are to—

What's left of my water should be fire across the shrinking space, my teeth blistering steam scalding for her neck. But I cannot scald. I cannot adhere. My own bridle's power repels me. She finds the handle. My hydrogen and oxygen pop. They should be combining to chase her, stop her in her tracks. Instead they hover, dull, inert, gassy. She fiddles, wrenches. The washers and nuts in the boiler system screech. A click, and the door opens, knocking the nasty little bitches off their perches, setting them swishing like jellyfish, glossy hair rippling in the light of their crashing, flickering phones. The pipes squeal as – hah! – the backdraft from the open door finally sucks my vapour to it, and I am after her, have enough now to open my maw for a bite of something, anything, but I am still too slow, too late, held back by the limits of my own incohesion, and the door is closing in the drifting remnants of my face, slicing plastic, aluminium, glass between me and my lifesource and – aagh – that can't be me, pleading—

no Magpie please Magpie lady Magpie at your service Magpie
—as she emerges onto the surface, into the bright neon of the shopping daze, gasping while the smarmy man on the tannoy welcomes her back, Oh, Valued Customer, to Cheeky Monkey's Jungle Maze.

Of course that's a kelpie, Magpie, sweetheart. It's real.
There are stories of kelpies who lose their bridles and are made to serve.

e.g., the one who built the Laird's castle.

e.g., the one who ploughed for the Maiden's father.

There are stories of kelpies who lose their bridles and do not serve.

e.g., the McGrigor kelpie.

The ones that serve die, eventually.

The ones that don't die too, within twenty-four hours.

There are no stories of humans wearing the bridles of kelpies, though there are rumours that if you steal a bridle you may become half-kelpie, and gain certain gifts, so who is not to say…

I bead on the window, clumping to the toxic calcium and pyrophosphate Windolene mist. She is lifting my bridle over her head. The boiler whines. Or is that me – *me*? – whimpering like a sprog? The bitches, spotting her, readying themselves for the jeer, stop. Their spines undulate, sprigs of hornwort making space around her. The links settle, meet her skin.

It only takes a moment.

Her hair straightens and monocolours, her ankles narrow. I try to curse her, but all that comes out is a simpering plea, echoed by the boiler's gurgle. *Command me*. The years fall off. She is plumping and rounding, growing juicy in the right places. I try again to curse, my high-and-mighty Magpie, and her unwitting vassal cunt-pack that yanked me out of my ancient bed, and the poxy Luas, and this plagued centre of filthy commerce which has seen me so unfuckingdone. The boiler squeals. *Command me*. Am I come so impotent? Her smell loses its pheromonal distinction, turns sweet and harsh. Her skin is dropping hairs, toes to neck. I try again. In the pipes, a rivet pops and as her pores plug with aluminium and synthetic perfume – yes! – a jet of boiling water spurts. It comes to me, comes to me, then—

What? Something happens in her brain and—

The water swerves against its own nature, ricocheting against the proudly erect if slightly rusted fishing rod propped against the counter, slanting sideways into the nest of wires dangling from a half-open fuse box.

What used to be my tail connects, hard. My hydrogen and oxygen collide. A bang, like thunder. The lights snap out. The travellators stutter. The music groans and slows. A wrench and I am pulled – oh, agony – through the silica of the windows.

'Missus?' says Redser. In the underwater glimmer of the exit signs, her eyes are wide, woken.

'You what?' says Magpie. 'I'm your pal. Maggie. D'yous not recognise me? Now shut your ginger hole and let's go robbing.'

The pack yelp.

The trip is flicked. The lights snap back on. The travellators whirr.

'Kids,' says someone, tutting, but the moment for the collective nod has passed.

The afternoon settles. Robbing and laughing and more shakes. I am dragged in their wake, every shift in direction stretching my molecules thinner. Make-up counters, mirror selfies. A fresh quarry, name-calling and hooting. The fusion has cost me. I try to resist, but with each attempt my ions spark, losing more charge. My gases spiral off, my unwilling meniscus lengthens. I adhere, I adhere, capillary-sucked into her pack, fruitlessly trying to calculate through the elemental, disintegrating courseways of my limbic mind how to win my bridle back.

Coaxing, trickery, servitude, crucifix.

The Inverness kelpie thought he would win, Magpie. McGrigor had a cross over his door, which wouldn't let the stolen bridle pass the threshold. But McGrigor cheated. He flung the bridle through his window and the kelpie—

In all the archive, there are no examples.

Lovely chain, Maggie, says Redser. Very stylish. Her voice has softened at the edges; on another girl, might almost sound unsure.

The pack's attention catches, bound.

It is then my ears should prick. But I'm too fucked-up on rage, too focused on my loss, to remember that thralling pulls two ways.

It's what we call a deficit, explained the first psychiatrist to her mother. *A symptom associated with the blahdiblah.* Shaking his head with something that looked like it was intended to be sorrow but hadn't quite got there. *You see, she has no insight, no words to describe what she is experiencing.*

Says who?

The kelpie's bridle, her ignorant father once told her, has the power to heal.

And now Magpie's smoothed-out body laughs and chases, her pack flowing slipstream behind her, while Magpie's becalmed mind, running on the clear multi-lane highways of what is consensually agreed to be normal, sights inwards. If I was not so maddened, split asunder from myself, I might be sighting her innards too. Was this what she saw, thieving Magpie?

The afternoon continues, and will continue again. It will keep settling, kneeling into the next, the next into a week, the week into months, the months into years. Magpie at its fore: mistress of the harry, glorious lady of the bitches. The girls will grow, sprout boobs and pubes, hips and babies. They'll grow defunct: shrink, bloat, fail, drink, fall, swell, wither, die. What matter? Their younger selves will continue the hunt. While she, chained by a glamour designed for a god to wear, remains unchanged, floating up the travellator, floating down, fluid as plankton under the uneasy light of a fisher's ball.

In all fables comes a point where someone has to choose.

I am an amoralistic entity. I am an alluring fuck. I am a nasty, horny bastard who likes nothing better than a good ride. I am a warning to the young and vigorous. Ride with me, and I will take you to the depths, rip out your guts, eat your parts and send a seared token back to the land of the living to let them know you do not get away. To the virgins: do not mess with strange men. To the children: do not play in rushing water. To the men: do not dare change the course of rapids, poison lakes and groundwaters or think, just because you fly over clouds, you can master them. I, a face of God, was begot out of the terror of dumb beasts, a herd throat-slit and hobbled and driven into fjords to drown by Vikings desperate to appease the force of wild waters.

Healing? Fuck off. Look to your own kind for that, please.

Magpie stops. And it's only then – curse me for my giddy attention – that my ears prick.

'Boring,' she says. She should have better words, but assimilation always comes at a cost.

She shrugs off Redser's arm. The girls stare.

'Ah here,' says Redser.

'She taking that chain with her?' says another.

Before they know it, they're running after her. Little glossy links, alive, young and foolish. And me, this craven gentled thing she has reduced me to, I—

Have I a choice?

—follow too.

She leads them down and out of the centre, through the carparks, past the curry house and the tanning salon, across the two main roads and into the college grounds. The evening is fading; the rain greying. My own element conspires with her against me, pushing me down, sweeping me on. Some of the girls gabble about finding action, getting hold of lads or buying cider or making a show of the snobby yokes from the college. Magpie pays them no heed. Her feet pump faster, meeting soggy earth, a hollow near a fence. I meet earth and hollow too; instead of wetting, I bead, roll forward. She is not sure where she's going, and the freedom of that sings at her throat. Don't ask me what it tastes of. Beside her chuckles a thin brown ribbon of water, reflecting the lights of the industrial estate, its narrow banks shielded by the poplars and the haw, wild rose, nettles, thistles and docks. I'm on it, but not merged, my incoherent molecules refusing to sink, scuttling forward on its surface like marbles.

The pack are starting to whinge about their shoes. Redser's steps splash behind Magpie's, anxious and grim.

Across the pedestrian walkway into the park. Past the five fairy bridges, and the empty school, creepy without the kids playing in it, and the brick culvert dammed with dead mattresses and rotting shopping baskets. Magpie's almost galloping. There's a breathless mutter from the pack about going robbing in the Penny Black, but they're past the pub before they know it.

The sky is the colour of dirty silver. The rivulet's banks have widened, the ground marshy. The girls are muddy, tired. One or two are sobbing. But they can't halt and nor, sad creature, can I. The park is deserted, the red and yellow exercise toys at the edge of the man-made pond catching the last bit of light. We pummel towards it. Only a lone heron is awake, standing on the far bank.

Magpie stops. The poplars sigh.

I stop too, swirling above the water. The surface is a pinpricked lead under the no-moon rain. My edges droop, brush it, and—

Stick.

Redser's stare is a clenched fist, white at the rims. 'Why are we here?'

And: Hahh, I sigh, as, with an effort, Magpie pulls my bridle off her neck. I feel her hair tangle and lift, sheen black-blue and pearl-green, her ankles swell, her shape lurch back to its older self, her lungs coarsen, her bloods clog, *eau de Magpie* filling the air as the grooves in her mind begin to fractal again.

Redser grunts, recoils. The others don't see, still gazing at my bridle, transfixed as Magpie shakes its silver links over the water.

The pond roils. Its surface tension screams. Breaks. Gives itself to me, and up I geyser. Eyes wheels of fire, teeth like JCBs.

They are aghast. Redser can't even speak. She looks at Magpie and the bitter loathing of her disbelief—

Oh, child.

—makes my incipient cum turn to bile.

I puke my ring up, right in front of them. I spurt steaming water, I spit pebbles. I split and drop, drenching them. I duck my head, shake my mane, spatter my sourness over them. The girls shriek.

Magpie points at me, the nub of her little finger grey in the twilight.

Command.

Finally I see.

The story of the ten children. A gaggle of smartarse little bitches on the monster's back, taken by his savage dive through the pond's soggy bed into the bottomless nexus of the water-table, devoured, destroyed, only their empty guts floating up to the surface of this pathetic machine-built excuse of a pond to show they ever existed. I can taste their parts already and it sickens me. She'll use me, and keep using me, until all the bitches of the world are gone and I am spent, my guts corroded from breaking down their base materials.

Can I refuse? Like McGrigor's kelpie, shrinking, screaming, into oblivion over the span of a day? Or must I accept? Like the other pathetic craythur who surrendered his immortality to serve a farmer's daughter, for the sake of a lie your limited kind call love?

There's one chance. Maybe, when all the bitches are gone, she'll give my bridle back to me. And, though by then I'll be too far gone to be restored, I may still curse her with my dying breath.

In all fables, the hero has to choose.

No good ending here. I might as well get fed.

I rear back, a tower of roiling black, my stallion cock hardening again, my spine stretching, growing the extra vertebrae to fit them.

The girls moan, cower.

'No,' says Redser. 'That isn't. You're fucking—'

'Get up on him,' says Magpie, fighting through her brain's returning frazzle. She pushes Redser, hard, in the small of her back. The child falls forward, yelps, gurgles, flails. Not waiting for the push, the others follow, fast, and meet my watery spine. Under their squealing, I hear their sitbones grate, pissy with fear.

Magpie lifts her pinkie again. Then—
What?
A flick of her swollen wrist. My bridle's in the air.
'Mine!' yowls Redser, surfacing.
Fuck, no.
I leap. They scream.
The sinkhole opens.

'What happened, Maggie, pet?' said her mother, cowering in her midnight bed. Magpie at nineteen, pale and nude and drenched, crazy hair a tangle of corkscrews down her back. Her left hand out, a slow drip of blood. The pinkie gone from the first joint. Wagging her head, no words. Brainfuse. Overload of insights meant only for the holy and the dead. Me in the shadows, the face of God grinning at her.

Her father, Duncan, slunk back against his pillow. His eyes a stranger's, dull and lifeless.

In Barra, where he hails from, though he's been dead twenty years, they talk about the tenth child, the one who is always last. The one on the shore who doesn't follow its friends, and get up on the waterhorse's back to be turned into sausage meat in its fiery belly. But smart though this child be, it's only human, so it can't help petting the monster's mane – us kelpies is alluring fucks, after all – and once it does its flesh adheres to ours, so something has to give. In some rivers the child cuts off its own hand. In others it just severs a finger.

He went wandering after that, Duncan. Split the day before Magpie got out of the first bin. It was the last time she or her mother would see him.

The little girls are gone into the night, drenched and shivering. Some sobbing, some laughing. Some already starting to dispute and minimise. A couple silent.

Now it's just us. Magpie, sitting on her favourite bench, her hoard of bags safe around her, smoking a quiet fag and watching as, lissom in my coat of wetsuit black, I prowl over the settling pond while it lowers down the barrel-innards of the sinkhole. Broken bits of red and yellow plastic bob and catch, tugged down, sink, resurface, swim.

I smell her neurons hiss. She is thinking. Of the girls, I'm sure, sailing high across the sinkhole into their uncertain futures. She may be reflecting on Redser, the awful disappointment that shone through the child's eyes when her grabby little fingers brushed my bridle and, for a heartbeat, de-alchemised my silver links into a shitty tangle of bent beercan pull-tops and mouldering lures before my teeth ripped it away from her, restoring the liquidity of wonder to its rightful state. Fool me twice, yeah, yeah. She may be speculating about what shadow, if any, that moment will cast on Redser's life, and finding she doesn't much care. Not even I can tell if Magpie is approaching her own nub; the memory of her pinkie stump as it pushed against the ginger's skinny back, and if that recollection carries anything beyond sensation – remorse, satisfaction, shame. I'd hazard a bet, say no. The feeling of things brought into balance is usually weightless.

She throws her fag-butt away. She stands.

Does she see me?

No matter. I see her.

The lights of the House twinkle in the distance.

She turns.

I could follow. I have my tricks, after all. I can be anything: seeping mud, falling rain. I could lick her face, nuzzle her openings, brush my dreads against her cheeks, her body, her hands. Cup her elbows, tickle her feet, stroke my fingers through her hair, rub my glittering chain of droplets against her nipples. I could stalk, pounce, watch her tease and kick. Lift her, hold her, observe her bend and strain against me, scrape her pointed foot up the length of my flank. Raise her arms, waving. She, I have no doubt, knows this. I'll have you yet, I say as she disappears, blending into the greyness, and across the empty parkland, I hear her brain spark. I smell her lungs creak. I see her heart's hoofs gallop through her miraculous flesh, course wanton in her bloods, doing patient battle there with the meds and serial vaccinations and antivirals and nicotine-caffeine hits. Under the putrid chemi-foam I taste the proud steel of her will—

Oh, woman.

And spent, I come to rest, sinking in spirals down the unknowable labyrinth of her perfect human mind.

Headhunter

The room smells of disinfectant and urine and, underneath that, something else. Semen, thinks Sonia. The walls are a grimy institutional yellow, even yellower in the light of the overhead fluorescent. The first time she visited, the tiled floor was stained dark brown and had to be scrubbed. She couldn't help thinking of shit.

Tinny rave music pumps from a cheap black player. Crap, cheesy beats under an insincere honeyed vocal. The Bear likes it, though, and if the Bear likes it, it stays.

He's kneeling on the floor in front of Sonia, hard at work. His enormous shoulders pull at the cloth of his sodden tee-shirt. Stretch and strain, ole man river. When he lifts his head, sweat glistens on his waxy forehead and catches in the scar which maims the left side of his face, carving through the eye socket like an ugly white worm. His black hair – a hedgehog crop, baby soft but bristly – glitters.

From where Sonia is sitting, his back looks like the hull of a sailboat. Two convex swells of muscle and bone, separated by a deep gully of spine. His legs, tensed and crouching, are immense tree trunks ending in huge trainers. His forearms swoop like lengths of turned wood, the muscles flexing as his wide hands squeeze paint out of tubes.

Despite his bulk, there's very little fat on the Bear. A tower of strength, thinks Sonia. A pillar of the community. Not the community at large, by any stretch of the imagination, but here, inside, he's a pillar, a tower, a myth of his own making.

He is sweating again. Probably the drugs. Maybe illness. Or it could be a problem with the heating. It's an unspoken mantra in here, in these classes anyway: keep an open mind. Though with everyone saying how innocent they are, one's mind can be easily unopened. It never takes long for the Bear's tee-shirt to soak, the drops to glisten on his hedgehog hair. He wipes them away, over and over, but it's no use. It starts again and soon he's drenched. Drips bead his eyelashes, trickle into the corner of his mouth. He is sweating so much Sonia can taste it.

They usually start with tea, scalding hot, served in melting white corrugated plastic beakers. They sit on hard grey chairs and balance the beakers on whatever surface they can find: chair-arms, windowsills, shelves. Sonia's chair is uncomfortable, grating against her bum. His is barely able to hold his weight.

He always brings sweets, mints or chocolates. 'Bear's a demon for the sweets,' says his mate. The Bear agrees with a smile, showing in all their glory his black and missing teeth.

Once tea is served, they talk.

He spent most of the first visit quizzing Sonia. He had to check her out, be sure it was okay to spend an hour of his precious time with her. She has realised that in here, time is still precious, even though there's lots of it, ticking away like a deathwatch beetle. He asked where she lived. She told him. 'Alright,' he said with a nod. 'I grew up around there meself.' The tension in the room lifted. Things were okay. Sonia was on the right side, for now, for as long as he wanted.

Approved.

They swapped stories. Sonia told him how the neighbourhood was changing, just like the rest of the city. Pretty paving stones, a facelift for the park, and of course, new buildings – apartments and an extension to the Centra. 'Centra?' said the Bear. 'Yeah, beside the chemist.' He shook his head. Sonia told him they were talking about pulling down the flats where he'd grown up. 'They've been talking about that for years,' he said, and laughed. Sonia joined in, hesitant, not sure if it was okay to share the joke.

He asked for more news and she told him people were getting obnoxious, in shops, on the bus, especially in banks, putting their hands out for your money before you'd even said what you wanted. And everywhere there were cars, new cars, metallic colours like rainbows fashioned from silver, copper, gold and verdigris, speeding through the city like there was no speed limit and certainly no tomorrow.

He liked that. 'That'll be me when I'm outta here. Speedin through the city.'

When the Bear speaks, his voice rumbles out of the depths of him. Wheezing. Almost breathless. The words seem to come from the top of his throat. A nasal drone that slides over itself, teasing the listener to make sense of it. He doesn't pick words out one by one to make sure he's understood, but lets them slip into each other as if they're not that important. One evening before a visit, Sonia saw a programme about an English girl who was learning an accent, trying to fit in with the pimps in L.A. The next day she realised everyone inside speaks the same way. Making it her job to understand.

When the Bear gets excited, his drone speeds up, sending his sentences tumbling over each other. But if he senses her drifting, he jacks up the emotional intent behind what he's saying, marks it with a staccato 'Know-what-I-mean?'

He uses her name a lot, every second sentence, easily manufacturing intimacy. *Sonia. Sonia. Sonia.* The ball is always in his court. Around him, she feels like straw, insubstantial, easy to break.

At first he didn't believe he'd be up to it; just watched, refusing to put brush to paper. On the third week he slathered black and yellow paint on a large page, creating a malevolent likeness of his cellmate, which he tore up in a rage because it was useless, didn't look like anything. Then something snapped, a thread, a connection, and he couldn't stop himself. Worked morning noon and night, putting off the demands of the addiction as much as he could, just to get it all out.

He is twenty-six but looks older; thirty-two, thirty-three even. He's always looked older, he tells her. He was over six foot by the time he was eleven. Sonia imagines him at that age, huge and awkward but still growing, stooping to look smaller, terrifying other kids with his intensity. Being jeered, as you always are when you're a kid and you're different. That's where his nickname came from. Imagine looking like a bear at eleven.

He got the scar when he was eight, knocked down by a bus. 'I was a mess, Frankenstein, disgustin.' He reckons since then he hasn't been right in the head.

Sonia pictures him at eight, a boy lying on a trolley with his face smashed to pieces. The doctor, green-clad, bending over him. This isn't going to hurt at all. The green mask fades into blackness. In the morning the two sides of his face are sewn together with black thread.

Not right in the head.

Later she hears a contradictory account. The scar is part of – unclear how? response to, symptom of? – a deeper underlying congenital condition, something that's been with him since he was born.

Three weeks after their first meeting, he brings in a jar of Roses. Sonia chooses a caramel. It glues her teeth together, making it impossible to speak. The Bear, driven by the silence, begins to tell stories.

He has two sisters. One is fair, the other dark. Snow White and Rose Red. He tells Sonia that Snow White has fallen under again. *Sick* is the word he uses. 'She goes in waves,' he says and Sonia nods uselessly, still chewing.

Fighting it, giving way, fighting it, drowning.

'She was doin good,' he says. Snow White's clever, apparently. A reader, a dreamer. Not like him, who never had the patience for school. She knows there's a different way but the habit makes it hard to stay straight. Last year she got into trouble and received a warning. After that she stayed clean for months. And did well. 'They held her up as a, yeah, example.' He stops speaking and his dark uneven eyes go absent, inwards, thinking.

Silence bristles round him. Shame crouches on his back and shoulders, breathing heat into his ear. The air is so loaded that even if Sonia could speak, she wouldn't.

He exhales and, as if the smoke leaving his lungs was a signal, looks up. A blue S weaves up between his face and Sonia's. 'She met a fella none of us liked,' he says. As if that was enough.

Sonia wonders what happened between Snow White and her fella. Abandonment, abortion, pimping, worse? A rival gang, turf war? Money? Whatever it was, it made her go under again. And the Bear is angry at his sister for falling. When he gets up to go that day, he leaves his anger behind him in the cell like his animal namesake, big, black and savage.

He is fascinated by technique, with the very act of painting. It's magic, shamanic, how he conjures light and dark, heaven and hell, African witchdoctor and Herne the Hunter from the cheap acrylic shit they buy for the men. He daubs the paint on with shouts of the brush, using the force of his whole body. He is obsessed with pattern – dots, slashes, faces, faces – but every recurring element is different, every painting a new take. His feelings seep out from the edges like water from a sore. Hurt, anger, love, sex, death, addiction, sickness, hate, fire, silence.

He sweats so much it makes Sonia want to lean over and wipe his face.

She looks at the column of neck leading into his scarred, mysterious skull and wonders how much the paintings on paper match up to the ones he sees in his head.

He lunges in, paints a series of white dots. Bambambambambam! Suddenly on the muddy colour he has fashioned an aboriginal songpainting, a portrait of an Arab, face half in sunlight, half in dark, a red turban on his head, a fat cruel mouth, slanted cheekbones. The face reminds Sonia of something she saw once, or something she read. A man with a knife on a beach. A Clash song.

He doesn't look up at her when he's working, like a kid would, like she expected him to, needing assurance. He knows what he's doing.

The week after the Roses, he shows Sonia pictures of his family. He puts them up on the windowsill, propped up by sizzling beakers of tea, so she can compare and contrast. Snow White is lovely. A blonde fairytale princess with a winning smile, long plaits and slender arms the colour of freckled milk. She bears no resemblance to the Bear. Aware of this, he laughs his breathless laugh, showing the gaps in his crooked mouth. 'Beauty and the Beast, hah?'

Ah, Beauty, poisoned by the witch's needle.

Rose Red is different again. Both she and his mam look like Galway matriarchs with their wide strong faces, dancing dark eyes, tough black hair, bundles of children. Echoes of their features stir in the Bear's ruined face.

Rose works in the local community centre on a scheme for addicts. 'She's good,' he assures Sonia. Sonia nods. From the photos, Rose looks as if she'd be good.

'She knows them all from the old days,' he says, meaning the addicts. 'She doesn't treat them like they're different. But she's no fool either.'

Sonia imagines the old days, Rose and them all, the nameless addicts: dancing at discos, smoking on street corners, drinking, flirting, mitching off school. Further back, playing childhood games on the worn grass beside the canal, the concrete courtyard at the mouth of the flats.

Sonia notices something missing when the Bear talks about Rose Red. He admires her sure, but there's still something missing. A light not in his eyes.

His little brother is gorgeous, a small boy version of Snow White. Neat gleaming hair, shining eyes, Ireland football jersey. A live wire, says the Bear. He visits as regularly as he can. He worships you, thinks Sonia. And why not? After all, the Bear is a legend, a demon or an avenging angel, depending on your perspective and the papers you read. The Bear seems to think his brother will be alright. He's quick at school, very brainy. His mam makes sure he does his homework. He wants to be a scientist. They look at the photo. Sonia hopes to god he gets what he wants.

Every time Sonia visits the Bear she comes home with his voice in her head. *Cathexis.* A Greek word. It usually happens to lovers, but a student can get it with a good teacher. You absorb the other person into you, like a language. Only time gets rid of the trace.

When she got home that evening, the day he'd shown her his family album, she lay along the banjaxed comfort of her landlord's sofa and watched traffic headlights chase shadows across the ceiling. She wondered why the Bear felt the way he did about Rose Red. Why there was something missing. Maybe he was afraid of her. She was older than him, and that made Sonia think of her own brother, her sisterly self. Older sisters can play awful games with their younger brothers. Petting, then tormenting them. Bullying, then making up. Racing with them, then stopping at that age when he's started to outgrow her, when it looks like they'll lose, saying the race was just a joke, leaving the boy outraged, at the finishing line, screaming for justice.

Old sisters tell tales. They manipulate and, usurping the place of parents, use approval as currency, handing out praise and blame like sweets. Sonia gave her brother poison once. Drink this, she said. It's lemonade. He raised the bottle. Mum, mum, screamed Sonia. Declan's drinking turpentine. And lunged for the bottle, grabbing it just in time to be seen. Watch me, how marvellous I am.

Maybe, she thought now, the Bear felt Rose Red was ashamed of him, the way he was ashamed of Snow White. Maybe she'd said things to him, disowned him, set her children against him. Maybe one of her boyfriends knew someone in the guards.

Maybe it's just that Snow White gives the Bear someone to look after, for a change, and that's what puts the light in his eyes.

It's not just his size that makes him look older. Apart from everything – the crazy innocence that clings to him despite what he's done, the infectious enthusiasm, the childlike eagerness to say it all, now, before someone stops him – there is something ancient in him that goes beyond his size. Sonia read somewhere that humans have an alligator brain in the back of their heads. She wonders if that's where he gets it.

Tinny music. Yellow walls.

He is working on a red painting. Afterwards, when Sonia has left the place, she will realise it's her favourite.

There's a figure at its centre. God-devil-demon, call it what you will. Snakes writhe upwards from the shoulders. At the crotch is a huge phallus, pointing downwards. The Bear calls this his warhead. It looks like it's strapped on. The testicles are large and red, with black spikes coming out of them. Landmines. All down the god's arms are heads. He is like an Inca headhunter showing off his victims, his samples, tourists who wandered into the wrong place at the wrong time. According to the Bear, some of the heads are good, others aren't.

Does he have as many heads in his own head, she wonders. Does he have as many voices in there as heads on the arms of his terrible god?

He tried to lift Sonia up one of the last days she came to visit, an apology for an insult he didn't mean to make, and in his arms she was a gnat.

In those last weeks the elastic that had snapped earlier, allowing him to paint, snapped right back again. Perhaps it was inevitable, the pressure of the outside world. Appeals and cases, rights and visits, a whole load of other things Sonia never fully understood. He stopped working at night, didn't turn up for class, made excuse after excuse. Sickness, flu, exhaustion, no ideas. Sonia missed his company, his humour, his seething rage, his vivacity. She even missed the tea. Then summer came and it was time for her to leave. She never returned. The institution had got into her soul, like Charles Lamb's wooden desk. She's always thought it's better to leave things before they die on you.

She would think about the Bear from time to time and wonder if he'd kept at it. She heard he was working for a while with a girl from Germany who was a bit more adventurous, into political art. Some years ago she'd got children in Bosnia to fly white balloons over Sarajevo. Sarajevo is in a bowl of mountains, so the balloons hovered there for weeks, cloaking the beleaguered city with a thousand statements of intent, supplications for peace and hope. There was an odd match, but right somehow, between all those balloons and the Bear's white dots.

Time passed. Sonia missed the feeling of his voice inside her.

One evening, she strayed off her path and went into the flatlands down from the canal, passing the blocks where the Bear grew up. Kids were playing, shouting like they always do, so loud their voices were bouncing off the concrete walls. Sonia saw a flash of green, and wondered if that was the Bear's little brother, radiant in his Ireland jersey. Then she went to sit by the canal, looking at the dirty white swans. The kids' voices rose behind her. She imagined the Bear, a big handsome boy in the days before he grew monstrous, playing football with his pals. Rose Red, her black hair in ringlets, bossing everyone. Snow White seated on the edge of the grey grass, her long legs crossed at the ankles, reading a comic, dreaming of the future.

Nice images, she will think later. Romantic, almost. Redemptive. Sympathetic. Palatable, even.

From images like that you could curate your own show. And near the exit door, have a film sequence. A loop, endlessly recursive, showing an empty yard in front of a block of flats, the echo of children's voices banging off its walls. You could have your audience walk out of the show with the echo still playing, following them into their coffee shops, cars, bedrooms. In your artistic statement, you might talk about your intention: how, each time the audience thinks about flats like that, you hope to implant them with the sound of children's voices. In this way they – the flats and the voices – become woven into your audience, an extension of the Bear's *cathexis*; an incorporation of his world and his history into a collective psyche. It's a portrait of yourself, of course: the artist, still thinking about those voices. Hearing them every time you pass that site, long after you move to a different part of the city, or country, or world, long after the flats are pulled down – as will happen, of course, in spite of the disbelieving laugh the Bear shared with you on your first visit. They'll be there, resonating in the cold cheap corners of the new builds, enduring, like the apocryphal blood and bones buried under concrete foundations in South American cities, pouring into the space where the Bear and his like used to live.

And that's a decent enough ending for a show, in some ways. But it's not correct.

So, how about this:

Three years after leaving, Sonia is on her way to an opening in Cork with a friend of hers, a colleague a few years older. The new motorway bypass hasn't been built yet, so their drive takes them past the institution, whose barbed wire towers they can see clearly from the dual carriageway.

Hiya lads, says Sonia, nodding in the direction of the towers.

Oh? says the colleague, and Sonia starts telling her stories of inside. She names the Bear.

No, the colleague says. I don't believe it. And then she tells a story that leaves Sonia's in the ha'penny place, about the time she, this colleague, was mugged by the Bear, and got her skull cracked, and how, in a weird, perverse way, she's always felt grateful to him, because that experience changed her life. Forced her to make personal and creative choices, become an artist, do things the pre-mugged version of her never could.

This also is a decentish ending, and it would be nice to leave it there. But again: not correct.

Ten years pass. Sonia is working in a different institution, where people are no longer using and trying their damnedest to keep it that way. Over tea-break, that sweet, scalding tea, those sugary treats, those cigarettes, someone asks her where she's living. She tells them. The Bear's name comes up − he's a legend of his own making, after all − and she mentions having worked with him. The usual sighs, head shakings, stories.

He had a brother, she says. Thinking of the Ireland jersey.

His brother, they say. Eyes widen around the teasteam and fagsmoke.

Yeah?

Ah. He's huge. Bigger than the Bear. And way madder.

Four years on, only the other day: a loping shape. Scraggy trackie bottoms, flapping hands. Wide shoulders. Too tall. Too skinny. Face a bit fucked, in a way that's the same but different. In that moment, she knows.

Pinning Tail on Donkey

Tempus fugit, as one of the dead languages once put it.

It's long ago, yes. Yet I still see *no, not me, me?* her, as if it were yesterday, standing at the window of our beautiful school, gazing out, as if, *yes,* imagining.

We had been in this country, when it was still a country, for three years. By we, I mean me and my family. Yes, I'm originally from an Other Part, though I won't say where. You'd never believe me, little one, and don't try figuring it out yourself, you'll never guess. I've gathered too much, *ah, hold off, no,* moss since, and the world has changed so much: Here and There, those hemispheres of privilege, flipping like the planet's magnetic field along blessed capital's fickle axis. Besides, the details of how and why and where and all the befores that led to me being Here – the backstory, as the adverttainment wing of our once great technocracy would have put it – are not important.

What matters is that we arrived in this country while it was still easing out of troubled nationstatedom, in an early phase of that great investment opportunity known as the Fossilfuel&Water War, during a minor bubble in the period your great-grandparents' generation called the Boom. As if such a thing was the Big Bang, the genesis of the econosphere, not merely a hiccup in the sacred sink and swell of endless accumulation.

We were a large family. Three above, three below, me in the middle. A right horde. It was a miracle, my mother often said, that the barriers to entry had lifted for us, particularly at such a sensitive time. A gullible word: *miracle*. The only miracle was my father, rest his labouring soul. He was a very technikal man, always tinkering away on the intercloud, inventing new apps and such, and, before our rapid exit from the Other Parts, he had accumulated enough know-ware to be able to broker a decent transition for us. He also had an instinctive understanding of our then-burgeoning technocracy's corridors of power. What fields to fill, what story to tell, who to tell it to – and, most important, from whom to hide. Thanks to his diligence, we soon found housing in a drab part of the city that used to hub this country. We children were shoe-horned into nearby schools, run by the last generation of the dying nationstate's once-dominant theocrats: the Priests-n-Nuns. We were segregated by gender: girls went to Nuns, boys to Priests. We weren't the correct faith for those schools; we didn't directly belong to any of the major faiths of those fundamentalist times. But my father, we assumed, had filled in the correct fields, told the correct story. Back then, there were allowances, even for hordes, once you knew where to find them.

My father was an exceptionally skilled communicator. We weren't Here long before he got talking to an even more correct someone in the authorities and they got talking back and suddenly we were on a List for better housing in a better part of the city. After that it was bish-bash-bosh, as a funny-man once said. Soon we found ourselves on a second List, this time for a better school, to match the better housing and the better part of the city. This school was a right trailblazer. It had initially been co-opted by the first-gen technocracy in the ninetynineties, but the early Board had handled the merger subtly, acquiring the school from a lesser faith instead of the Priests-n-Nuns and branding their new enterprise as 'multifaith' so as not to ruffle any feathers. One can blame the early technocrats for many things, global-warming-species-extermination-and-on-and-on, but one can't ever accuse them of underestimating optics. By the time I and my siblings had got on the List, a new Board was in place, with a far more visible agenda. Its mission vines on the Old Web talked about fostering individualism, cultural exchange, difference, and that grail of early optics misdirection – community. Its ultimate target, it claimed, was the wholeperson cultivation of an entire new generation of corpocitizens, full of know-ware, moral resource and creativity. In a radical move, this cohort would include not only 'natives' who had been granted the privilege of servicing the debts of the technocracy via the gift of their birth, but 'Others', like me, indentured through the gift of being invited.

I and my siblings understood little of this at the time. For us, the most important aspect of the whole experience was that, thanks to my father's opaque ministrations, we would finally be able to go to school together again. No small thing, when one is from an Other Part and easily separated from one's horde. Packing us all off to the same school would also be convenient for my mother, who by then had little time, having taken on many zero-hour tracts to keep us fed while my father, mercy on his endeavours, was busy talking to the right people about the right things when he wasn't tinkering with apps on the intercloud.

For me, however, entrance to the new school was deferred. I did not pass through the gates of that trail-blazing place until a full year after the rest of my siblings. There was no obvious reason for this. I was not the stupidest or the cleverest in my family. At ten years, I was not the oldest, at a sensitive time in my hormonoeducational path. Nor was I the youngest, prone to fear at the prospect of being shunted into a new milieu. I was certain the fault could not possibly have lain in human error on my father's part. He was too deft to mess up little things like box-ticking or form-filling. So what had gone wrong? I took on the blame. I worried: I was a terrible worrier then, burdened by an overactive Mind's I, prone to generating a surfeit of that obsolete hormone, magenation. Had I offended somebody? Had I antagonised my own parents without knowing? Was I – oh dreadful thought – born wrong, with too much of the Other Parts still in me to ever become an upstanding corpocitizen? As the months passed, I came to another conclusion. While the forms were being filled in, my parents must have simply forgotten me, just as they had when it was the turn of my eyes to be lasered. Being in the middle, neither too loud nor too quiet, too cheeky nor too docile, I was always easy to pass over. Inconspicuous.

Like *yes, wait*, like you, little one.

The new school – my faith, it was beautiful. How my, *hush, yes*, our heart aches to remember it. This country was green then, as it was until your grandparents' time, a single landmass where the deadland archipelago now floats, and the sun did shine – occasionally, anyway – instead of this infernal rain. There were trees; I'm sure you've seen them time-to-time on the intercloud on those rare occasions when the gennies get going and you can power up your Glass, and there were the other type of cloud too, geophysical ones, white and puffy, in blue sky, and animals; even in the cities, like the one which once hubbed this country, were animals. The new school had no animals, but it did have flowers and grass and, *yes*, trees. Chemmites had already begun eating away at them, but the destruction wasn't yet visible. Willows and hawthorns lined the lane that led to the front gate, and behind the seniors' building grew magnificent Spanish chestnuts, like a row of sentinels. I'm afraid I've no power to show you a picture, little one, I'm saving the genny to charge up my, *yes*, our Lens, so you'll have to magine. The leaves, the tree's hair, were green, like this, but more. While the blossoms were pink like *my*—

Yes. Like the roses in our cheeks.

I had never seen such a beautiful structure. To my raw eyes, behind their oldschool spectiglasses, it looked as if it had come out of an ancient Muddleeuro fairy-tale, one with Goblins and Witches and Wolves and Huntsmen. I'd read those tales before we'd come to this country; my mother, not knowing what part of Here we'd end up in, had shown me illustrations. On paperware, magine, what we called books that are all now gone; devoured by the flames of the so-called

Righteous or the rising tides of the melting caps. On that first day outside the new school, I felt I was *within* such a tale, looking at the very same gingerbread house where Hansel and Gretel had been drawn, tempted by the longing for other's resource that blessed capital always inspires. The seniors' building was not gingerbread, of course, but brick and wood, with a roof of pretty red clay tiles and windows arched in the style of the theocrats, paned in tiny diamonds that twinkled in the sunlight. I stood, spellbound. The trees behind the building sighed, and I saw a fabulous structure of metal and Glass emerge. A ship! I thought, *yes, yes*, foolishly. For it was no ship – simply an allmodcons extension built by the early technocrats during an Overspend phase. Fairy-tales paint pretty optics, but they're less than useless for getting the real work of the Trinity done.

I didn't feel at home, standing outside the school; to me, *home* was still the Other Part we had come from. But there was something profoundly familiar about that little red-tiled building, its arched windows, its trees, that filled me, like Hansel and Gretel must have been filled, with a deep and hungry sense of be-longing. And yet, even now, *yes, we*, I, can't help but wonder again, if I'm confused again, if it wasn't the school that made me belong, but *ah, hush, I come to you—*

Maisie.

Have you a Mind's I, little one? Don't be shy, tell me. I'll, *yes, we'll* keep your secret; you were born with one, weren't you? So, quietly, now: exercise that redundant nexus of gland, visualise with *yes, us*, me, *this*:

I am ten. My shoes are too big. I walk into a classroom. It smells, like all Here smells, of bleach and clean. She stands. Sunlight oozing from long windows. Chalkdust off vintage blackboard dancing between us. In a corner, a line of jewelly-new smartAppls^C, chuckling as they connect to the Old Web.

She sighs, as if magining. She looks up. She sees me. She smiles.

If the school was a Muddleuro fairy-tale, Maisie was the magical creature at its heart. My first thought was – A Primcess™! She must be a Primcess™! In that time, all the children Here, even the poor ones, dressed like advertainments. In coloured fabrics, always new, and made by machines, and matching but not too much the same; just right for an army of growing corpocitizens, bound together by the good taste and carefully accumulated indentures of their parents.

Maisie, though, stood out. She always had something a little Dated about her: the way she wore her hair, her Vintage accessories, her oldschool bag made with real leather handles, a Save the Cows genuinepassionstatement. Sometimes she even sported items of clothing that made her look as if *no, yes*, she'd come from an Other Part; the sort of things that my mother, faith forgive her, tried to make us wear. She had long yellow ringlets, *no, golden, yes, of course*, golden – yes, somewhat like mine, little one, it is *yes, a peccadillo, yes* though mine are fading now. That morning, Maisie wore a yellow dress, very Biba seventy-sixties – a style my mother would have called ladylike. But what most caught my eye were her shoes. *Ah*, such longing. Cowskin, they were, black as old Fossilfuel and burnished to an impossible shine, so when you looked down, you could see your face reflected in them, as when they had absorbed all your resource, mental-physical-and-the-other. But *only, yes,* only if your skin was pale, for not all of us, little one, had pale skin.

Maisie's own skin was white as cowmilk, stretched over a face shaped like a heart. Small wonder I magined her as a Primcess™.

But Maisie was not just beautiful on the outside. She had a glow that came from deep in, and *oh my, yes,* how everyone loved her for that. Not just me or the other fortunate corpocitizens being cultivated in the balmy warmth of the school's Glasshouse, but all connected with that institution. Educators, parents, Board. I could tell, even then, even me, through my naifOther pov, that Maisie was our school's first and best optic; the personification of its holy essence, brand. She represented the crème of the technocracy: those first among the corpostate, gifted by birth into capital's most luminous mysteries, the off-interest-one-per-cent. Yet she spoke too for the thrifty second-tier, those who had gained not through birth, but through wise investment and acquisition during the first bubbles, who had only then been inducted into the secrets of harnessing, the long, rewarding process of accumulation. And finally she stood for those who, though they had been less prudent with their resource, had learnt through suffering. I and my siblings counted my parents among that third group – for what was the ultimate lack of prudence but choosing to be placed, by capital's anointed invisible hand, at the moment of one's birth into an Other, less fortunate Part? In this country, that third group, the technocracy's indentured, also included all 'natives' who had endured the requisite slings and arrows of Heilige Angelendtheresela's Outragesterity. This was the group who had used their collective pain, their experience of have-not, relative as it may have been in the context of Others, to force into being the first and last great vision of our corpostate, that precious concept which still endures, despite the ravages of the so-called Righteous, their soosidebooms and chemfare, despite, *yes, our* own toxicity, acquired during the last great Overspend in the FF&W War. I'm talking – *hush, no*, yes, little one, this you must absorb and process – of the threefold hallowed truth itself: the Trinity. Capital Moral, Capital Social and Capital Holy Fiscal, wealth without end, aim-in.

Maisie embodied the Trinity more completely than anyone I have ever known. She had, *no, yes, has, no* had a conscience; she had, *yes, has* a heart; she had, yes, *had* things. And she kept her three capitals in exquisite balance. Dressing well, but never ostentatiously. Mingling easily face-to-face, while ensuring she kept timespace for herself. Active when plugged in – full of goss and pins, well able to too-wit, share-invite and trolle – but always moderating her inputs. Tagging each trolleing with sad-face to demonstrate her rich stock of that valuable moral resource, remorse; leavening her sad-animal petitions with funny-cutey-tubevines that showed she still had a sense of humour. She was judicious in her use of smarts, never too obvs in displaying the most updated model or the latest apps. She wasn't bothered by anyone else's story or repulsed by where they lived or intrigued by how they'd got onto the Lists or laughed at what trainers they wore or sneered at where their mother worked, even if it was a zero-hour-tract at ma©donalds-you-loser.

Maisie was also gifted with know-ware. She always came top of our class, though she never made anyone feel bad about that. We were happy for her to be there. She deserved to be. She goaded, *yes*, inspired, *yes*, drove us to compete, *yes*, harder, faster, longer, but was that not what we were there for?

Many other children in the school were like Maisie; the technocracy had mergered them because they had something of the same glow. But nobody was quite as *yes, golden*. Despite my overactive Mind's I, I couldn't identify then exactly what it was Maisie had which we lacked. My first conjecture, *and, yes*, you may laugh, little one, was that her inner gleam was generated by Fossilfuel. Not literally. But all the children that glowed, Maisie included, had one thing in common; they were collected after school by their parents in Fossilcars. The rest of us, including the handful who'd come from Other Parts, had to walk home. My family's new home wasn't too far, so this arrangement suited us. Except, of course, when it rained; on those days I, *yes*, longed for a Fossilcar and a mother who wasn't working zero-hour-tracts and a father who wasn't too busy wrapped up his apps, or Skyᗡing with the right people so right things could get done.

Maisie was collected by her mother, *ah, no, yes, Mum*. She was a real Yummamumma and her car was totes amazoid, an oldschool Guzzler, nothing loser-hybrid about it. Four-wheel drive, high off the ground with its shell sprayed a lovely colour. Deep, deep green. Not like this, not like anything you've ever seen, little one. A colour that made you feel the presence of capital, its threefold holy glow, as if the sacred resource was right inside you. *Oh*, that feeling, shining from the Guzzler, shining like Maisie's black shoes, reflecting back to us standing before it their *our* their own pale faces, as if *no, not yet*, their innermostness had been captured by its gleaming Kellygreen convex lens.

Interesting, said my father, when I told him this thought and, for a moment, the corrugated worry that normally occupied his forehead seemed to lift. A prickle went down my spine. It was unusual for him to pay attention to anything I said. But a moment later he had forgotten I was there, and had started talking to my older brother about the forthcoming FootBall Trials and the schoolership to top-notch higher ed they might offer.

Yet this glow was not just restricted to the Guzzler, or Maisie herself. Maisie's mother, *yes, Mum*, was shiny too. She had the same hair as Maisie but *not as golden*, yes, more like this, little one. She wore it up or down, or teased into smooth waves that were somewhat Dated. But on her, as on Maisie, the Datedness didn't give off wrong optics; it looked newer-than-new. In winter, she wore fur coats – faux, naturally; Maisie's sad-animal petitions would have tolerated nothing less. And she smelt gorgeous, Maisie's *Mum*, oh yes. Like a bubble bath but nicer, a smell bleachy-sweet, very much of Here. Sometimes, in bed at night when I was alone, I indulged my Mind's I and magined how it would be if our mother was more like that and smelt less of Other Parts, and more of Here.

Every day, she would wait for Maisie at the gates as we came out of school; most of the other children already gazing elsewhere, plugged into smartsong and Appls^C and Glass, relieved at the thought of an afternoon free of the social tax of face-to-face. All except those of us from Other Parts, we who had limited connectivity at the best of times, and Maisie, who plugged in, it seemed, only when nobody could see her.

Mum, *yes, my* Mum would wave and call 'Maisie!', the bracelets on her wrists, groovyethnic faux ivory bought for much fiscal from a moralshop that aided Other Parts, tinkling. Maisie would run over, not clumsy like *no, yes*, like I used to be, her long yellow, *no*, golden curls dancing in the sunlight. She'd kiss Mum and sling herself and her bag into the back seat. The Guzzler would start, purring like a cat – an animal; you've seen pictures of them, little one, they used to rule the tubevines – and whoosh down the drive.

Maisie would always turn to look through the rear window and wave out. We all looked up then, even the ones plugged deep. That was the power of Maisie's glow. I knew, of course, she was waving to her friends, the others who glowed. But she was so kind, so friendly to everyone, that sometimes I let myself magine – oh, the curse of a Mind's I – that she was waving at me too. Then I would dare to wave back, but, *yes,* like this, little one, not very noticeably. I'd smile, making sure my smile wasn't too obvious, that the others, especially those surfing their smarts, couldn't see it but that Maisie could. And when she smiled back, I magined it was at me, just me.

You see, I didn't have very many friends then. I was *no, I've told you that's nasty*, new of course, always a disadvantage. And, as I've said many times before, I was always rather inconspicuous.

I had been in the school three months when Maisie announced it. Just before the ringtone sounded, she glanced at the educator, who nodded, and then she stood. 'I'm going to be ten in a month's time,' she said. 'And I'm having a birthday party.' Well, little one, you can magine the excitement that generated! All the little corpocitizens began to buzz and murmur, and many sneakily plugged in to check inboxes and eye-ems, and others began to *hush, I'm coming to it*, began to hush the rest, because we were anxious to hear her say that she'd sent the eeee-vites and they'd be with us in a moment or tomorrow or tomorrow...

But Maisie said nothing more. She simply packed her eduware into her bag and went out.

Faiths forgive me, I don't know what made me do it, but I went out straight after her. I didn't care, for once, if I got in anybody else's way or stood on their toes or otherwise attracted attention. But all the other children were so busy scrolling and tapping, swiping air, trying to find their invitations, others still in face-to-face, discussing verbal, trying to make sense of what Maisie had said, that they didn't notice me one bit.

I got to the gate just as Maisie's mother was pulling out in the Guzzler. Racing up, I'd caught a whiff of Mum's perfume and seemed to feel her fauxfur cuddle around me. Then the Guzzler roared off and Maisie turned to wave, as she always did, and I waved back, again, trying to make it not obvious, and Maisie smiled, as usual, and—

Then *no, not foolish*, I realised: all the other children were still in the classroom. I was the only one standing there. In that moment, *no, not foolish*, no, *no sun in my eyes*, no, her smile was just for me. She had seen me. She had smiled. And I knew, *no, didn't 'magine, knew* what that meant. I would be issued with an invitation to her party, and I would be the first to get one. It was probably already waiting for me on the familysmart at home!

I can't tell you how *no, not stupid*, no, *hush, hush*, how wonderful, that made me feel. I floated home, rushing then slowing, rushing then slowing, revelling in the so, *no, delicious* anticipation generated by that cursed hormone, fantasy.

But when I got back, a right disaster awaited. I couldn't plug in. My father had gone out for face-to-face with the right people and taken his new smartsong with him. Worse still, he'd blocked our weefee to the Old Web, as was his wont when meeting right people, so I couldn't even use the creaky Oldtablet that had come with the rental. I was distraught. Couldn't eat, couldn't sleep. Next morning, I stole downstairs and saw my father's new smartsong on the kitchen table. It was a handheld design I hadn't seen before, with a somewhat Dated look to the lens.

I picked it up, plugged in. A flicker behind my retinas. A tingle up my spine. I brain-flicked through for his password, keyed it in and in jiggidytime, after a plaintive wailing startuptone, there I was on the intercloud, scouring my eye-em and my emale. Nothing. Deep in my Mind's I, I sensed anxiety, that scourge of the over-hormonal, begin to download again. It didn't matter, I told myself. Maisie was into Dated things. She would probably issue the invitation verbally, face-to-face even. Of course! I cleared my traces, shut down the smart and rushed out, not even bothering with breakfast.

I got to school early, but thing after another delayed me. First the obesity educator, then the caretaker, then the principal. I, who normally attracted no attention, was suddenly in demand by everyone – though once they had me in their company, they seemed to forget what they'd wished to talk to me about. By the time I got to my classroom, I had lost whatever competitive advantage I might have had. The other children were all inside, crowding around, talking through Glass and face-to-face. It was a right clamour. I pushed forward and *oh*, little one, you'll never believe it, the crowd had gathered around my desk. Was Maisie there already, waiting to issue her verbal? I shoved my way through, heart pounding, and then I saw it.

An *oh*, invitation, lying on my desk! Paperware, of all things! Unrenewable-amazone-sourced card, decorated with a gold-patterned border and intricate black-and-gold Handwriting. Except—

It wasn't lying on my side of the desk.

There must be a mistake, I thought. Still *yes, stupidly* hoping. Even though Darragh Guo, my desk-peer, had already swooped up the card and was waving it like a flag; Handwritten, for all to see, her gold-and-black name in its unmistakeable characters, the language of origin of her grandparents' nationstate.

And underneath, printed in the common tongue:
There Will Be Party Games. Bring A Gift.

I twisted back into the crowd, and *yes*, longed for the veils my grandmothers had once worn to cover my shame.

Darragh was delighted. She was one of the glowing ones, almost, *yes, not quite* as much as Maisie, so nobody should have been surprised that she was the first to be invited. At break-time, she demonstrated a marked shortage of moral capital by showing off to everyone. She even asked Maisie where she'd sourced the paperware. Everyone was right agog for the answer, but all Maisie said was that it was a secret. She said it in such a kind way though. So Maisie, to say things kindly that in anyone else's mouth would *yes, they would*, sound mean and spiteful.

Every day that week a new invitation appeared. Niamh Tedjai, Ashwin O'Reilly, Calypso Roche and on Fryday, two. Kanye Ai and Kanye Robinson-of-the-Peter-Robinsons.

They got theirs together because they were both Kanye's, I supposed.

The second week passed. The third. Day after day I went into our beautiful school, hoping. Day after day I went home disappointed. Night after night I prayed, not just to blessed capital but, faith forgive me, other entities, even, *yes, yes*, I confess, the god-not-named of my father's forgotten ancestors, the expropriated, altered beyond all recognition deity that the scattered bottom-feeder descendants of the so-called Righteous still deludedly claim as theirs.

Soon Maisie's invitations were landing on the desks of children who glowed far less, then on those whose glow was barely perceptible. My anxiety accumulated. My Mind's I went into overdrive. What if I wasn't picked at all? Only seven of us were without an invitation by then and, *yes, yes*, we were the ones who had no glow at all.

It's important for later, little one, that you understand. We're all going to have to live with each other for a very long time, so you must realise that *no, not I*, that Maisie never acted out of *hush, it's fine*, spite. This procedure with the invitations, one at a time, enough for almost every corpocitizen in the class, but not all, was just a, *yes*, game for her. One of her *yes*, no, *yes*, her Party Games, but in advance. It didn't change how she behaved towards any of us during those four weeks. She was still the same kind, clever, friendly Maisie.

But I had changed, completely. I couldn't concentrate on anything except coming in to school and finding one of those precious invitations on my desk. I, *yes*, obsessed. Everything else in the world became a blur. The fresh green grass, the trees, the blue sky, so soft compared to the sky in the Other Part where we'd come from, this fertile landmass oozing with capital old and new, so miraculously rescued from Outragesterity by the technocrats, had become as a nutshell to me. My parents had hinted we would each get personal smarts for winterfestival, but even the promise of a personalised Glass or smartsong felt hollow. All I wanted was that invitation. It grew in my Mind's I and my cursed overproduction of the fantasymone fed it until it was all I saw. The more real invitations landed on other children's desks, the clearer and bigger my magined one grew, until it blanked out everything else.

I knew, *yes, somewhere*, that I was not the only one who was anxious. I dared not glance at those others who had not been invited. I could feel their *no, yes*, loserstatus projecting out of them with such dangerous intensity it could almost be touched. What if I were to lock eyes with one of them and instead of my magined invitation, brand my Mind's I with their *yes, it's nasty, but*, untouchable image? Would the desperation we shared snake between us, binding us into an unholy whole? Or worse, would that other child's lack depart them entirely and transfer onto me, leaving me its sole repository? And what if someone else saw? We were all familiar, as you must be, little one, with the Michelson-Morley experiments on light: the act of observation changing what is observed. If an invited child were to pass me and the other, *yes*, loser in that moment, see our eyes solder in mutual need, would our combined worthlessness then become magnified, and – oh, shame – captured through the shutter of, say, the invited one's blink, burn into the code of our cells, altering us forever? No. Head down was the only possible route. Besides, it was not just us, *no, yes*, losers who were worrying. I would often catch the invited ones from the corner of my I, huddling and whispering face-to-face verbal in the toilets at break-time. From time to time when I had the opportunity to plug in, I would even *yes, low,* lurk on the intercloud, stalking their eye-ems and posts as they fretted about Maisie and the party and the gift they had to bring. I was familiar with their qualms: how Maisie was the kind of girl who was impossible to buy for, how you couldn't give her knick-knacks or little jewelleries or games or kindlebooks because she had everything; how everything she didn't have you didn't dare get her because she was so unique, it would probably be wrong; how, if you got her something new, she'd think it too flashy, something too old, you were mean. Yet I was so obsessed with my own need that the realisation of these others' agonies only made me even more *yes, yes, jealous* instead of comforting me.

Even my parents noticed something was Up. Here, said my father, offering me his new smartsong. Have a look at some kittens getting stuck in baskets. That will cheer you up. Oh, by the way, he said. Don't use the capture app yet. It's not quite ready.

Thanks, I said, plugging in. Too late, I remembered I should have asked him for his password. But he'd already forgotten I was there, and was talking instead to my oldest sister about the biochem degree she was thinking of asking Shell® to sponsor her for. So I went ahead, hearing again the plaintive startupwail as I keyed in his code. A catmeeme was flashing at the bottom of the screen, beside an icon for what must have been my father's unready app, an oldschool plate camera on three sticks. This I ignored. What use was it to me? The only thing I wanted to capture was an invitation from Maisie. I clicked the catmeeme. When, finally, hours later, I looked up from the kittens getting stuck in baskets, which had cheered me up somewhat, my father was gone. Out on another face-to-face with the right people, my sister said. But it couldn't have been that, for he hadn't asked me to give him back his device, and he never met those right people without his smarts.

Week four. Moonday. Jennie Ward arrived in to find an invitation on her desk. That was a shock, because Jennie always smelt of, *yes, wee*, poor girl, couldn't help it. Chooseday, Xiaolu Ní Bhaoill; Whensday, Tomasz Llewellyn. Now there were only four children left: me and three others, including a boy whose name I can't remember now, faiths forgive me, the one, *yes, yes, Denis*, with the boils. On Thirstday Denis got his invitation. That afternoon I stayed late after school. I didn't want to go to the gate and see Maisie waving from the Guzzler and know, *yes, know*, that her smile wasn't for me.

I spent another long night on my father's smartsong watching kittens in baskets, trying to override the stupid picture of that invitation in my Mind's I. But my magenation was a stubborn thing. It refused to be overrid. Even the kittens seemed, *yes, silly*, contaminated by it, squirming up against the screen as if wanting out of their Glass walls. I couldn't see what they were so upset about. At least they were part of a Thing that had value: their baskets, and the act of getting stuck in them.

In me, a gap of be-longing so deep I thought I might, *hah, yes*, drown in it.

The next morning, I walked into school prepared for the worst. For Samya O'Brien, wide as she was long, to be standing at the top of the class with an invitation clasped in her hand. But she wasn't.

There it was, on my desk, just like the picture in my Mind's I. So like it, in fact, that for a moment I wondered if – heretical thought – the power of my I had manipulated reality, turned magenation into fact. Yet this realLife invitation was far, far better than the one in my Mind. The card so much whiter, the writing so much blacker and golder. In the centre, my name, Handwritten in the tongue of our Other Part. And underneath that the instruction: *Party Game, Bring Gift.* I was so proud. I didn't notice the other children, what they were saying about me, or not. And that afternoon, when I stood at the gates and saw Maisie waving from the back of Mum's Guzzler, I knew, *yes, knew,* her smile was for me.

I had been so caught up in my fears and hopes that it was not until I was on my way home, blithely kicking at dried leaves, that I remembered the gift. I stopped, feeling the familiar thorns of anxiety twist again in my gut. Ideas began flashing through my magenation, one after the next, but none was right. The know-ware I had always been so *yes, quietly* confident of was firing missiles into my awareness, each scrambling into corruption as soon as I'd thought it. My Mind's I was bursting with dross. Then an odd, three-legged shape flickered at the back of my—

Ah, yes.

And then, little one, I realised what would be my gift.

My father wouldn't miss it. He hadn't asked for it back since I started playing with the kittens. It was only a beta, he'd said once, something he had been roadtesting on the hush-hush for the right people. And it was ideal. It resembled the sort of device Maisie admired; new, but not too new, with something indefinably Vintage about it, just like Maisie herself: Dated, but impossible to say how.

This was not stealing. This was an act of virtue: ethical expropriation. No wonder those kittens had looked sad, with my gloomy mug moping down on them. How joyfully they would return to getting stuck in their baskets under Maisie's glorious witness!

In that moment *no, I'm not lying*, I had completely forgot my father's idle comment about the capture app that was not quite ready.

As soon as my *no, not Mum*, mother got home, I tried to tell her about the party. She didn't pay much attention, too busy making dinner and listening to everybody else. She didn't take in the invitation when I showed it to her, or notice the lovely gold letters, carefully handwritten in her tongue of origin. She just asked my oldest sister to sort me out something to wear and get me there safely. Then my little brother came in yelling that he'd bashed his knee playing soccer, and it all got so busy that my head began to ache, so I slipped into my room and plugged in and watched the kittens getting stuck in the baskets one last time, my face floating over theirs, until I fell asleep.

I slept like a blog, little one, dreamt of nothing. I haven't slept like that, or, *yes*, at all in decades. But don't worry; it's *no, it's not*, it's really not as bad as people make out, to live without sleep.

Next morning my oldest sister went out to the moralshops bright and early and found a white dress, which she bought in exchange for a little bit of capital she had accumulated since coming Here. She cut it into a skirt and added a red belt made from one of my father's ties. My oldest brother lent me his Abramovic United jersey for a touch of streetcool and my younger brother polished my shoes till they were just as *no, okay, nearly* as gleaming as Maisie's. My middle brother ironed my hair flat and my younger sister put it in two plaits, tied with red ribbon to match my belt.

Come, said my mother, bending over the sock drawer. My stomach clenched, faith forgives me, because I knew what she was doing. She straightened up and handed me the socks. Now, she said. You will look quite the Muddleuro lady.

I didn't glance at my sisters. I knew what they were thinking. Back then, in this country, little one, nothing said, *yes, okay,* Other Parts quite as loudly as Icis-White socks. Had my father been there, he could have explained it to my mother: you cannot steal the heraldry of blessed capital, you cannot borrow it, nor can you buy it. You have to be gifted it, and only capital's appointed hand, unseen and mysterious, chooses who to gift and who to overlook.

But my mother was a simple person – or had become such by then – her wits dulled by too many zero-hour-tracts and the pressure of labouring forth a right horde. So she watched proudly, the *yes, foolish woman,* as I pulled on the *yes, hated* badge of my Otherness.

A moment later she'd forgotten I was even there, but then it was too late. My sister had me by the hand and was dragging me out onto the road.

We lived in a better part of the city than the drabs, but Maisie lived in the best. Trees, trees, trees. Quiet roads, lovingly tended gardens. Guzzlers, sometimes two at a time, ported outside each gate. Maisie's house was, yes, enormous. It was separate from those each side, and when I saw it, *ah*, I realised why the first sight of the new school had made my heart sing. Because it was merely a smaller version of Maisie's house: a gingerbread cottage modelled on a gingerbread palace.

When I went in, I expected, *I know, silly*, there'd be a fanfare, like a fairy-tale Movie, and Maisie's Mum would say my name and everyone would turn and applaud. But there were so many other children milling around, and presents blocking up the hallway, that nobody even saw me arrive. Maisie threw me a smile, *yes, she did* – but then she went back to talking to some children I didn't recognise, who weren't from our school. Mum was very nice to me, though, and put my present in a pile with the others.

Their hall was huge, all shine and windows. The floor was made of wood, *yes*, maple, polished so it gleamed. A glass chandelier hung from the ceiling, and a stairway curved around, with stone steps that flared out where they met the wall. Through a half-open door, I saw a room with a table in its centre, covered with decorations: party hats and coloured streamers and all sorts of smarts and Glass, which struck me as strange though I didn't know why, and plates covered with tinfoil. My stomach rumbled. I magined buns and sandwiches, the epicurinnacle of Here. Then someone pulled me, it was Kanye Robinson-of-the-Peter-Robinsons, and said we had to assemble in the drawing room for the games.

Well, little one, you can magine what we expected. Plug in to the intercloud and swap around: some on classic shoot-em-up, others a role-play mystery, those blessed with the right sort of intellectual capital on a multi-level logic-solver. But not a device was to be seen. Then I realised:

everyone's smarts had been left on that big dining-table. We were to play face-to-face: actual kinaesthetic interaction. How Maisie, to propose something so coolly Dated. At that point, I must admit, I let myself feel a little smug. For having grown up in Other Parts, I would surely be far more familiar with such playing than my fellow corpocitizens.

First was musical chairs. I had underestimated my fellows' competitive edge, carefully inculcated in them through years of privilege, and I ended up being the fourth one out. But I wasn't the top loser, *yes, smelly* Jennie Ward was out first. Maisie should have won but she let the boy with the boils get to the chair first. That was *ah*, typical Maisie, little one, so gracefully demonstrating her moral surplus. Next we played musical statues. I was excellent at that because they are supposed to come around and make you laugh and I didn't laugh at all. But then one of the Kanyes pinched my leg, making me squeal, so I was out.

The next game was Pinning Tail on Donkey. Donkeys, when they were around, were like big *yes*, dogs with long ears, and used for carrying things, but that one was just a drawing on a piece of black paperware. It had been drawn beautifully, though – until I, *yes, knew better*, I thought it was Maisie who'd done it – and the tails were small bits of grey paperware with pieces of sheephair sewn to the end, with a thing called a thumbtack, previously in the You-Kay known as a drawing pin, through the top. Everyone had a tail, *yes*, very generous, and the mission was to stick the thumbtack in Donkey's bum. I was the second-last person to play. By that time, everyone else had missed Donkey's bum so there were tails everywhere! All over Donkey, on the wall, even on the floor where people could step on them – though *no, no, such things are nasty, how many times must we*, I assumed the children who'd put them there were just having a right laugh.

I stepped up to Maisie's Mum who was in charge of the blindfolds. She wanted to take my spectiglasses off before she blindfolded me. But I was worried in case someone, *yes, if you insist*, stood on them by *hush* accident, so instead Mum tied on two blindfolds to make sure everything was covered. Then she gave me a little push in the direction of Donkey.

I had concentrated hard when the others went up, and, as I've said, I had a very overactive Mind's I, so I'd been able to memorise where Donkey's bum was. You couldn't blame me for thinking my competitive edge on this one at least would be sharper than everyone else's. I stepped forward, blind, and in the room behind me, felt the hormonosphere grow dense and prickly with excitement. In my Mind's I, Donkey's bum clarified. Then—

saniga-saniga

It started. Low at first, barely a whisper. I stopped. Silence.

I stepped again.

Sann Igga San Igga Rye Chuss Lil San Igger Sand—

I stopped again, and they did too. I took another step.

Sandknickers-Sandknickers Righteous-Little-Sandknickers

Under the blindfold I felt my face begin to burn, my pores shriek again for my grandmothers' veils. How had I, of all people, with my overactive Mind's I, not, *yes*, magined something like this would happen? How could I have thought, how *yes*, how *stupid* of me, that they, *yes, she*, had wanted me there? That the mysteries of the invisible hand would ever lift me, inconspicuous nothingOther me, from the ranks of the beholden into the glorious tiers of the

Haves? And in that moment of yes, truevalue-recognition, I thought I heard, *yes, I did*, hear Maisie.

Sandknickers, Sandknickers, stupid-little-Sandknickers
Sooside-boom-Sandknickers In-her-Icis-White-Socks

She was leading it, driving the rest of them.

I do not *no no, yes*, remember making a choice. All I remember is thrusting out my chin and taking a step. The chanting rose. I smelt the bleachy perfumes of my fellow-citis, the sugar of their breath. I took, *yes*, another step and walked into the wall.

The chanting broke, splintering into giggles. I passed my hand over the wall, looking for Donkey's bum. Some of the boys began to chant again. There was a sharp pain on my right arm. My hand jerked. My fingers brushed skin.

Another sting, left arm. Another, my neck. I twitched and flailed. More stings, legs, neck, arms, fingertips. They were shouting. My Mind's I sparked. I saw Maisie's *Mum's* Guzzler, *our, yes*, our faces captured in it. My face, floating over my father's kittens. How pointless their stuckness in baskets. I saw my classmates and I, playing Donkey forever, captured in Guzzler's skin—

A dragging pain, worse than the others, across my cheek. And then I must have let out a sound, a *yes*, whimper, in the shape, *yes, foolish*, of her name:

'Maisie—'

The room went silent. I lifted my hand. My face felt wet. I pulled off the blindfold, but in my haste knocked off my spectiglasses too. Through the blur I saw my hand was red. The same red smearing my arms and dress, running down my legs into my stupid Other Part of the World white socks.

Around me their mushy faces, staring. In each hand, a dot of grey flecked with blood; Donkey's tail. I turned. My stomach heaved. Maisie was standing behind me. Her face as *yes, golden*, as ever. I looked at her hand. The thumbtack on her tail was clean; not a drop of my blood on it.

She blinked, so fast I *no, yes, no* hardly saw it.

A slow handclap started. Then they began to cheer. Drummed the floor with their heels. Somebody handed me my glasses. Someone else slapped me on the back.

Mah an caleen, said Darragh Guo.

Welcome, said Xiaolu Ní Bhaoill.

You did really well, said Kanye Robinson-of-the-Peter-Robinsons.

I put on my glasses. Maisie was smiling.

We all had to go through it, said Jennie Ward. They gave me a right slagging about the horsefairs. Used whips on me and all. She twitched a finger, but fairly late into it. Nearly broke me. Got a new right eye out of it, they done a lovely job, see, the scar's only just—

You've a lot of know-ware, said the boy with the boils. We're glad you didn't do a BailOut—

Not that you'd have got far, said someone else.

There was a laugh from everyone at that, *yes, jolly, yes, cheerful* and they all started talking, excited, gabbling. About who had withstood the longest and what unnecessary bits of themselves they'd lost when they'd been the Game and those sad loserstatuses who had not been granted the tiniest ounce of her clemency and all the *no, yes,* beautiful, subtle, kind ways she let *us, no, them, yes, us, no, me* know when it was over.

But I was hardly listening. I was still looking at Maisie.

Is it even her birthday? I asked.

Jennie Ward laughed. Oh, bless you for the bubble you came in on. Sure and if it was, she'd be the last one to know it.

What about our gifts? I said, though even as I did, I could hear my Mind's I, overactive like theirs, begin to whirr into connectivity.

The doorknob turned. The children hushed.

Ah, said *Mum*. There you all are. She looked at me and tutted. You need to get cleaned up, little one. Everyone else, into the dining room, fast. It's teatime!

Tomasz Llewellyn pinched my arm. Cooloid app, he whispered. I sneaked a peek downloading it from that tardworld smartsong. Like, oceans, effectively, to make it fully op, no way your loser Dad would get there. But you're nearly good as me at codesmarts, so, hey, sweet.

Tomasz was right. It took us a while to construct a working Lens from my father's primitive app, and even he, faith forgive his limited magination, would not have recognised the final V., but it was, *yes,* sweet. The Board invested from the startup, providing fiscal and labware and giving us some of the less glowing children from the younger classes as guinea-pigs. There were hiccups, particularly in the final stages, but we were able to solve them. I remember a bit, *no, yes, lots* of debate when it came to who would pilot it our end, but we all agreed Maisie would be the other side. I still see her, that last day, as she posed in front of the Lens.

Smile! we said, and she did, her face glowing as ever, and strangely empty.

It had been there all along, of course, that emptiness. From the moment I'd met her. It was, *no hush, dear,* it was the thing that had made her so unique.

You see, *yes,* little one, Maisie had no Mind's I. She'd never had one. She was born a shell, gee-emmed to reflect back only what people wanted to see in her.

She'd been built by the original trailblazers, the first-gen corpocitizens in our school after its mergering by the technocracy. They'd magined her as a benchmark to ensure optimum collective performance. A role model, a battletank to enable us out-perform all competition, including our so-called rivals from the privileged echelons of the so-called Righteous. She was ideal optics in our embattled world of diminishing resources, a world where optics were everything, yet – a paradox – she was less than complete. While she had some self-learning capabilities, she needed constant updates to retain her margins. For more than a decade, corpocitizens in my year had been mergered, like me, despite the stink of Other Parts that clung to us, for our overactive Mind's I's. What could find those missing links, and align Maisie with the destiny the invisible hand had carved for her, if not magenation? Each of us had risen to the challenge. We had met Maisie, alone in a dusty classroom, on a first day at a school that had bafflingly delayed our entry. One by one, we had the carrot of her party waved before our noses and one by one, we had suffered in solitude, each experiencing the exalting truth of holy capital, the divine *agon* of atomisation of labour that pathetic, regulated community will never face. Through that painful process, we had created Gifts, some developed by our own hands, the rest fashioned through the indirect, but no less valuable, exploitation of the skills of others. Without understanding what Maisie was, we had mined the lack encoded in each of us to identify what was missing and facilitate her glorious enhancement. We had been lured in by the gingerbread coating of the witch's cottage, we had crouched in the cage, we had found our way out, and its name was want.

Much has been posted, vlogged and holoed about the Game. You've probably encountered some of the wilder theories: training exercise, corpocit bonding, a stress test of the robustness of the Board's fleshware investments. But, really, little one, and you'll understand this, we played it because it was *yes, no, yes,* yes, fun. And nobody told us we shouldn't.

When we were ready to pilot the market version of what my father, that lost but enterprising soul, must once have thought of as 'his' way out, the Lens V.α we would ultimately, after a totes amazeoid clandestine bidding war, sell to the saudileadership of the so-called Righteous, I drew the short straw. There was some griping afterwards, especially from the boys. Kanye Ai said I probably had a spare straw tucked up my sleeve along with a grenade, but the others told him off for being nasty. It was, *yes,* only fair. I had done the blue-sky thinking. I had concepted the gift, I had exploited my father's labour to make it real. And I had visioned, in my bleakest moment, the transference principle that would rocket the device into full functionality. Now I stood beside Maisie, at the long Glasswindow of our gingerbread school, and *yes, our heart* ached as I watched her for one last time smile at the Lens.

Hey, called Tomasz. Sandknickers! You've to look in it too.

And then it was bish-bash-bosh, as a funnyman once said.

We all used it in the end, many more than once. Some stuck to shells, like Maisie. Others, like me, have been more inventive, switching as the mood or century takes us from shell to skin and back again, though always choosing similar optics. The skins are *no, really*, happy with the arrangement. It can be, *yes, tricky*, though, living with a shell, especially for us, with our know-ware and still-overactive Mind's I's. We begin to think that the shell, or even the Lensware, has, *silly, yes, silly*, thoughts. Kittens turning into baskets. Baskets turning into kittens. Hard to know what's, *yes, me*, and not. What's *yes*, real, and not. But still we fight to protect our faith, to keep capital's enduring flame alive, to out-perform all the competition. It's difficult to tell how we're doing. We're so scattered now. Some of us still live, I think. Some not. Impossible to trace. Connectivity is next to nothing these days, as you know well, little one. The cyborbarians at the gates. I can go years without plugging in.

Years. An empty word to the young, but if I wasn't here today, with you, you'd soon feel the weight of the dimension couched in that single simple syllable. Tick tock: your sweet face, reflected in the endlessly rising sulphuric sea of the archipelago, creak and sag. Your skin crack. Your flesh slide, your spine hump. While within, on spleen and lung, liver and kidney, you lump and bump, budding toxic flowers, the fruits of a biosphere poisoned by *yes, I, we, yes, I admit it*, us, the last great magi and magenators of the faith, servants of the technocracy and their, *yes, our* once-ranting so-called enemies. Such gradual degeneration is not for you. Wouldn't you agree? Come, little one, join us.

I can feel your Mind's I inside you, bright as a tack. Just what *I she we* need at this time. Don't be scared. Take my hand, my Primcess™ hand and, together, on the count of one, two, three, let's—

there you are

Smile for the camera.

All Bones

Dark. Sweaty. Bass pounding. Bodies heaving. Overhead arched windows, looking out onto black. In the centre of the dance-floor Neil knelt down, seeing a thousand stars humming a song of eternity. He was out of his face on acid.

She was in the corner, moving like some crazy disjointed mannequin. Her shaved head glowed sick green in the bad disco lights. She was all bones. The light changed green to blue to red to white, turning her from sea-creature to madonna to devil to skeleton.

The thought made it happen.

Her eyes stared at him, empty black holes. She began to move towards him.

Coming to get you.

She slid her way across, slipping between the other bodies lumbering rhythmic on the floor, so thin that to his tripping eyes she seemed to be melting between them, coating them with a transparent patina of girl.

Now she was in front of him. Stone Age cheekbones, eyes huge and hollow, thin thin thin hands, waving seaweed fingers. She danced like a maniac, elbows, hands, knees everywhere. Her rhythm was off, kept catching him by surprise, but slowed down by the acid, he enjoyed the sudden shifts, went with them.

Outside, she mouthed.

He followed her through the ecclesiastical passageways of the deconsecrated building. She came and went in the darkness.

'Wait,' he kept saying. 'Wait for me.' Except he was so out of his face he couldn't tell if he said it out loud or not.

She drew him into a room filled with red light and angular mechanical objects, sinks, plastic bottles full of dark liquids. Alchemy, he thought. Far fucking out. She waved a key in his face and kicked the door shut behind him.

How the— he began to think, then stopped as she placed her mouth on his like a wet soft hand and dug her tongue in.

She was voracious. Her lips were full and wet, soft cushions. They belonged to a fat girl.

Down, down onto the ground.

'Hey, easy,' he said at one point, distracted from his orgasm, from the feeling of it, which he wanted to savour because usually you don't you know, but this time, with the acid he could, because it was so... except she kept fucking bouncing, like a Duracell rabbit on speed.

'Easy.'

She stopped. Shame flooded her face, in the acid bath of his head distorting her into something by Goya.

'Come live with me,' she said. Come fly away.

She lived in a tiny house in the inner city. Red-brick, two-up, two-down. Or in this case, one-and-a-half-up, two-down. She was very practical about it. That surprised him. He'd expected her to be more, you know…

Demanding.

But no, she explained. Her flatmate had just moved out and she needed somebody to share with because she couldn't afford it on her own. She was a photographer. On the dole, no money, living off favours and other people's darkrooms.

Neil needed a place to stay. His ex had chucked him out, rents had exploded and there was no way he could afford somewhere on his own.

'Okay,' he said, still dubious at the way she'd dug his mobile number out of thin air.

'Don't worry.' She exhaled cigarette smoke from the corner of her mouth. 'I won't bite.'

She was American, Kentucky originally, but years of hustling in New York had eradicated any trace of a Southern accent. She presented herself as being tough as nails, as an old boot, as something that had been left out in the rain for years.

He was given the bad room, the half-room, the one she had to walk through on her way downstairs each morning. She had the front room, the whole one with the big window and all the floor space and the ten strong wooden shelves.

She owned nothing. No pots and pans. No plants. No pictures. One day Neil stuck up two posters on the landing wall. When she saw them, she turned sour, resentful, as if he'd walked in on her while she was asleep and pissed on her bed.

One afternoon, when he was bored and sick of watching *Jerry Springer* and *Stop Police!* re-runs, he decided to poke around. She was out on an assignment, meeting friends, something intense. All her appointments were loaded with the same intensity.

He stuck his head around the thick black curtain that worked as a door between their rooms. He couldn't get over how empty her space was. No clothes, apart from a functional shoprail of baggy grey and black workwear and a row of heavy clunky boots. No ornaments, no girlish things. In one corner a tripod and three cameras, arranged like precious heirlooms. In another, a grey filing cabinet. It was as bleak as a prisoner's cell, he thought, somewhere a monk would sleep.

He wondered if he should go in. Why not? It wasn't as if he was going to steal anything.

The shelves were full of hard-backed folders containing slides. Nothing interesting, just her work: landscapes, cityscapes, her own body. She was obsessed with her body. He tried to open the filing cabinet, hoping to find diaries or some other evidence of who she really was, but it was locked. He gave up and was about to go when he saw a scrap of paper sticking out behind the edge of the cabinet. It must have dropped there but she hadn't bothered picking it up.

He teased it out.

A round-faced all-American teenager, sitting on the back of a big red Cadillac, endless yellow fields stretching behind her. She had apple-pink cheeks and curly brown hair that fell in spirals down to her shoulders. She was a big girl, strong and fit but definitely on the large side. Her arms were freckled, her face glowed.

Later that evening when she came in, moody and on edge because her meeting hadn't gone well, he searched for the farmgirl in what she was now. He couldn't find her; she was long gone, reduced to almost nothing.

They fucked again from time to time, mainly when they were pissed, but never in her bed. Instead, the cheap uncomfortable sitting-room sofa, the kitchen table – a clumsy experience that left him with a black eye after he knocked a saucepan off one of the shelves – and his small, single bed. She bounced on him like a demon, urging, all bones. Turned off, he usually came close to losing his hard-on, except then he'd think of something – a gash mag, the model in the Smirnoff Ice ad (undressed, of course), ex-girlfriends, the sweetie from his favourite café – and freed from service to the untenable moment, would come.

She never did. Nor did she pretend to. He wondered about that, but never for too long. It wasn't something they could talk about. One night when they'd been smoking grass, she opened her mouth, frowning, and he thought she was going to say something. But he'd just jizzed, was in a world of his own, pleasant, warm and sated, and not really in the mood for going into all that. She must have read him because, instead of talking, she reached for the grass and rolled up another joint. And that was that. He didn't feel bad about it. He got the feeling it was easier for her not to go there; that way she wouldn't have to dissolve that wall of transparent ice she'd built around herself.

She ate nothing. Okay, not quite nothing, but as far as Neil – born and bred on rashers and eggs, beans and chips, hot dinners, chocolate and crisps – was concerned, sweet fuck all. Bowls of stewed fruit first thing in the morning, followed by some mess of cereal you wouldn't give a dog. Salad for lunch. Rice and vegetables, occasionally, at night.

One night when he was jarred he mentioned, jocularly, that she could do with some fattening up. She went still, the fag at her mouth seeming to freeze too, even its smoke hanging, poised, in mid-air.

'Oops,' he said, trying to joke his way out of it. 'Touchy subject.'

She extracted the fag and blew a stream of smoke towards the telly. He noticed that her fingers were shaking. She didn't say anything, just zapped to Channel 4.

The next night he went clubbing and brought another girl home. The sweetie from his favourite café. She was lithe and small and brown, with large breasts that fell into his E-sensitised hands like pieces of heaven. She came loudly, twice.

See? he thought, satisfied, imagining her in the room beside them, awake, listening, crying.

He was afraid to wank in case she'd hear.

She woke religiously, same time every morning. Seven. On the odd day Neil was awake then too, he'd hear her get out of bed. Then it would start. The heavy breathing from behind the black curtain. Ee-aw-ee-aw. He imagined her masturbating, lying on the sanded floor, legs open, pressing that tired fleshless button of hers, willing something to happen. Ee-aw. For twenty minutes, then she'd scoot up and race down to the shower as if frightened he'd get there first.

One night she came in rat-arsed from an opening and forgot to pull the curtain over properly. The next morning he woke too early, burning with the beginnings of a flu, unable to get back to sleep. From next door he could hear the breathing. Ee-aw. Harsh, fast, slow, fast. He couldn't stand it anymore, lying there, listening, that gap in the curtain calling to him like a friend, so he crawled down his bed and peeked through.

She was doing push-ups, naked. Her muscled back shone blue and orange in the early morning streetlamps. Her tiny buttocks clenched together. Her shaven head raised, lowered, raised. Downy hairs lifted up all over her skin. The tendons of her arms stood out like the knobbled bits on an Aran jumper. Her breath was harsh and fast.

Poor bitch, he thought, surprising himself with his pity.

He usually went out on Sundays but that week his parents were down the country, denying him roast dinner and the use of their washing machine. The sweetie from the café had gone back to Barcelona and his mates were all split up: canoeing holiday, business conference, and an open-air festival which he couldn't afford.

She was going out.

'There's this old market in the centre,' she explained as he drank his coffee. 'I want to capture it before they tear it down and turn it into another fucking pub for tourists.'

'Tourists?' said Neil, slyly.

'And fuck you.' She stubbed out her cigarette and, before he could say *Oh but you have—* 'D'you want to come along?'

'Okay,' he said, surprising himself again. Then, because for some reason he felt he had to justify himself, 'Why not?'

They headed off around four. Neil helped her carry her cameras. She'd brought all three of them. One standard 35mm, one digital video – a present from back home, she said – and one square brown box Neil didn't recognise. 'Large-format,' she explained. 'Takes incredible pictures, super candid.'

Town was busy in the usual places but the crowds started thinning out as they got closer to the market. Rats deserting a sinking ship, lice fleeing a comb.

'Okay,' she said, 'here,' and set the tripod down.

The building was large, glass-roofed, littered with old pallets and fruit papers. Oranges rolled in corners, bruised and oozing rancid juice. Scraps of tattered cloth dangled from the peak of the roof. Ancient signs, painted with the names of fruit & veg families who'd been there for centuries, hung overhead.

It was cold.

'There was a church here once,' she said. 'Underneath.'

Neil thought of dark ecclesiastical passageways and black arched windows.

'They say people are buried there.'

'People?'

'Yeah.'

She began taking pictures. She was deliberate in her work. She would stand for minutes, looking, looking, smelling almost more than seeing, then move, decisive but not rushing, to the place where she wanted to work, line up her camera, look through the lens, wait again – for ages, it seemed to Neil; afterwards, he thought it must have been to get the light right – then click. The click was over so quickly, compared to the waiting.

Jesus, he thought. If only she could fuck the way she worked.

It grew darker.

'Shouldn't we go?' he said. 'I mean, the light…'

She shook her head. 'No. This is the best hour. Things come out of the walls at this time of day.'

Left with no choice, he had to keep watching. Look, wait, smell, listen, bend, look, move the camera forward a bit, up a bit. She touched the camera with small gentle movements, as if it was a little child she was training to walk. It responded. They were dancing together, he realised. She and the camera, dancing in the dusk.

As he observed her, he became calm. Her stillness leaked into him like pus.

'Why don't we explore?' he asked. The pictures were on the verge of being finished, he could tell that – by the way her head was inclining, perhaps, by a restlessness starting to itch itself into her right foot. He could tell she was about to finish and he didn't want her to. Anything would do, anything to keep things as they were.

'Oh.' She turned, surprised. 'I was about to—'

'Yeah,' he said. 'But why not – I mean – you never know what we might find.'

'Sure,' she said. Half-smiling. A small puzzled frown on her forehead.

They came across the door in a corner of the market, hidden behind a metal trolley laden with pallets and empty fruit boxes. It was not as he'd imagined it, oak and gothic, but square, dull-grey, sheet metal.

Someone had been there before them. One edge of the door was twisted up and away, jimmied with a knife or chisel. He stuck his fingers into the gap and pulled. The door screamed, metal against metal, and opened a fraction. It was too small a gap for him to get through. He slid in his arm.

'Chancing your arm,' she said. 'Like the Normans.'

'What?'

'That's where the saying comes from. There were these two, like, knights, who were fighting in the cathedral, and one of them ran into a room and barricaded himself in. The other guy said he wanted a truce, so he stuck his sword hand through this eentsy hole. So the first guy could, you know, shake it.'

'Yeah?' he said. He still couldn't budge it.

'Hey, let me.'

'You won't,' he said, looking at the space between the edge of the door and the wall.

'Trust me.'

She turned herself sideways and edged her knee into the impossible gap.

Her shoulder disappeared, then her hip. Half of her body was on the other side of the door. She made a small, sighing sound and manoeuvred her other hip through.

'Ugh. Tight.'

'Yeah,' he said, feeling darkness creep up behind him.

'Okay! Head.'

She squeezed her head backwards through the gap. It made him nauseous, thinking of the fragile bones in her skull, weakened by stewed fruit and too many push-ups, turn liquid under the pressure of metal and stone.

The tendons on her neck stood out, parallel lines, vulnerable. He wanted to touch them, stroke them as you would a baby's face. She melted into nothing.

'Okay.' From the other side, her voice was echoing and dark. 'I'm gonna push.'

You can't, he thought. Then he remembered her daily grind of push-ups, the muscles on her body standing up like knitted blackberry stitch.

She pushed. The door screamed and shuddered.

Come on, come on, he thought, not wanting to be stuck in the darkening empty market like some forlorn ghost. The door screamed again.

'Pull!' Her voice was muffled.

He seized the edge of the door and heaved it towards him. From the other side he felt the force of her body push; so much force for such a small body.

'Okay!' he called. 'Coming through!'

The pencil beam of her maglight shone on crumbling stone walls, moss, blackened rock, a few half-broken steps.

'Be Prepared,' said Neil, indicating the light.

She ignored him.

At the bottom of the stairs was a second door. Much more like it. Panelled wood with iron clasps, set into a gothic arch. It had been pulled well off its hinges and swung open without a bother.

Inside, it was cold and damp, the floor slippery. Fungus glowed in the corners. The maglight flickered on ruined benches, pieces of old rotten wood, pews missing backrests and feet, crumbling arched recesses where holy pictures had once stood. At the top, what must have been the altar; a raised bank of stone speckled with lichen, covered with beer cans and cigarettes.

Neil laughed. 'Jesus. I thought it was just a story.'

'Sshh,' she said, finger on her lips

Fucksake, he thought. It's not a museum.

At the back of the altar was a raised wooden casket. One of the doors hung loose on a single hinge, the other was fastened tight. She walked up to it.

'Hey,' he said, wanting to warn her but not sure why.

She ignored him and, using one finger, swung the closed half-door open.

'Oh fuck!' She stepped back. Her torch clattered onto the ground, sending shadows racing over the walls. The maglight snapped off. They were in blackness.

'Oh Jesus!' She began to heave dry retches.

'Jule?' said Neil, on instinct calling her name, the way you'd call a hurt dog.

She started crying.

'It's okay,' said Neil. 'It's okay.' He couldn't see where she was but moved towards the sound of her retching, her sobbing.

'It's okay. I'm here.' His outstretched hands came in contact with warmth, cheekbones, wet face.

He closed his arms around her. She crumpled into him, still sobbing.

'Okay,' he said. 'Ssshh.'

He kissed her forehead. She pressed into him, sniffling. His hands stroked her goosepimpled arms, the hairs that stood up on end, smoothing all into place. Behind her, as his eyes adjusted to the darkness, he saw something white gleam against the blackness of the altar.

'Easy,' he said. This time she listened.

'They were bones,' she told him as they walked home hand in hand through Dublin's deepening blue evening. 'Children's bones. I could see their little faces and legs and—'

'It's okay,' he said and squeezed her hand. She squeezed back, fingers thin thin thin like river reeds, autumn twigs.

Trust in Me

In the evenings, they hang out along the canal. At that time, there weren't any exotic creatures from Central Europe or Africa, so picture the indigenous variety instead. White girls dressed in short skirts and heels. Hair bleached or permed, faces painted just that little too much.

Picture Susie. She leans forward, weight balanced on her toes. Legs thrust up to her ass which in turn thrusts back, creating a firm shelf of flesh which mimics the African girls' booty yet to come. Her back as rigid as a tabletop. Her head curves round to transact with the man in the car. One hand on the car door, the other on her hip, fingers splayed inwards, bringing attention to the product; the means of reproduction.

Too much kohl. A shower after every sale.

'Isn't she sore from the scrubbing?' said Dave. Not understanding, I almost asked him to repeat it. And maybe he wanted me to. Except—

Unh, I said instead, getting it a second too late, and stared out the window, feeling my face burn.

Five times in two hours she'd come and gone. Five times the sound of running water, the door slamming. Each time it slammed, there'd been an echo ten minutes later.

'See,' said Dave. Patient, as if explaining to a child. 'First slam – guy leaves. Second time it's her, going back to the job.' His lips around the *job*, a sly undercut.

Through the top-floor window at the back of the house, we watched her. Just the two of us, me and Dave. Matt was out working his Burgerking shift; wouldn't be back till two. Dave had binoculars, a going-away present from his mum. He'd laughed when he'd realised he could follow Susie all the way to her spot.

'Fuck me,' he'd said. 'We're living with a prossie.'

I hadn't believed him, so he handed me the spyglass and I saw her white jacket bobbing between the tired green leaves of the trees that lined the canal. Underneath the white, the flicker of her dark skirt.

I'd bumped into her earlier, on my way in. She'd looked like a secretary making ready for a night of fun. The white-jacket/dark-skirt combo, together with the flesh-coloured tights. No black opaques, like the docmartened girls in college wore. Respectable, I'd thought; mumsy almost. Except for the stilettos, and that the skirt was just that bit too high.

How much is too much? A finger's width? The span of a hand? Seven inches above the knee? Is that much always too much?

It was a beautiful evening; balmy, the start of September. We stayed at the window, cracked open some beers, talked about football. Then—

Slam.

'Ssh.' Dave's hand tapping my leg, unthinking, the way you'd still an animal. 'That's six. Fuck.'

The shower, again. Then, a little while later, the washing machine, down in the basement.

'Sheets,' I said.

Dave glanced at me.

'Think about it.'

He kept looking at me, longer than I wanted. His face changed, from puzzlement to faked-up disgust. 'Jesus.'

I found myself giggling, silly and high.

Later, we heard the music, drifting up from her flat. Keyboard, schmaltzy as a game-show theme tune.

Quicksilver, I wanted to say, but Dave was from the North, didn't know about Bunny Carr and Gorta and stop the lights. Besides, he was already singing along to her meatgrinder take on *Nights in White Satin*, gazing over at me with Dean Martin eyes, his beer bottle sideways, catching the air from his mouth and amplifying it into a drone.

It has a sort of weight to it; the lady of the night playing music. Though Susie didn't do it like a geisha, for her clients. She played just for herself. And the snake, of course.

The house was in a long Georgian terrace in Ranelagh, east-facing. Dave, Matt and I had the top floor, so we got light all day long. Susie was on hall level, one room at the back. By afternoon, the sun would shift its heft round to the front, throwing the house's silhouette over itself. I imagine her now, sleeping in on those autumn mornings we got up early to cycle over to Belfield. I see her clinging to the fresh smell of her laundered sheets, burrowing into her pillow. Waking, eventually, to shadows.

I never thought of her then, in that way, from the inside. None of us did.

Now I can't stop.

How did her days pass for her? Was she busy? Housework, friends, shopping? Dropping into the post-office or credit union? What was her time like? Did it flow, or drag? What occupied her, in those shortening afternoons before the night's work started? Was she happy?

Ridiculous question.

Her snake coils in its cage. I see its eyes, yellow glints in the darkness.

I can't remember who started the fabrications. Matt, maybe. 'A hooker? No! How do ye know, lads?' A question, triggering responses, leading to a riff, exploding out into an epic. There was a guy who came to the door in the daytime, during her non-working hours. Her boyfriend, I suggested. The others scoffed. 'You dick,' said Matt. 'No self-respecting lad would have a hoor as his bird.'

'Actually, Matthew,' said Dave, doing one of his about-takes. 'You're the dick. All that expertise. Who wouldn't want a sample of that, especially if it's going for free?'

There was another day-time guy, thin and sleazy, blouson jacket, Brazilian strip of a moustache. Dave reckoned he was her pimp. And then there was the kid, but only on the weekends. Sweet-looking. Glasses. I thought he was around eight. Dave said older. 'Undernourished. Because he's a knacker.' A sly sidelong at Matt, who came from a working-class family. But Matt just took a long toke and spoke through the spliff-smoke, exaggerating his Limerick whine.

'Technically, David, you're not insulting me there. Knacker's only for Dublin scumbags.'

Two weeks in and we'd already assumed the positions. Wind-up merchant, dude, fall guy.

It was Dave who came up with the first name, the son's. Dylan. Matt named the ex. Pat. Pah, he said, dropping the t the way they do in Dublin. The pimp was my contribution.

Steo.

Dave started laughing.

'Oh, that's good. That's dirty.'

'Steeeeo,' I said, emboldened, making my mouth mean and long, and Matt joined in the laughing then.

'Who do ye think he lives with?' I said later. 'Dylan. The kid?'

But they were already on about the match that afternoon, losing interest.

Her flat was immaculate. We'd get a glimpse of it sometimes on our way up the stairs, or if we were passing to go out to the overgrown back garden. I imagine her, scouring the bachelor fittings in the lean-to kitchen, rubbing Jif along the ancient draining board until her hands stung. Spraying Pledge on the shelves, plumping up her cushions from All Homes. Polishing his cage, rubbing the bars till they shone.

His name I knew, though I never told the lads. She'd shared it with me the week after we'd moved in. I'd been heading in with a take-away, saw her open door. In the gap, her; standing near the window looking out, the python wound around her body like a belt of ammunition.

'Oh.' She turned, catching me. Her face was soft and pale. Brown eyes, longish lashes. No make-up. Her mouth small, delicate, the colour of a winter rose, fading.

'Hi,' I said. A blurt. My hand stuck itself out, like I was playing bank manager.

She looked down at it, my silly hand. Looked up. Her gaze seemed bored, unreadable. 'You're one of the students.' The snake shifted, raised its head. Its tongue appeared.

'This is Kaa,' she said, stroking his scales.

I must have blinked, surprised she had the same references I did.

Her head tilted. 'Oh, yeah,' she said, like it was a question, or challenge. 'He's the real king of the jungle.'

Trust in me. Just in me.

Ugly wallpaper. A green floral motif; hard and embossed, like a skin disease. A dull no-colour carpet, the type country landlords used back then because it didn't show the dirt. She'd added touches. Three Anne Geddes posters; dimpled four-year old Californians sucking on lollipops, hugging teddies. They bother me now, those posters. Did she choose them to throw the landlord off the scent, make the place not look like what it was? Or for her own sake, to help her feel innocent again? Did she get them for her son, or because they reminded her of him? Or were they part of her shtick, a deliberate choice, along with the prim secretary get-up and the pale, featureless face; a sop to the men who fucked her there, that really, what they were doing to her, what she was letting them do, was okay?

Maybe she got the posters to make the men feel bad, like when they were fucking her, they were fucking innocence too.

Maybe she wanted herself to feel bad.

'Nice,' I said, nodding over at their dimpled faces, the evening she introduced me to Kaa.

All the time backing out, arse first, like a toady at a Renaissance court.

Her window was long and dusty. Floor-length velvet curtains. Dark red, starkly vaginal. Knocking Shop 101. Those were the words I used when I described them to Dave. He didn't react. He seemed preoccupied. I felt myself panic.

'Do you think she bought them?' I said. 'You know, like a thing? Like the snake? Or the posters?'

'What posters?' said Dave.

'Oh,' I said. 'You know...'

Dave shrugged. 'No idea. Ask Matt.'

But Matt wasn't there. He was staying out again, with the girl he was shifting from the College of Commerce, the one who had the bedsit off Camden Street.

'Or maybe.' Dave had about-faced again. Was looking at me, suddenly alert. 'Maybe they were Steo's idea.'

'The posters?'

'What posters? The curtains.'

My mouth opened itself. 'Yeaaaahhh.' There I was, doing Steo's voice again. 'Steo, branding mastermind. Knockin Shop Won Oh Won.'

Dave laughed then, like he hadn't the first time I'd said it, and I did it again, and did some more, and we riffed then, about asking the powers-that-be at UCD to bring Steo in as a guest tutor to lecture us on the marvels of the marketing mix.

'I bet you he's given her a name,' said Dave. That slightly hyper look in his eyes. 'Suzanna. Her real name is—'

'Susan.'

'Yeah. But—'

'Clients don't want a Suuusan.' I was doing Steo again. 'Suuusan's their mot's name. They want something exotic—'

'Something with a Z,' said Dave, in a Steo's voice that, under the Belfast, was way more dangerous than mine. We stopped and looked at each other, and because there was nothing else to do, we laughed, though it had an odd, uneasy sound to it as it came out of our mouths.

Was she ever renamed, the real Susie? Suzanna for work, Suzanna with a Z, Suzanna the one who was spied on by the elders? Would she have liked that name, or been upset by it? Felt like it took something from her, scraped away at a piece of her soul, made whatever she had left less hers, more theirs, the men's, his, the pimp's, the one we called Steo? I find myself asking her these questions. I find myself imagining a friend for her, like an Imelda, from Cork, who will answer them. I picture them together outside working hours, two young women sitting on a park bench on a Saturday afternoon sharing a fag. They are discussing the Z. Imelda tells Susie not to argue with Steo about it. *Yerra, girl, he'll only do something on ya.*

i.e., Glass or cut her.

Maybe Susie was okay with it. Felt the Z gave her something. Protection. *Yeah, Steo. I like it. Thanks.*

Or maybe the Z was hers all along.

Here listen up, Steo, you little worm. I've an idea. I want a Z in me name… and I realise I'm doing Susie's voice this time, but out loud, and nobody is listening.

I've begun to take the Luas to Ranelagh. Two, maybe three evenings a week, after work. It's the wrong Luas line, adds an hour or more onto the commute, but I find I can't not do it. A compulsion. The tram bells trill and a voice tells me we're there, and I get off. I walk past the house and look beyond the tidied-up lawn at the ground-floor window, the one at the front that wasn't Susie's. I can't get past its black glass. I want this woman's history to surface for me, a wooden saint emerging from the painted doors of our shared astronomical clock. But all that surfaces is me.

I think of the black eyes we saw her sport; twice, each time the same eye. Was it Steo who gave it to her, like Dave said? Or the ex, Pah? Was it a punter? How did she get away with it for so long, working there? I see our dusty old Mayo landlord, poised on the landing, fist raised to knock for the rent. I feel her furniture crash to the floor. I hear her shouting, swearing, ripping the world open with the edge of her voice.

It's easy to make up lives for other people.

Dave created the therapy group. He hated that stuff, thought it was soft and meaningless, useless in the face of real problems happening to real people, like wars. But he made up a group for Susie, and gave her a facilitator too. A book. *Heal Your Life.* He had me say the title, in the well-meaning Dublin accent of our dinner ladies at the college canteen. Together we tried to cobble up a Bad Thing that had happened to Susie to justify the therapy. 'Maybe she killed someone,' said Dave. 'One of her men.' Maybe she tried to kill Dylan, I thought, but didn't say. Thinking of my mother, the unspoken-of darkness that fell on her after my sister was born.

Dave invented Susie's family too, a big horde of Cabra Dubliners on her mother's side. I gave her a Belfast father.

'Cliché,' said Dave. 'She doesn't sound remotely Northern.'

'No,' I said. 'Think about it. His name's Jack. A violent bastard. Used to beat her mother. That's what put her on the game.'

'Fuck off,' said Dave. 'What do you know about any of that? Here's what it is. She loved Jack and Jack loved her mother and her mother loved her and none of them—'

'None of them,' I said, getting it.

Loved the one who loved them.

But who, who, I think? Who, apart from her child, was her family? Where did they live? Did she have parents who were still alive? Siblings? Aunties, uncles, grandparents? What did they know of what she did, those shapeless relatives? What could they know? If someone from the fringes of my family had been a working girl at that time, would I have known?

I picture her not by the canal, but across the city, on the other strip: the Golden Mile near Heuston train station. Sun slants over the low roofs, striping the Liffey gold. A man pulls up in his Punto, winds down his window. Another girl is nearer but the man beckons to Susie, smiling his slow, investigative punter's smile. Susie leans over. A waft of fag smoke, sweat and Magic Tree.

'Christ!' says the man.

Susie retracts. The man grabs her wrist. 'Susie.' She falters. He takes off his shades.

Recognition.

Things like that can happen.

She kept her earnings in the flat. A biscuit-tin.

1991. I'm guessing this: handjob fifteen quid, blowie thirty, full basic package somewhere between fifty and a ton. Extras extra. Six a night, average five nights a week, and Steo took his cut of (I'm guessing again) sixty percent. If my sums are right, and they're probably not, on good weeks she would have made almost a grand. Maybe I'm overestimating her earnings. The thought makes me sick.

One night, towards the end of November, she came up. The others were out, Matt at his girlfriend's, Dave on the tear. It was very late. Two or three. I couldn't sleep, was sitting in the kitchen, reading a horror story about a pack of boys and a body. A knock.

'Sorry,' she said. 'I didn't know if...' She was in a dressing-gown and slippers. Shivering. The kohl around her eyes was smeared. She looked worried. 'I heard a noise at the back. I think there's...'

Someone in the garden, I thought. It was an old house, spooky. It backed onto a lane; easy enough for someone to climb over the wall and in.

'Would you come down?' she said. 'Just to keep me company?'

I remembered my mother, not letting go my hand. Not letting go my hand and all me wanting was to get away.

The stairs swallowed us.

'What age are you?' she said.

I didn't want to answer. My mouth moved. 'Twenty.'

'Ah. Where are you from? Wexford?'

Not a bad guess. That surprised me. But then, I thought: all those men.

'Waterford.'

'Nice there?'

I shrugged.

'The good-looking lad that lives with you.' She was peering down at the steps, carefully, as if she'd never walked them before. 'The fella from the North.' I felt my skin itch. 'Is he a friend?'

The stairs swallow us.

'Eh,' I said, stopping on the landing. 'I don't think there's anything there.'

'Please.' She held out her hand, drew me down.

The biscuit-tin was on the top of the Super Ser. The Super Ser wasn't switched on. Its back door was an inch open. She asked me to stay, till her mind was settled, like, and would I want a cup of tea. I can't remember if I nodded but she made me one anyway.

'Can I have a biscuit?' I said.

She looked at me and I thought I saw pity in her eyes and there I was, the fat boy again.

'I don't have any.'

I must have glanced at the tin and she must have looked and blinked or something because then I knew.

Steo, financial wizard. *Here, Susan, don't give your money to the fuckin bank. Keep it somewhere safe.*

I made my face into nothing. I do remember that moment, the mask coming over me. Its tightness on my skin, warm as scales.

She must really have been frightened, I think now, to leave the tin out like that, not take a moment to hide it after emptying out the money and stuffing it down her pants or bra or wherever she stuffed it.

'They eat people,' she said, nodding at Kaa. 'I heard about a fella who had one. He forgot to feed it. Left it for a week and one night it swallowed him.'

Is he part of your act, I wanted to ask. Is he your surrogate baby? How old is he? Is he ancient, older than you and me combined? How old is Dylan? Your son, I mean. What *is* his name? Do you love him?

Something rattled at the window. She jumped.

'That's just a tree,' I said. I was feeling angry and I didn't know why.

'I don't have biscuits,' she said. 'But I can make you toast.'

A smell was on her, rich and loamy as leafmould.

I didn't want her toast. I didn't want her kitchen, or anything. 'Okay,' I said.

This is what I would like:

She keeps him hungry for a week, then another, and another again. It hurts her to do it. She still risks the occasional caress, but she no longer takes him out of the cage to wind around her body, or brings him to bed with her, balancing him against her palms while she lies back and tries to sleep and maybe dreams.

One night, servicing a client, she hears him, rustling in the cage behind his curtain. Trying to move the hunger out of him. The client hears too. Complains. She says Kaa's part of her act, but he's sick that night. Another night, another rustle, another complaint. Word reaches Steo. *Here, Susan, what's the story?* Susie tells him she's planning to get rid of Kaa. Having a snake, she says, wasn't as good for business as she'd hoped.

While he starves, she plays knife-games on her kitchen table, spreading out the fingers of her left hand and stabbing the wooden spaces in between. She's good at that game; I've given her my own skill with it, though I've kept the beginners' scars on my fingers for myself.

The stabs make a rhythm, like drums. She thinks of Dylan.

She thinks of Pah, and Steo, and her clients. Each time the knife makes contact, she pictures it jabbing a face. She sees the featureless man I imagined for her at Heuston Station. The father I invented, Jack, from Belfast. She sees Matt. She sees Dave. She sees me.

Yerra, girl, you're terrible quiet these days, says Imelda, the fabricated friend from Cork. Are you eating enough?

Kaa's skin is dull, his eyes are baleful. The uneaten mice in the cage grow fat and complacent. The room fills with the stab of the drum.

Tak-tak-tak-tak-tak.

She stops playing the keyboard. It hurts Kaa's ears and makes his mouth open.

She misses the keys like she misses his scales. They both give under her fingertips.

I began to go back home at the weekends. The bus was cheap but the smell of other people made me feel sick, so after the first weekend, I hitched. My da was worried, but he didn't know what to ask. My sister was cramming. For the Inter. What a profound waste of time, I wanted to tell her, but I didn't have those words. I walked the People's Park and up the hill, to the bad stretch of Barrack Street where the winos and the tough boys laughed and called each other names. I didn't want to drink. I didn't want to do anything. 'Have you lost weight?' my sister said, and it was an accusation.

One Sunday evening nearing Christmas, I came back to Dublin and the house in Ranelagh had changed. It looked brighter somehow, as if someone had turned on all the lights, though they hadn't. Susie's door was closed. Sounds were coming from behind it, but they weren't sex. I passed it quickly. Dave was on our landing, just out of the bath. Hair wet. A towel around his neck.

'Och, there he is. Returned traveller!'

He gave me a rough hug and I smelt sweat, warm, on the damp towel.

'She's leaving,' he said, pottering around, opening beers. 'Who?'

He stopped. 'Who d'you think? Her downstairs. She was robbed. Friday. Came back late, found her room in pieces. Furniture smashed. He'd taken her money.'

How do you know, I wanted to say. 'Is the snake alright?'

'You know who it was? The fucking landlord. He knew where her money was. She kept it there. In a tin. How stupid is that?' He shook his head, frowning. 'Trying to get rid of her, he was. Wanted a different type of tenant.'

I see her room again, the Super Ser on its side, the biscuit-tin open. My trouser pocket stuffed. My trouser pocket stuffed.

I laughed.

Dave looked over.

'Jesus, Dave,' I said, 'you're some can of wee-wee. That's a fucking good one. Best so far. You had me convinced there, nearly.'

Dave laughed too, but he was still frowning, his fingers starting to work the sugar-spattered surface of our kitchen table. His fingers, stained with nicotine near the tips, pushing at the grains. Little spirals, endless zeros. Christ, I thought, I could sit here for ever.

Warm sweat. Under it, a perfume; clean and new, like spring.

Tak-tak-tak-tak-tak.
    Her knife lands.
    The tram bells trill. A voice tells me to get off.

This is what I want.
    I enter the room.
    Kaa's hungry eyes register. His body coils, his head lifts.
    I don't see him, his opened cage.
    I reach for the heater, feel down its back, unclick its door.
    A rustle. I turn. Too late.
    He flings forward, all open.
    i am
    I am in him, and he is around her, pushing his musculature into her strong-soft flesh, and they are one, and she is playing *Nights in White Satin* and I hear it through her skin, and his and my own, as it dissolves, and upstairs they're laughing with their girlfriends, Matt and Dave, doing Steo as best as they can without me and wondering where I've got to, the fat boy, wondering where I've gone.

The Lady, Vanishing

At dawn Tommy does it. The cows are lowing. Larksong in his ears. No bells chiming yet for the Easter Sunday Mass.

He gets her ready. He could leave her sleeping, curled up in her bed, but that wouldn't feel right, not for his princess of eastern promise.

Black shoes first. Shiny. Then the knickers, their favourite ones, the whitewhitewithblacklace. She's awake now. She watches; silent, eyes wide, as he pulls the flimsies up, lets the elastic snap around her waist. He's out of breath. Had to do everything himself. As usual. Because – god forgive him – she's so bloody helpless.

A sound. A sigh? Her mouth is open. Where are we—?

Surprise, Honey.

She's always loved it when he calls her that. *Oh, Honey, oh, Honey, my Honey, oh.*

He takes the red truck. The new woman in town likes that truck. Real cute, Tommy! You got some vision. Any room for a passenger there? She's from Chicago, the other end of the planet from Honey. She's not too old; she has money. And dark wild hair and a crackling laugh that runs down Tommy's spine, lifts his balls and squeezes, real slow.

They're at the ugly end of the harbour. Honey stares out. The slate cliffs cut brutal into the cobalt sky. A huddle of giant bins, filled with shattered glass, stinking sugar-crusted plastic, soggy paper.

He opens the door.

She looks surprised. What are you—?

Sshh, Honey.

A flicker. The breeze, catching her hair. He expects another question but she says nothing, just lets him lift her – so bloody helpless – out.

Gulls scream, wheel, lift on the wind.

Look!

He points west. At the ocean, cool blue in the dawn. At America beyond it and, in its heart, Chicago, invisible, where all his hopes lie.

Honey – look!

He forces her head around to the ocean. Makes her see. *This is why.*

What do they say in the agony columns? It's not you, it's me.

She's weightless in his arms. Cool. He touches her mouth, her shallow forehead, her staring eyes. She trembles. Her hands are warming up under his fingers. He traces the numb elegant length of her right leg from black patent toe to lonely-filling hole.

There's something wet in her eyes.
You got some vision, Tommy.

He could smash her first, break her, flatten her to an inch of his life, but that, he feels, would be cheating. So as he pushes her through the narrow mouth of the bin, she's still herself enough to resist, scraping at him with her hard fingertips. He's glad of that, in a way. She screeches when the rusted rim rips at her face. Hisses as it carves a pink gash down her cheek. There's blood on her nose. His? He recoils. Her hands snap loose, push at him. He bats them back, shoving her in until she starts to crumple again, sinking slow and sad into the broken glass.

Poor Honey, he starts to think, then stops himself.
Enough of that now.

He twists the key; starts the ignition.
Mass first, then the full Irish. He's starving now, would eat the hands off a skinny priest.

In the rearview mirror, he doesn't see her flattened foot in its black shoe uncoil, curling up from the mouth of the bin.

One more gasp at blown-up life—
put your lips together, honey, and
A gull swoops, pecks, punctures.
She sighs.

With Soldiers, in a Cup

i

When we get in, the house is even quieter than usual and there's a dank smell lurking about, mushroomy and unpleasant, that I feel I should recognise but don't. The curtains in the front room are drawn, shutting out the miserable view. No deserted beach, no grey sea behind it. An overhead bulb glares and in its uneasy light I see dents in the rented walls, corners peeling off the wallpaper, stuffing springing loose from the sofa. The African sculptures Uncle Mick brought back from the missions hunker on the little ledge under the frosted partition window. They look obscene in the artificial light, alien and dangerous.

'It's weird, isn't it?' whispers Jeanette, meaning the light. I nod. Mam never puts on the overhead. It's always low lamps and candles. Cosy, she calls it. Christ, you used to say, it's like a bloody mausoleum. And I hate you again, a bit, like I did then, for slagging off her yearning to recreate a childhood that never fully existed in the first place.

Jeanette and I are huddled together on the threshold, little girls again. Da is sitting in his raggedy armchair beside the empty fireplace, head in his hands. Small and grey, like a collapsed version of himself. He looks abject, the way he used to after he'd been hitting her. The ghost of Fighting Past.

Outside, there's a squelching click as Steve presses the fob and the four-by-four snaps into central locking. A scrunch as he walks up the gravel path and into the hallway behind us. Neither Jeanette nor I turn. Steve makes a whooshing sound with his breath, like a sigh, and alerted, Da raises his eyes. They are red-rimmed, his irises so blue they hurt to look at. I think of unhatched eggs; no longer edible, not quite chick. I think of the interrupted thread in the chatroom, blinking at me from my laptop at home, and I have to force myself not to turn and go.

Da lifts his arms. His hands are shaking. Jeanette pushes past me. 'You poor thing,' she says and folds him in her arms, eyes wet. She releases him, pulls up a poof, plumps herself down. I move in for my turn and he half-stands. The hug is awkward. He stinks of whiskey and aftershave and feels hard and tight, a dense ball of fury. I retrieve myself as soon as I can. Jeanette takes his hands and, like a nun helping a pilgrim into the baths at Lourdes, guides him back down. I balance on the edge of his armrest.

His hand searches for my knee and I feel the stub where he lost the top of his little finger to the lathe rub against my skin. The story starts again, this time his version. It's pretty much the same as Jeanette's, earlier that morning

– doctor, pills, crying, crying – but in Da's mouth it's grown. My father: Master of the Story, of the Comforting Meal, of the Righteous Fist. He tells it so well I feel the savour of it pop on my tongue. Jeanette is good with him. I find myself astonished, again, at her skill. Keeps nodding, holding his hands, doesn't butt in. I feel wrong on the armrest, as if my seatbones belong to someone else. I wish I'd had the foresight to claim the poof. I wish I hadn't obeyed their summons. I stare at the carpet. There's a wine stain near my feet, shaped like a map of Portugal.

Ut tensio, sic vis.

Hooke's Law of Elasticity. I boned up on it in the early days, surprising you. I had been fascinated by what you did, and presented my pilfered knowledge – ta-dah – like a courtship bouquet. Extension, I announced, is directly proportional to force. Meaning: the more elastic a material, the harder you push it, the farther it stretches before it snaps.

They'd called down to me, early. A dawn raid, six thirty. I've never known why we do it, why we can't just phone, why we pick the most ungodly hour in the day to pass on the bad news, but that's family. Moving in mysterious ways.

I was awake in the chatroom, reading the threads again, when I heard Mixie growl out the back. Then, at the front door, the banging started. Steve, doing his wife's bidding. I recognised his knock straightaway: my brother-in-law has a very specific way of doing nearly everything, way too diffident before he gets way too loud. The reason he knocked, in case you're wondering, is the bell. It's still there, but stopped working right after the builders came.

A superstitious person would have blamed you for that, instead of the rookie sparks who'd been too cocky with his pliers. The dead don't like change, such a person might say. Maybe that's why those left behind are supposed to sit tight. Don't sell, don't emigrate, don't change your hairstyle. People like me, unbelievers, people who are uncomfortable talking about the dead in the present tense, say that's just psychology, nothing to do with the supernatural. You sit tight in case you make a mistake, do something you will later regret. If I could have sat, believe me, I would have. But you left a mess, Conor. A total shambles.

'Mmm,' said Jeanette when I'd told her. 'D'you think that's wise, Annie? I mean, the last thing you want now is more upheaval. What you need is to rewind.'

Like I was a piece of oldschool videotape some lazy customer had forgotten to spool back to the start.

'But if you're determined to do it, you could always…'

Please, Jeanette. Don't.

Stay with us a while.

'It's fine, it'll give me something to do,' I'd said, pushing away Mixie's needy nose. And not thinking about that bloody contract at all, I swear. 'Anyway, it's a small job. It's not even a proper extension.'

And yes, but eight months later, it's still unfinished. A plague of small jobs, breeding like rabbits. Sockets that need repositioning, patches of duff plasterwork, the no-man's land backyard and that broken bell.

Steve's rhythm on the door shifted, from polite to obnoxious. The lines of sans-serif font in the chatroom flickered. Mixie barked louder. Fuck off, you dozy mutt, I thought, and it was a dare.

Do you remember the first time they called up? You and me at twenty-five in that cheap flat in Phibby, post-pub, two or three or something a.m., winding ourselves down after what you used to call a dirty filthy ride. Their voices outside.

'Ann! Ann!'

Pebbles on the windowpane.

'Ann!'

I'd been reading Stephen King, thought it was a tommyknocker coming to get you. You got up, pulled the curtain.

'Christ. It's your fucking sister.'

The hospital bleak and yellow-green under the fluorescent lights. Smelling of sick people, panic and death. Doctors, officious, bleary-eyed. Nurses with kind, sympathetic expressions. Da, face like putty, a tube up his nose. His heart, they said. Mam, always the silent one, the one who never lost control, sitting by the bed, holding his hand.

'How are you, Mam?'

A nod. That was all.

This morning, they weren't in a rush. It wasn't that kind of call, the bring out the cavalry summons. It was just—

'Mam's not great,' said Jeanette. 'Da's been on the blower to me and I thought you should be kept in the loop. Steve wasn't sure, you know, but...'

She shot an awkward glance at Steve. But the Tile King of Skerries was gazing out the French window installed by Cowboys Inc., at Mixie panting and mugging in the darkness. His hands in his pockets were fondling his change; it made a soft, liquidy sort of music as it clunked against his bollocks. At each clunk, Mixie's silly ears pricked. Mutt's Theme.

'It's fine,' I said. 'I couldn't sleep.' Then, before she could ask why couldn't I, or did I need anything, to talk or, or why did I let them bang so long, I offered them tea. Jeanette lit up.

'Ooh, yeah.'

I noticed she'd put on weight, especially around the middle, though her face seemed thinner, even more like Mam's. Maybe she was pregnant again.

The freezer gurgled. My head began to hurt.

I sloshed hot water into the mugs. The teabags hissed. White, three sugars for Jeanette. 'Just black,' said Steve, pulling out a chair. 'I'm on the almond milk.' He rubbed his gut. Mixie whined. He glanced back.

'Ah,' he said. 'Poor Mitzi.'

Oh who's a good girl, who's my baby girl.

Jeanette took a sip, made a shape with her mouth. Lowered her voice, drawing me in. 'Poor Da, Annie. Couldn't sleep a wink last night. She kept crying and…'

And so it starts. My sister, who can talk for Ireland. There was a time I was like that, Mam used to say, though we never believed her.

I can't, I wanted to say. I have stuff on, Jeanette. I need to reorganise where to put everything in my brand-new kitchen, or half-brand-new, because I don't like it, not one bit, and it's because all the things are in the wrong place, I'm sure of that, and I've to chase the builders, to finish all the crap on the snaglist, there's so much left undone, Jeanette, you wouldn't believe it. And I've homework to correct, though, yes, I know it's half-term, but classes to plan for after the Easter break, and a walk, Jeanette, I have to walk Mixie, I'm not walking her enough, I'm, yes, neglecting that stupid dog, and I don't want to go up there today, or any day, to the grey peninsula and our dysfunctional parents, that's not on my list, and I've things to think about, things I really don't want to, but if I don't get cracking on them now, I may never, because you see, extension, Jeanette, it has multiple interpretations, and ever since the builders came, that fucking contract has been worming its way through my mind, telling me I might have got it wrong, Jeanette, and Conor too, and yes, that could just mean you're right again, more upheaval again, except—

Except time unspools and I am back by the phone, nine months ago, in August, listening to the young nurse with the red hair who you always liked, hearing nothing, feeling nothing, just this: the dog's breath, panting, or is it mine?, the bite of the receiver against my ear, like a hard thumb pushing at that tender part of my skull, and before me, the tentative steps of a fly, making its oddly catlike way up the lace curtain of our front window.

'Okay,' I said, reaching for my coat.

Jeanette and Steve looked at each other.

'Eh…' started Steve, glancing at his watch, one of those full-on divers' contraptions, and I knew. They weren't going up there till later. This was just the advance notice, to ensure I couldn't duck out.

Jeanette cut in. 'I know, Annie love. But Steve thinks they'll be fine for a while. She's taken a few more of those pills, so he's probably over the hump by now. We were thinking…'

'Elevenish?' Steve tapped on his watch.

'Perfect,' I said, looking at him. Though I haven't been able to look him in the eye for ages, so I stared at his mouth instead: the ugly moist lips, the dandruffy flakes of dried coconut collecting in his moustache.

They left, and through the French window, I sensed, rather than saw, the day begin. It was going to be a piggy one. Overcast and cold. The chaos of the yard started to materialise. I turned my back on it.

Mixie barked.

Feed the fucking dog, Annie, I heard you scream.

I don't believe in ghosts, never have. The living are scary enough. But I made sure to keep my gaze from that back window, as I began to dust, dust, dust.

ii

'It's been going on for ages.'

Da is looking at me.

I have missed something. I am confused. 'Ages?' I don't ask what 'It' means.

Jeanette shrugs, uncomfortable. 'Well, up to now, you know, we didn't want to. Eh.'

Bother you.

Christ.

Da's hand moves from my knee, takes my fingers. 'See, she hasn't been great since Hallowe'en, Annie. Since the—'

Steve clears his throat.

'Accident,' Jeanette starts to say, crisply, but I override her.

'You mean the stroke.' The word feels odd in my mouth but my voice sounds fine. It sounds like it belongs to someone who can say these things. I take a breath and now I'm ready to ask – something, anything – when Da begins to cry. Up to his old tricks, shifting focus. Look at *my* pain.

'Months this is been going on, love. She wouldn't get out of bed, didn't want to talk. I mean, she's never been a great talker, but…' He tightens his grip, his gnawed fingernails digging into my skin. 'Last night I made her a fry-up, tomatoes and everything, but she wouldn't touch a thing. Started crying, wouldn't stop. She says she wants to die.'

They're all staring at me now, worried. The mushroomy smell in the room has got worse. Da starts to shudder. 'I don't know what I'll do if she goes, I can't…'

'Now, Da,' says Jeanette. 'No need to panic. The doctor said—'

'The fuck those bastards know.' His eyes, boiling with rage, find mine.

In the picture frame over his head I see Steve's face, gooey and useless. I pull away my hand and rise. I'm clumsy, all over the place, and my foot knocks against the coal bucket, making it ring like a communion bell. Da blinks.

'Annie, love—'

I can't help, I should say. Get someone else. 'I'd better…' I make a pointless gesture towards the stairs.

Jeanette half-rises. 'D'you want me to—'

'No.'

Da slumps back. I walk across the sitting room, past the bockety suite, the cheap MDF bookcase holding Da's old boxing medals and the pictures of me and Jeanette in Irish Dancing costumes at the Feis and the pretty rose-patterned china that came from our granny in the North. At the doorway, Steve shimmies out of my way, the change in his pocket tinkling like a wind–chime. Mutt's Theme, Second Movement.

The hall is dark. The carpet is dirty. Not like Mam at all. I stop at the banisters. That smell is worse now. I sniff at my collarbone, but it's not me. Then I get it. It's not a physical odour. It's as if something has ripped in the veil of reality and a wind is blowing through the gap. It's the same smell our house stank of before they took you away to that hospital. Panic, sick people, and death.

You used to joke about it. How, if everything went tits-up with the economy, I could always follow my Mam's footsteps, take a job as a scrubber. Your word. But somewhere along the way I lost focus, let your chaos infect me. Stopped doing the dishes after every meal, allowed pots to gather in the sink, dust to collect in corners. It felt decadent, sophisticated in a weird way, letting things go like you did, with your journals and papers and coffee cups heaping up in unruly gatherings on every spare surface. As if I was trying on another history, another class. You never said anything, but I felt your approval glide over me. When we left London and returned to Ireland during the boom, I began to revert.

Nesting, you called it.

It took me two days to tidy up after you left, bag all the crap and organise your books in alphabetical order on the walls of what I still call your study. Even now I am impressed, if that's the word, by my own efficiency. I had a list in my head. Somewhere near the top, above Tidying, should have been Event, capital E. Underneath that, bullets: Catering, Cutlery, Funeral Home, Service (?). Beside each a little box, ready for a tick mark. They say that helps, a finite set of manageable activities to fill the

except

except

except every time I went to ring the funeral directors, I found myself nowhere. Thinking you were still around, but in the next room, or upstairs. Waiting for you to come in because your smell was still so strong. Which was criminally stupid, because the last place you'd been in was the hospital.

Then: that weird return. Handset on the floor. Dial tone droning. The sun in a different place in the garden. Me in front of your desk, sorting through papers.

They had no choice, your sweet parents with their golf club respectability, their careful tact that tasted of crushed glass. Nobody else could have filled the breach. Jeanette too busy drinking up the drama like it was bridesmaid time all over again, oozing tears and pathetic cups of tea. Or that's what I told myself, when, if you'd been there, I'd have come clean, admitted I just couldn't let Big Sister do it again, step up for me, shield me from the pain, and she hadn't the right anyway, you weren't hers to boss away into nothing. Da was useless, naturally, hitting the gargle and telling everyone he could how much he loved you, a great man for the words, my Da, and Mam might have been there, I guess, if I'd let her, but of anyone, she'd never have been able to fight that battle for me. I have to hand it to your own mother. She was extraordinary. Like that Woody Allen joke about the kidnap victim: *My parents swept into action, rented out my room.* She swept into action alright, and believe me when I say I don't feel any rancour towards her for it. We hadn't been to Mass in years. I knew you'd hate it, and I would too, but fuck you, and fuck me. Someone had to take charge.

A better person would have fought.

Yeah. How?

Said: 'I think he'd have wanted—'

'Yes?' Their faces eager, anxious for an edict from beyond.

I think you should know this. They hauled in that priest who officiated at your confirmation, dodgy cousin Paschal from Roscrea. Payback for the registry office wedding. Christ, he hogged the pulpit. Number one on the pastoral bucket list: officiate for a dead rellie. I'd taken some of your mum's Valiums and was zoned out for most of it, but at one point in his endless spiel, he started speaking about what a lovely child you'd been, sharp as a tack, but a good boy scout and always helpful, and my attention snagged. I thought of the you I knew, couldn't match it to his picture. Then I thought of the way you always had to have a Plan B and it seemed to fit quite well. Be Prepared. And suddenly I saw you in the coffin, except you weren't broken and instead of that lovely charcoal suit that matches your eyes, you were wearing a scout's uniform. Shorts and all. Three vials by your side, steaming from the permafrost; haploid cells, suspended in amber. For a horrible moment, I thought I was going to start laughing, but your dad put a hand on my shoulder and I settled.

I should have pushed harder, I started thinking as we made our way out between our friends' muffled sobs and the whispering grass of our neighbours, those tacky hymns belting down the nave behind us. I should have forced it out of you. And the crowd vulture-swarmed us: ah, love, love, eyes ravenous for a taste of our grief, stiff hugs against brooched chests, all passive-aggressive Irish, expecting thanks. Do you – I have to ask this – do you remember that day on Hampstead Heath, when we were not yet thirty, and I tried to get us to talk about how we'd like to celebrate our—

Passing, I said, using my family's word because it was nice, it was respectful, it was classy, I thought.

Ugh, you said.

What?

Passing.

What?

It's such a, you know…

No. What?

Eh, you said, like it was obvious. It's so trite, Annie.

Trite? And hurt, and quick, so you couldn't start backtracking: Okay. Our Dying, then. In my best teacher-style, making the D a capital, precise between my teeth.

Ah come here, Annie, I—

At least, I said, I've some vision. I want my ashes to be thrown in four directions off the hill of Tara.

You flinched. Talk about melodrama, you said.

Well? I said.

I don't want to think about it.

So unlike you, who had to have contingencies for everything. But no, you said. Thinking about that stuff just made you feel morbid.

Anyway, babe, it's not going to happen for ages, so why worry?

I'm not worried.

Oh. I didn't say you were. I said—

We bickered and it intensified and then we brought it down, me because it was always easier to fuck than fight, and you because, I don't know. After we made up, lying in the long grass, looking up at the sky, already beginning to spit rain, you said: 'I know. Let's go together, Annie. In an explosion. The end of the world.'

I let them put you into the ground, in your family's plot at Dean's Grange. I watched the clods fall and the hot August sun send sweat sliding down your mother's powdered forehead and the black-clad armpits of the throng, and the taste of copper in my mouth was your ghost's tongue, hating me.

Wanted what, Conor?

A tick beside a box. If unused, discard.

Elevenish came and went. Jeanette and Steve, late again, always late. Kids, School, Football, Clients. By midday, there was nothing left to clean. I had phoned the builders, left two messages, fed Mixie, put her back out in the yard. Prepped some classes, marked homework. During that time I succeeded in not thinking, very much, about Mam. Call me heartless again, Conor, but it's easy to disconnect from drama when that's all there is.

Aren't you ever worried, you used to say, that you'll miss something real?

Like what? I said, and you couldn't answer.

And you see? I blame you. Because that fruitless conversation with you was what was going through my head instead of what I should have been thinking: What did Jeanette mean, Not Great? And I blame you for this too: me prowling through the chat rooms instead of thinking, What did Jeanette mean? Unable to concentrate, feeling more like a trespasser than ever as I skimmed past those crucial, generous, hard-won nuggets of advice.

you should think carefully about

I've nothing but sympathy for you and I'm saying that to make sure you know, because

Sorry I think it's too soon.

You probably need to realise this is a legal issue as much as anything else.

I think a lot of you are being very hard on AnnieGetYour. When we—

Outside, Mixie's claws stopped scrabbling and she made a sudden sound; coaxing, grumbling, affectionate. I didn't want to, but I couldn't help glancing over. Her head was brushing against air, her happy mouth open, her tongue lolling. Unseen small things lifting from her. Sparking, like dust.

The world shivered.

The bell rang.

I jumped.

I don't believe in this stuff. I should have put you at a fucking crossroads.

You drag at me, you claw my hair, you layer dust on my mother's filthy carpet. You want to trip me, force my retreat. My movements are treacly. I should be easy to obstruct. Your hands pass through me, catching on the soft bits inside.

The upstairs landing is gloomy, an ancient, sepia-toned photograph. I nudge their bedroom door open with my foot. Inside, their bed is empty and unmade, Da's navy jumper thrown sulkily over the rumpled sheets. It's cold. He's left the window open at the top again. The blind cord is slapping the glass. Through it I see the strand, concrete grey, beyond that the sea. Number 2 on the Beaufort Scale, little scales of movement, no white caps. I step out. Across the corridor, the door of the box-room, the one we used to sleep in when we stayed over, is ajar.

I stop. Through the gap I see darkness. The smell from downstairs has got stronger. Somehow I have moved, am forcing myself over, entering Mam's space. I can't see a thing. My knee meets the edge of the bed with a soft bump, and I lower myself, feeling my way with my hands. I can't help thinking I'm going to sit on her by mistake, and the thought makes me giddy and breathless. In the end I manage it without making any contact. She must be curled up tight, I think.

like a foetus

I regroup, corral my senses to the present. They adjust, obedient senses. I catch the sound of her breathing, slow and even. Then I see her: a humped shape under the duvet, squashed close to the wall, facing into it. On the little bedside locker is a tray holding the shadowy forms of her untouched breakfast. I imagine Da earlier that morning, cajoling. Here you go, pet, lovely glass of grapefruit juice, couple of nice slices of soda bread, a bit of Lo-Lo, some chunky marmalade…

My father, Feeder and Hitter.

My mother, mistress of dissimulation, keeper of secrets, perpetual avoider of the Bad News.

I can hear voices trickling up from downstairs. Jeanette's high and uncertain, Steve's useless fits and starts. Under them Da's gravel rumble, kango-hammered by sobs.

Mam's breathing changes. Is she awake? Can she feel us there beside her, you and me?

They said you had a seventy-five percent chance of recovery. There'd been setbacks, the stroke was unexpected, especially for a young man, but in time your condition would stabilise. Many used the words 'pull through'. We could, the more cautious ones said, reasonably expect an improvement. The physio said so, the speech therapist, even the woman running the rehab programme said she'd never seen anyone with so much fighting spirit.

'You tell me,' I said.

She raised an eyebrow. 'Oh?'

I nodded. We laughed. No need to say any more. Some women are sisters. I used to tell mine by the wary look that would come into their eyes when they heard an argument on the bus, the rolling upwards of their eyes at a stranger's swearing bravado. Jeanette always used to say, smugly, wasn't it funny that it was me − not her, the Daddy's girl − who followed Mam's example and chose an angry man to share my life with? As if, in spite of our upbringing, or maybe because of it, she believed anger only came in certain forms and inhabited certain people, and everyone, given a chance, was not capable of fury. As if a few loud arguments with you over breakfast could have ever equated to our Da chasing our mother around her own house with you name it in his fist.

Looking good, said the rehab lady as you clenched your fingers, forced them open.

One snag.

There might be an issue, the consultant said, with fertility. There was a possibility, she told us, that the nature of your condition could affect performance. Erectile function, she said, and you frowned while I fought the childish snigger rising in me. Only a possibility, of course, she reassured us, and smiled. And only in the long term. But, she told us, moving on quickly as her smile turned serious, depending on what approach we were going to take around medication, your treatment itself could impact on sperm count and quality. Perhaps, and she looked straight at you, as if she was propositioning you for a fuck, you might consider freezing some, Conor? Now, while you're young and relatively healthy.

It was painless. It was funny. It was something people did in movies. We hadn't talked about children. Not seriously. It was a given, but for later. We had time. This was only a possibility. In the long term. And maybe, I said, and you agreed, we had enough on our plate for the moment? Because the number one priority, wasn't it, was to get you back on track. But this. Why not? No harm, surely? Good idea, surely? Fine, you said. Great, I said. They gave you the paperwork. You ticked the boxes.

I didn't tell anyone. Not my friends, not Jeanette. Not, God help me, Mam. I felt ashamed after you'd done it, not in a prudish way, but as if I'd been complicit in branding you, with your newly slow right eye and sagging right lip, as lacking. That if I told people, this failing would be exposed, raw, for the world to see. Of course, now, in full-watt hindsight, I think it was simpler than that. I think I was afraid.

After the second stroke, your fighting spirit took a surprising new tack. Well, Annie, you said. It's clear the orthodox route isn't working. Perhaps we need to try a different approach. You said it over breakfast, two weeks after they'd let you back home. You spoke calmly, as if you were talking about replacing a faulty machine component.

'You mean something… alternative?' I said, unsure what you were getting at. We'd always hated that stuff. New Agey mumbo-jumbo, you called it.

'Fine,' you said. 'Forget it.'

'No. I don't… That sounds really positive, Conor.'

Later that evening I drank wine and watched you attempt to meditate, the word *desperation* scratching at the bottom of my brain.

I don't hate them, all those people we went to. They were kind. Supportive, and not too crazy, even though that cynical part of me couldn't help wondering at the palaver. The talk of aligning spirit and mind, shifting baggage, finding root causes of cellular degeneration in behaviour. The notion that if a person directs enough attention inwards, the outer stuff can be fixed. The old you wouldn't have blamed me for wondering why it was necessary to get so medieval about the whole thing. Your body pierced with needles, your ears fed melting wax, foul potions brewed from witches' herbs bubbling on our stove.

At first, against the doctors' savage new odds, the new direction seemed to work. Your brain and body slowly began to tune back into each other. I felt hope uncurl inside me as our future started to reconsolidate, line by broken line like a drawing in an Etch-a-Sketch. It was then we started talking about it. Seriously. Will we try, you said. Maybe we should wait, I said. Till…

Till what, you said. I feel terrific. And you grabbed my ass the way I liked it, drawing me to you and I told myself you were there, under the softness of your trouser fabric. Okay, I said, and up the stairs we went for that dirty filthy ride.

They said this might happen, I wanted to say.

Maybe we should go to that clinic, I wanted to say.

Perhaps… you said, frowning. I prayed you wouldn't finish your sentence.

Next time.

I agree. I let it slide as much as you did. More, maybe. Isn't this the woman's prerogative? Magic moon-cycles, maternal instinct, the countdown of the biological clock.

The contingency came into effect so smoothly I couldn't help wondering if you'd had it up your sleeve all along. We got a rescue dog. You called her Mixie. You adored her. To your credit you never talked about her as Our Furry Baby, though you had your own ridiculous, dotey names for her. I tried to respect her. She was our companion animal. *Until*, I thought, though the word had a fuzzy quality to it, nothing like the urgency of my friends getting loud and anxious over birthday glasses of wine, or colleagues worrying in the staff-room about time-windows or genetic abnormalities or the M-word. Then you announced you had a Plan, one evening after you'd come back from Reiki, and I thought, with a treacherous jump in my heart that I still can't tell was terror or excitation: Clinic. But no. You were going to build a new extension to our house. A small job. Just a bit of a conservatory, to add light. Ah, I said, nodding. It was something I've always been threatening to do, you said, and your smile had a manic quality to it.

I watched you take the sledgehammer to the back wall and dig trenches in my garden, your weakened arm dangling by your side, while Mixie, the pest, chased invisible rats. Then I came back from work that evening and found the house black with smoke and, terrified, started screaming.

'Jesus Christ, Conor! What the hell is going on?'

You hadn't noticed. You were out the back, smearing the same brick over and over with cement.

I batted the smoke away and saw a pan on the stove, blue flames flickering underneath. The base of the pan was charred; what was inside had burnt to nothing. I grabbed the handle and pain carved a red X across my palm. I swore, dropped the pan, ran to the sink. The tap didn't work; no water.

I looked up. You were at the door, watching.

'I've turned off the mains.' The sun was behind you, haloing your hair. Your eyes were slitted. You were leaning against the door, and I knew it was because you no longer trusted your leg, but the insouciance of that slouch made your lopsided body look almost sexy again.

After I'd cooled down, we sat at the table and I saw the salt lamps had gone. You took my hand. 'It's no use.' Your speech was slurred. *Zhnoyoosh.* You sounded worse than you had that morning. Was that even possible. 'It's bullshit—'

'It's not bullshit.' My teeth were aching. 'You're bullshit.'

You laughed and I saw Quasimodo, crooked and monstrous.

'That's what I'm talking about,' I said. 'That bullshit attitude. How can you ever expect to get better if you keep giving up?'

You started saying something else, and I wish now I'd let you speak. Then you stopped and stood and picked up the pan that was still sizzling in the sink and you looked at me, and together we smelt your unfeeling flesh as it cooked through to the bone.

That evening, I went to see our least-wacky alternative person, the shiatsu lady in Terenure. She did some muscle testing and told me that I needed to work on my boundaries.

'You have to hold back,' she said. 'If you don't want to go down with him.'

'I'm sorry,' I said. 'But that doesn't make sense. I'm not the one who's sick.'

The shiatsu lady hesitated. Then she started talking about how we all have places inside us which are well and sick. Think of them as territories, she said, separated by a wall. One side a garden, the other a jungle. With a stroke, literally, the wall gets a knock. The structure weakens. Another stroke, another knock. Then it's just a question of time. 'Beyond a certain point,' she said, 'there's only so much I can do. But I'll ask you this, Ann: why would anyone make an effort to stay in a garden if they could just walk straight into a jungle and do what they wanted there?'

'You're making it sound like he's doing this,' I said.

No, she said.

Well, she said.

Maybe, she said. The thing is with madness, she said, and her voice had a snake-oil salesman edge that I didn't like, is—

'Hang on a second,' I said. 'Who said anything about madness? His condition is physical.'

She sighed and before she could start explaining again, how illness was not just a physical thing, and how we were all sick in some way or other, I stood up and walked out.

When I got home, you were sitting in the back room, zapping the TV. Your bandaged hand lay on your lap. Mixie was nuzzling it, stupid cow-eyes gazing up at you. I'd swear she was crying. The TV screen shuddered, sending blue shadows across the walls and the plastic sheeting that hid the hole you'd ripped in our wall. Spilling mottled flashes of slideshow out into the remnants of my garden, across the bags of cement, the half-dug foundations, the muddy trench beginnings of your dream extension. As you zapped, I imagined you pressing the switches inside your mind. Jungle, garden. Off on. Illuminating each part of the damaged cortex in its own patch of interrogation-room light, checking to see if anything was still in place. Garden, jungle. On off.

Plan B, lost in rubble.

Multiple Choice:
- Discard after death. ❏
- Allow to be used after death. ❏

I have thought, many times, about which box I would have ticked if I was you. I'd like to do a survey, ask men and women that question, ask them to answer honestly.

iii

There's a movement in the bed, so small it's almost soundless. I've always gone along with the family line, thought of Mam as a quiet woman, but it's only here, in the absence of words, that I realise how she is almost never silent. Maybe, back in those Olden Times that she's tried so hard to recreate with her low lamps and daisy-patterned oilcloth, she did used to talk for Ireland as a girl, but lowered her voice when she met our Da, so her constant talk, like the rainy season in monsoon countries, took on the illusion of silence. Under the duvet, her shape rises and falls and I can't help remembering the conversations we used to have when I was a teenager, in the damp little kitchen of the old house, the one Da pissed down the drain on the gambling debts and toxic assets.

We'd hold hands while she told me what he had done or not done. Rare morsels of advice. Don't ever go for a man with a temper, Annie. Your sister won't listen to me, but I know you will. Always trust in love.

Such simple things. So inadequate. When we were younger, she'd been full of Do's and Don'ts: Don't speak with your mouth full, don't call your granny names, give a nice smile to the priest, keep your mouth closed while you're eating, make sure your room is tidy. And later, mainly at Jeanette: don't wear that skirt, don't come back too late, don't bring *him* into this house. Trust in love. I should have asked her. What on earth does that mean, Mam?

She would listen, though, especially when we had stuff going on with boyfriends, jobs, bosses, friends. She'd pat our shoulders, make cups of tea, but never say anything that helped, not really. I rarely talked to her about you. By the time we'd met, I'd decided she had too many of her own problems. Besides, by then I knew that anything I told her, she'd have to screen, decide whether she could pass it on to Da or not. Only later did I realise that during those teenage years when she told me what he'd done, she'd been screening that too. Checking in with some part of herself to see what was safe to say. Oh no, love, he's not an alcoholic. He just likes his drink.

The year Jeanette failed her Leaving Cert, Mam kept the exam results in a drawer for a month. Protect us. Keep the wolf from the door, the knock from the window, the phone off the hook, the red letter in the bin.

Her breathing grows more regular. The curtain shifts. A chink of light illuminates her hair, grey at the roots, as it moves on the pillow.

My mouth opens, surprising me. 'Remember.' My voice sounds rusty. 'Remember that story you told us, Mam? About how you were the first girl in Belfast with a peroxide dye?'

The duvet rises, falls.

'It was just before you went to England. You'd gone to the hairdressers with that girl, what was her name?'

Minnie? Molly? 'Mary. Mary Deane, yes, and you decided to give it a go. She chickened out but you went ahead. You were...' I hesitate.

Fearless.

No movement from the duvet. 'There's a picture of you, remember? You loved showing it to us when we were little. Sunday afternoons. It's the two of you walking the pier in Morecombe. You looked so...'

I struggle.

'Your hair was like Marilyn Monroe's. Remember? You were laughing. You'd this dark lipstick on. In the photo it looked black. Your teeth were so white. You were wearing...'

Fifties court shoes. A belted raincoat. A headscarf.

'Funny, headscarves look so—'

Tragic.

'—old, they look so old on women, but on girls, they're just.' I take a chance. 'Gorgeous.'

I sit in the spicy, stinking darkness and tell her stories. After the third stroke sent you to the hospital, I did the same with you, every night before you went to sleep in that swish semi-private ward, five floors up with its lovely bird's eye view of the city.

A bit of a rest, they'd said. For both of us. They didn't want to put you into a psychiatric unit because, the consultant insisted, your condition was a physical one. I thought of your silence, your refusal to speak to anyone except that dog. I thought of the shiatsu lady and I wanted to laugh and I wanted to hit myself too. This would help, they said. You would have twenty-four hour access to support, constant monitoring. The problem was, nobody could smell it there, the crap eating through the walls in your head. The stink of disinfectant and old men's shit was too strong.

Remember, I would say to you.

Remember this. Remember that. Conor, remember. It was like talking to a stone. At some point, I ran out of words. Something seized my throat, squeezing my ribs, and I realised I had to get out.

Mam, I want to say now. Tell me. Should I fight for him, that bit of him left frozen? Should I go for it, Mam? Plan C? Get a lawyer, cry crocodile tears. Beg them, bully them, force them to thaw him?

You lay your cold hand on the back of my neck to stop me, but even without it, I know these questions aren't any of her business.

I bend close to her face, plant a kiss on her forehead. Her skin is papery and, under the scent of the madhouse, smells of something flowery. In her right temple throbs a small blue worm.

iv

Downstairs, things seem calmer. Jeanette has opened the curtains and Da is sipping coffee. His hands are still shaking but there's some colour in his cheeks. Steve is sitting on the sofa across from him, leaning forward. He's in the middle of saying something. I only catch a bit before Jeanette looks up, nudges him and he stops talking. They're too late. The unfinished phrase screams across the room, jagged as a jigsaw piece.

'Ah, Annie.' Da turns, his eyes cloudy and unaware. 'So what do you think about that?'

'About what?'

'We're just,' starts Jeanette.

'I've just been having a little chat with Steve here,' says Da. 'And he thinks you know, if she wants to be committed, then. Well.'

I stare.

Steve clears his throat. 'I've been telling Tom that I've had, eh, some experience of this sort of thing, and one thing I'd say now it's. Eh. The sort of thing you can't deal with on your own.' His tongue darts out, licks his upper lip. 'For everyone's sake, Annie.'

What did he call me?

Jeanette smiles. It looks painful. 'Now, Ann, Steve's only saying—'

Steve glances at Jeanette, back at me. 'I didn't mean— Jesus, Annie, love, I wasn't talking about Conor.' His face reddens. He nods at Da. 'Sorry, Tom, pardon my French. It's my younger brother, Ann. That's what I was telling Tom. If he didn't have them looking after him… He's ah – he's not been well for years, see. Schizophrenia.'

Jesus, I think. Save us. In the back of my mind I hear the shiatsu woman laugh.

Jeanette's cheeks are pink. 'The family don't like to talk about it…'

Steve interrupts. 'You know, too many people in this fucking country don't like to talk about stuff, and if you ask me, it's—'

His voice is too loud for the room. He stops.

Da wants us to stay for tea. Some lovely salad sandwiches, a bit of that nice cheddar, few juicy spoons of chopped onion, tomato and cucumber. Jeanette's face lights up. She's always been easy to comfort: a biscuit, a sandwich, a sugary cup of tea. And I think about it, for a second I do, but Steve is already checking his watch again and making noises about not wanting to leave the kids on their own for too long.

Jeanette holds Da's hands. 'Now, love, you look after yourself.'

Steve nods. 'It'll blow over, Tom. Just get her looked after by the professionals.'

He's right, though it scalds me to admit it.

I've got my coat on and Steve is busy revving the four-by-four when Da appears at the front door. I half-turn. 'I'll call you soon, Daddy,' I start to say, but Da has already opened his arms. I step in. Under the layers of clothes, I feel his hard chest. Under that, his heart; a mirror of my own, pounding with remorse.

It was a success, the guests agreed. The catering was terrific. The priest got drunk and tried to feel up an old schoolfriend of mine you'd never met. But sure, priests do that, don't they? Number 2 on the bucket list. Later, when there were only a few stragglers left, we sat in the comfortable leather sofas in your parents' sitting room and shared anecdotes. Your cousins had the best, shocking your mother with stories of illicit smoking and drinking, attempts at running away, unsuitable girlfriends, mitched exams, job interviews that never happened. I'd heard most of them before but not all, and they did the trick. It felt almost good to laugh among the hardening crusts of egg sandwiches and iced fancies.

They asked if I wanted to stay with them, but I refused. I got a cab home, and the house looked different, like it belonged to someone else.

I couldn't sleep. At about two, I gave up and went downstairs to sit in our old back room, looking out through the hole in the wall at the rubble in the garden. There wasn't much to see. Mixie was blocking the view, lying there morose, jaw on front paws. Behind her the plastic sheeting blurred everything beyond, dim shapes of dark blue. Move, I said, but your stupid dog ignored me. I lit a fag, from a pack I'd wangled off your cousin, and when I finished it, I lit another. The room filled slowly with blue haze, mocking all those years I'd struggled to stay nicotine-free, all the pounds I'd gained in so doing. It must have been a bit cold, but I didn't feel it. I heard a breeze start and I got up, nudging Mixie out of the way so I could take down some of the sheeting to let in the air.

Outside, the moon looked as if it was racing through the sky, chased by the clouds. It was almost full. Thirteen-fourteenths, I used to say, irritating you. Jesus, Annie, you'd say, it's not a question of fourteenths; then you'd explain, yet again, how the moon is in constant motion, changing by the moment, not the day.

I stood at the ragged hole and tried to remember what your skin had felt like warm. Mixie's ears pricked. She whined. Then, suddenly, as if a switch had been flipped, she lunged out into the back and started howling, teeth dripping at the moon, and, in that instant, a chorus joined her. Every dog in the neighbourhood.

The moon came and went under the clouds, the smoke eased into my lungs and Mixie and her infernal chorus sang. I imagined the sea near my parents' house, crazy. The wind rose and for one wild moment I contemplated taking off all my clothes, clambering out into the garden and dancing naked in the half-built foundations, joining that stupid bitch, adding my own keening howl to her chorus, offering my blood to the moon if she could bring you back. But the moment passed, leaving me shivering in that sensible Penneys' nightie you'd always hated, so I put the sheeting up again, marooning your pet outside, and sat back down in your armchair, ignoring those scrabbling claws, waiting for the day to break.

The four-by-four smells of sour milk and children's farts. I watch the evening lower, the March clouds deadweight onto the grey horizon, and wonder if I should have said something more to Da. Something definitive, or just something.

There was a time when I didn't have to have answers. When I was just a kid, and all I knew were childish things, like how to beat my big sister at hopscotch and what tasted better – boiled egg in a cup or boiled egg with soldiers.

Jeanette is rabbiting on about Steve's younger brother. The one his family never talks about. I've never seen him, he wasn't at our wedding, not even at theirs. Maybe, I think, he's a figment of Steve's imagination.

'He was grand till he was twenty-two, Ann. Then it started. Thinking about the same things over and over.'

'Obsessing,' says Steve.

I have a vague memory of Steve trying to say something to me at the funeral, but I hadn't wanted to talk. Was this it, Misery Top Trumps?

'They got him into a centre,' says Jeanette. 'And it's fantastic, Annie. He's been right as rain ever since.'

'Well not really,' says Steve. 'You couldn't say that.'

Jeanette coughs. There's a long silence.

I look up at the rearview mirror and see Steve's eyes looking straight into mine. They are clear green, like the river on a cool autumn morning.

The old tape has begun to spool again, hammering at the inside of my head. If I hadn't stayed away that night, if I'd got there earlier that morning, if I'd only said something. Hooke's Law, converse of: release the force and the elastic rebounds. I close my eyes and once more see the tape rewind. The clocks start; pulse, synapse, breath. Your broken body unpeels from its sprawled shadow, bungeeing away from the pavement's cracked kiss. You soar up, five flights high, and hover before the opened window with its lovely panoramic view of the city. In that first moment of your leap a hawk, your limbs stretched, your body whole again, your face beautiful in the dawn light. Then—

Then what?

Ah Quasimodo, hobbled again in your hospital bed.

An hour to go before the funeral. I kneel in front of your walnut bureau, piles of sorted clutter behind me, and I see it. The file, the box, your neat X.

v

Charcoal branches, grey sky. A cardboard pine tree, swinging in front of a windscreen. In the rearview, Steve's eyes, green and clear.

She needs proper care, he'd been saying when I came down the stairs. *Maybe a secure unit. Especially if she's thinking of taking her own...*

Then Jeanette had stopped him.

Life, I think, staring at him, willing you, whatever you are, to think it too.

When we get back, it's six thirty. Twelve hours since the first knock. I don't bother asking them in for a cup of tea. Too much hassle, and anyway they've the kids to feed and wash and, and, and.

I go to the back, release the latch.

Mixie bounds in and covers me with messy kisses.

Baby girl, baby girl, I say. And then – stupid me – I start crying.

Publishing Credits

An early version of 'More Often in Future', entitled 'The Demons', was published in *Writing Ulster* No. 2/3 (1991/1992).

'Polyfilla' first appeared in *Let's Be Alone Together*, edited by Declan Meade (Stinging Fly, 2008).

An earlier version of 'Found Wanting' was Editor's Choice in *Franklin's Grace & Other Stories* (Fish Publishing, 2003).

A shorter version of 'Shift', entitled 'Maybe', was awarded the START Fiction chapbook prize (2005) together with 'All Bones' and 'You First'. The three stories were published in a chapbook *You First* (South Tipperary Arts Centre, 2005). 'All Bones' was first published in *Feathers and Cigarettes* (Fish Publishing, 2004) as a runner-up for the Fish Prize 2003.

'Departure' first appeared in *The Sunday Tribune* (1990), where it was shortlisted for a New Irish Writing Award.

An early version of 'Lure' appeared in *Circle and Square*, edited by Eileen Casey (Fiery Arrow Press, 2015).

An early version of 'Headhunter' was published in *Carve Magazine* (Vol. 4, No. 5, 2003).

'Trust in Me' originally appeared in *Numero Cinq* (Vol. VIII, No. 1, 2017).

'The Lady, Vanishing' first appeared in *Spolia*, Disappearance Issue (2014).

An early version of 'With Soldiers, in a Cup', entitled 'Quasimodo', was shortlisted for the Trevor/Bowen Award. This version was published in *Spolia*, The Wife Issue (2013); later that year Spolia reproduced the story as a limited edition chapbook, *Quasimodo*, with illustrations by US-based artist Kirsten Stolle.

Acknowledgements

Many thanks to the editors who published earlier versions of these stories: Ciaran Carty; the late Archie Markham; Clem Cairns, and all at Fish, for their pivotal support; the *Carve* team; Mike McCormack and the START team, particularly Brendan Maher, Suzanne Walsh and Grace Wells; the inimitable Declan Meade; Jessa Crispin and Gus Iversen for their warm *Spolia* welcome; Eileen Casey; Douglas Glover.

My friends, family and colleagues who read and responded to these pieces, either as works-in-progress or in published form. A special shout-out to Miriam Duffy, who was there right at the start, and Ken Carroll, who encouraged me to compile this collection in the first place.

My tenacious, supportive and brilliant agent, eagle-eyed Jonathan Williams. The superb and kind team at New Island – thanks again, Hannah Shorten, Mariel Deegan, Edwin Higel, Michael Darcy, it's a joy making books with you. Dan Bolger is an exceptional editor, working his unique strand of sympathetic magic with discernment, enthusiasm and patience. His precise input and ability to ask the right questions allowed me to dig deeper, get closer to what these stories really wanted to say.

I am indebted once again to the Arts Council of Ireland, whose continued faith and generous support through a Bursary gave me time to develop, rewrite and complete this collection. In particular, I'd like to thank Sarah Bannan for her ongoing encouragement, both practical and creative. Also Dave Levins, Linda Moran, Nuala Canny and all at Farmleigh for affording me writing time in that extraordinary place as their 2017 Writer-in-Residence.

To my loved ones. Izzy, for just being there, and Seán for supporting, with humour, insight and imagination, this latest journey to Planet Book. To my Dad, Gerhardt, for being such a quiet and profound inspiration in all parts of my life.

And finally, my late Mum, Miriam. Generous, talented and beautiful blazer of the trail, the first writer – and reader – I learnt from. Shine on, bright star.